# ALREADY

# TRAPPED

(A Laura Frost Suspense Thriller —Book Three)

BLAKE PIERCE

# Blake Pierce

Blake Pierce is the USA Today bestselling author of the RILEY PAGE mystery series, which includes seventeen books. Blake Pierce is also the author of the MACKENZIE WHITE mystery series, comprising fourteen books; of the AVERY BLACK mystery series, comprising six books; of the KERI LOCKE mystery series, comprising five books; of the MAKING OF RILEY PAIGE mystery series, comprising six books; of the KATE WISE mystery series, comprising seven books; of the CHLOE FINE psychological suspense mystery, comprising six books; of the JESSIE HUNT psychological suspense thriller series, comprising nineteen books; of the AU PAIR psychological suspense thriller series, comprising three books; of the ZOE PRIME mystery series, comprising six books; of the ADELE SHARP mystery series, comprising thirteen books; of the EUROPEAN VOYAGE cozy mystery series, comprising six books (and counting); of the new LAURA FROST FBI suspense thriller, comprising five books (and counting); of the new ELLA DARK FBI suspense thriller, comprising six books (and counting); of the A YEAR IN EUROPE cozy mystery series, comprising nine books (and counting); of the AVA GOLD mystery series, comprising three books (and counting); and of the RACHEL GIFT mystery series, comprising three books (and counting).

An avid reader and lifelong fan of the mystery and thriller genres, Blake loves to hear from you, so please feel free to visit www.blakepierceauthor.com to learn more and stay in touch.

MURDER (AND BAKLAVA) (Book #1)
DEATH (AND APPLE STRUDEL) (Book #2)
CRIME (AND LAGER) (Book #3)
MISFORTUNE (AND GOUDA) (Book #4)
CALAMITY (AND A DANISH) (Book #5)
MAYHEM (AND HERRING) (Book #6)

**ADELE SHARP MYSTERY SERIES**
LEFT TO DIE (Book #1)
LEFT TO RUN (Book #2)
LEFT TO HIDE (Book #3)
LEFT TO KILL (Book #4)
LEFT TO MURDER (Book #5)
LEFT TO ENVY (Book #6)
LEFT TO LAPSE (Book #7)
LEFT TO VANISH (Book #8)
LEFT TO HUNT (Book #9)
LEFT TO FEAR (Book #10)
LEFT TO PREY (Book #11)
LEFT TO LURE (Book #12)
LEFT TO CRAVE (Book #13)

**THE AU PAIR SERIES**
ALMOST GONE (Book#1)
ALMOST LOST (Book #2)
ALMOST DEAD (Book #3)

**ZOE PRIME MYSTERY SERIES**
FACE OF DEATH (Book#1)
FACE OF MURDER (Book #2)
FACE OF FEAR (Book #3)
FACE OF MADNESS (Book #4)
FACE OF FURY (Book #5)
FACE OF DARKNESS (Book #6)

**A JESSIE HUNT PSYCHOLOGICAL SUSPENSE SERIES**
THE PERFECT WIFE (Book #1)
THE PERFECT BLOCK (Book #2)
THE PERFECT HOUSE (Book #3)
THE PERFECT SMILE (Book #4)
THE PERFECT LIE (Book #5)

ONCE GONE (Book #1)
ONCE TAKEN (Book #2)
ONCE CRAVED (Book #3)
ONCE LURED (Book #4)
ONCE HUNTED (Book #5)
ONCE PINED (Book #6)
ONCE FORSAKEN (Book #7)
ONCE COLD (Book #8)
ONCE STALKED (Book #9)
ONCE LOST (Book #10)
ONCE BURIED (Book #11)
ONCE BOUND (Book #12)
ONCE TRAPPED (Book #13)
ONCE DORMANT (Book #14)
ONCE SHUNNED (Book #15)
ONCE MISSED (Book #16)
ONCE CHOSEN (Book #17)

**MACKENZIE WHITE MYSTERY SERIES**
BEFORE HE KILLS (Book #1)
BEFORE HE SEES (Book #2)
BEFORE HE COVETS (Book #3)
BEFORE HE TAKES (Book #4)
BEFORE HE NEEDS (Book #5)
BEFORE HE FEELS (Book #6)
BEFORE HE SINS (Book #7)
BEFORE HE HUNTS (Book #8)
BEFORE HE PREYS (Book #9)
BEFORE HE LONGS (Book #10)
BEFORE HE LAPSES (Book #11)
BEFORE HE ENVIES (Book #12)
BEFORE HE STALKS (Book #13)
BEFORE HE HARMS (Book #14)

**AVERY BLACK MYSTERY SERIES**
CAUSE TO KILL (Book #1)
CAUSE TO RUN (Book #2)
CAUSE TO HIDE (Book #3)
CAUSE TO FEAR (Book #4)
CAUSE TO SAVE (Book #5)
CAUSE TO DREAD (Book #6)

# CHAPTER ONE

Ruby Patrickson had been looking for love for a while, and it wasn't going so great. That last date had been awful. But there were plenty more fish in the sea. Besides, she had time. She was only twenty-five. Prince Charming was out there somewhere, and in the meantime, she could kiss a lot of frogs to see what they might turn into.

Ruby sighed to herself as she looked at the stack of dishes by the sink. It had been a long day at work, and she didn't even want to think about cleaning up. It was going to have to wait. She turned to her favorite dating app instead, where she saw she had a message from a new connection. Opening it, she saw a flirty conversation opener that made her bite her lip and smile. He wasn't shy, whoever he was. She giggled quietly to herself as she typed out a response, leaning over the kitchen counter on her elbows, adding in a couple of winking faces at the end of her message. He was cute, at least assuming his profile image was accurate. She was more than interested.

A sound outside made her frown a little. The condo was normally quiet at this time of night. Half the residents in this sleepy little Wisconsin town were retired and the other half, so it seemed to Ruby, were young families. Everywhere she looked, it was either proud parents with fat toddlers or old couples leaning on each other to walk.

Maybe that was a little something to do with her current lack of a romantic life, but Ruby wasn't going to analyze it too hard.

Still, it was odd for someone to be out in the hall this late, after Ruby had finished her shift. She often felt like a criminal sneaking into her own home, trying not to wake anyone as she fumbled her keys in the lock. Now, someone was out there making enough noise that she could hear it through to the kitchen.

She straightened up and wandered back out toward the front door, idly. She paused just beside it, glancing through the peephole. The hall lights were on, triggered by the motion sensors as she had walked in. Probably triggered again by whoever was out there a moment ago. There was no one there now.

The lights went off while she looked through, leaving Ruby in darkness. She frowned. That was odd. If someone else had only just

1

retriggered the motion sensor, why would the lights turn off? It wasn't a power cut. Her own lights were still on.

There was a soft sound somewhere behind her, making her freeze. If there was no one out in the hall, and the sound she'd heard was coming from inside her apartment, then…

She looked around wildly, spinning so fast her auburn hair whipped around her shoulders. She half-expected to see some serial killer from a movie standing behind her, wearing a hockey mask or a sack over his face, wielding an axe. But there was no one there.

She sighed, taking a breath. *Come on, Ruby, get it together,* she told herself. *It's probably just the building settling.*

Or that giant pile of dishes in the sink finally starting to give way.

She passed a hand over her forehead, shaking herself mentally. What a stupid thing to get all nervous about. She'd been living alone for only a few months, since moving away from the home she shared with her sister. It was her first time. She was bound to be a bit skittish from time to time.

Still, she was a grown woman, and this was just being ridiculous.

Ruby heard a buzz from her pocket and reached for her phone, leaning against the door and grinning as she read a response from her new suitor. He was suggesting they meet up tonight. It was tempting, but she was tired. Better to string him along a bit, get him to take her out on the weekend for a drink or something. Ruby liked the flirting part. It would be over quickly once they'd actually been on a date—or stumbled into bed together. Then it would quickly dissolve—in her experience so far, into either a lack of contact altogether or an arrogant assumption that she would be there and ready the next time he wanted to see her.

No, she'd drag the flirting out a bit first, get her fun out of it. She smiled to herself again as she typed out a reply, imagining him reading it.

She stood from the door and pushed herself away from it, wandering around the corner into her bedroom. Just at the threshold, she froze again, then turned. Had she heard something else? Another creaking floorboard? Something shifting in the darkness?

The kitchen light was still on, and nothing was casting any kind of unusual shadow. The room she could see was empty, just as she'd left it. Next door was the living room, still bathed in darkness. The door was only half-open. But there was no one in there. This was all absurd. Her heart racing—it was stupid. There was no one there.

She looked into the darkness for what felt like a long time, straining to see something, not quite brave enough to go over and turn on the light and see it properly.

The whole time she had been looking, the house had been silent. Ruby shook her head, tapping on the solid wooden doorframe for reassurance. There was nothing there. There never had been anything there. A settling floorboard. Maybe even just someone moving around upstairs. That's all it was.

She forced herself to turn again and reach for the light switch, heading into her bedroom. She slung her purse on the bed, reaching up to shrug a wool cardigan off her shoulders. She would get changed into something more comfortable, then make food and eat in front of the TV. And then, she thought, she'd be better off getting some sleep. She was obviously far too tired, her brain making up ghosts to scare her.

Ruby reached for the bottom of her shirt, ready to pull it over her head—

And a noise, an unmistakable noise right behind her, made her spin around, bringing her face to face with terror.

He was in her home—in her bedroom—reaching for her—reaching out something toward her—

Ruby looked down, down at her own stomach, unable to understand for a moment. There was something in his hand. His hand was against her stomach. The thing in his hand was a knife.

He had stabbed her.

Realization brought pain. Ruby tried to scream and only managed a strangled gasp, trying to stumble backwards away from him. She couldn't think. Couldn't move. It was like her limbs were trapped in ice. There was pain, terrible pain, a feeling of wetness below her stomach. She backed away from him and then stumbled and fell.

The knife was in his hands again. Ruby put her hand to her stomach, felt the warm liquid falling over her hands. She kicked back desperately, trying to find enough purchase to crawl away, to kick out at him. He leaned over her, his face a grim mask. She kicked out and he barely reacted. Ruby could only hear her own breathing, heavy in her ears. The pump of blood in her veins, improbably loud, like she was more aware of it now than she ever had been before only because it was spilling out of her.

"No!" she said, her scream coming out as a strangled wheeze, as he drew back his hand. Then he plunged the knife down again, and Ruby's attempt to push him away failed, and the last thing she knew was the bitter tear of the knife through her skin before she lost her grip on everything.

# CHAPTER TWO

Laura Frost stood in her living room, holding the toy rabbit and wondering why it was in her hand. Why she'd pulled it up out of the bag she was holding. Why she'd even bought it at all.

Laura sat down on her battered old couch, heavily, as she always seemed to lately. The whole living room seemed almost haunted since she'd come home and found black paint smeared across her wall as a warning. A warning to stay away from Amy Fallow, the six-year-old girl she had once managed to rescue from her father's abusive clutches.

But her father was Governor Fallow, and he had enough clout to pull enough strings to get his daughter back. It was a fact that had weighed heavily on Laura's mind every day in the couple of weeks since. She'd been strictly forbidden to try to contact Amy in any way; her superior, Division Chief Rondelle, assured her that an investigation was underway and they were doing whatever they could.

Whatever they could. It didn't seem like much, given that Amy was still in the lion's den.

Laura opened the shopping bag she'd carried back to her small apartment, reaching in to pull out the items inside. She'd only intended to go out for essentials. A new shirt, necessary after a recent case in which she'd had to tackle a suspect to the ground and managed to rip the fabric of the one she was wearing. Rondelle seemed to be throwing her into every group investigation possible, keeping her busy while there was nothing in particular to work on with her partner, Nate.

Which was good, because Nate kept trying to ask her questions she couldn't answer whenever they were alone together. Questions about how she always knew where to be and when. There were things she didn't want him to know, both for her own safety and the sake of their friendship. A friendship that was quickly dissolving all the same, no matter what she seemed to do.

And being kept busy going after local suspects in conjunction with other law enforcement agencies was also a bad thing. Because even if it was keeping her occupied, it was in no way keeping her mind off the issues that plagued Laura and kept her from sleeping through the night. Amy, and how badly her father might be hurting her either now. Lacey,

Laura's own daughter, and the custody hearing that was rapidly approaching. Nate.

The fact that she was still distracted was clear from the other thing that had been in the bag, besides the shampoo and the new shirt and the cleaning spray.

The soft, plush toy rabbit, which Laura had been utterly unable to resist after seeing it in the store.

She stroked the silky fur absentmindedly, running her fingers along the toy's long ears and touching its button nose. She hadn't even known, when she bought it, which little girl she had in mind. She could give it to her daughter at the custody hearing at the end of the week, if her ex, Marcus, would let her. If things went badly—a possibility she couldn't quite let herself entertain fully, because it might send her off the deep end—it might be all Lacey had of her mother.

Marcus had been cooperative lately. Letting Laura see her daughter for a couple of hours at a time. Even letting her take her out, away from his watchful gaze. But would that last, if the judge ruled that Laura had no right to see her at all? Would Marcus pull back and stop her from seeing Lacey entirely?

The only thing Laura could see happening after that was the bottom of a bottle. A spiral that would be the worst she had ever been down. She'd been so strong lately, keeping up her sobriety even in the face of awful revelations. Nate's impending death, delivered to her not by a vision but by an ominous shadow that gave frustratingly few details, was one. But Laura had thought of her daughter's face each time and managed to keep going.

But was this rabbit for Lacey? She couldn't even be sure herself. There was also the possibility that she'd bought it with Amy in mind. The last time Laura had seen her, she'd been clutching a toy rabbit just like this one. Laura had driven by Governor Fallow's house a few times, despite the instructions from Rondelle, and found it heavily guarded. He'd employed a couple of bodyguards to stop anyone from entering the home without his permission. Still, there might be a way. Laura pictured herself driving up to the back of the house, somehow, throwing the rabbit over the fence. Or, better: giving it to Amy when her father was finally arrested, and the little girl was free.

The smile that played across Laura's face at that thought was wiped clean by a sudden stab of pain in her head, so strong she could barely stand it. She gasped out loud at the sign of an incoming vision, a pain she couldn't control, a pain that warned the vision was going to be about something happening very, very soon—

*Laura was floating above the room, looking down. She found herself dropping, like she was suddenly prone to gravity in her visions. With a heart-wrenching jerk she stopped at what might have been her own shoulder level, looking ahead into the room. A room she recognized all too well.*

*She'd been here in a vision before. She'd been here in person, too. It was Amy's bedroom at her father's house. The room where she should have felt safest in all the world, but she didn't.*

*She was in there now. Cowering on the bed with her hands over her ears. Laura could only just glimpse her face, red and wet with tears. She was shaking. She had pulled all of her toys in front of her, as if to create a barrier between herself and the rest of the room. Laura's heart broke, watching her. She was so afraid. So young and yet so afraid. Because she knew what could happen—what would happen, when her father came into the room.*

*What was she hearing that made her want to cover her ears? Laura tried in frustration to look around, but the vision was out of her control. She could only watch Amy crying, powerless to reach out and comfort her. Even if she could, it wouldn't matter. This was a vision of the future, not the present. Laura had no physical body here. No ability to interact with or change anything. It was only a window, and she could only look through it.*

*She found herself turning, her view shifting until she was behind Amy, as if she could move through the wall itself. Now she was looking at the closed door of the room. She realized she was holding her breath, trying not to make a sound. Straining her ears.*

*And then she heard it.*

*A heavy footfall—a stomping noise coming up the stairs.*

*Below her, Amy whimpered. Laura felt like she was hovering above her as a guardian angel, a protective force. But she knew that wasn't true. Whatever would happen to Amy right now, there was nothing Laura could do about it. Not until the vision was over and she could spring into action in real life.*

*But there was no way to control the vision. No way to know when it would be over. No way to stop herself from seeing what she was about to see. Even if she wanted to, Laura couldn't close her eyes now.*

*The door thundered open, ripping back so quickly it seemed like it would come off its hinges, hitting the wall behind and bouncing back. Framed in the doorway was Amy's father, Governor Fallow.*

*Laura felt a scream building inside of her, wanting to tear out of the throat she did not have here. Fallow was angry, his face contorted*

7

*and twisted into an evil mask. His hands were fists. His body was heaving up and down with ragged, uncontrolled breaths.*

*Most frighteningly of all, he was covered in blood.*

*It was splattered and splashed all over him. His face. Great bursts of it on his shirt, once white, the sleeves rolled up messily to the elbows. His fists were awash with it, and Laura saw also that there were tears in his own skin, contributing to the blood. Like he'd punched something hard enough to hurt himself.*

*Something that had splattered blood up over his forearms, with so much force that it had sprayed far wider and higher as he punched on.*

*"Amy," the Governor said, his voice raw and cracking, like he'd already shouted and screamed enough to damage his throat. "Amy, come here."*

*She only whimpered and sobbed, her pathetic hiding place belied as much by the noise as by the fact that he could easily see her. Her distress became louder as he walked closer, a deliberate stride that had inexorability written through it.*

*"Amy, I'm your father. Come over here right now," he said. His voice was almost strangely calm, though it snapped through the air like the tongue of a whip. Like cracking thunder. So heavy it was inescapable.*

*Laura didn't have to see the rest to know what would happen next.*

*She prayed she wouldn't have to.*

*And when the darkness from the edges of her vision flooded in to cover the rest, to cover the approaching form of the Governor, for once she was grateful that she didn't have to watch it to the end.*

Laura gasped for breath, unable to hold back the visceral response the vision brought upon her. She dropped the rabbit she was holding on the floor, her hands flying up to cover her mouth and hold back the bile that wanted to come up her throat. Hot tears stung her eyes.

She'd seen so many people die in her visions, in so many awful ways. She'd seen gunshots, stabbings, strangulations. Innocent people. Even her own father, wasting away in a cancer ward.

But of all the things she had seen, this was the second worst. And the worst thing had driven her so deep into the bottle, she'd spent years clawing her way back up and fighting not to drown.

A drink was the first thing on her mind, even now. It was an immediate, gut-deep response. A desperate need to drown out what she had seen and forget. To never have to think about it again.

But there were two things that stopped Laura from walking right to the nearest store and buying a bottle of the hardest liquor she could find.

The first was that it wouldn't work. She knew enough now to know that, no matter how far under she buried herself, eventually she would have to come back up. The memories, the nightmares, would still be there waiting for her when she surfaced. And this time, she might not just lose her relationship and her daughter and her home. She could lose the things she had left—her job, Nate, the hope of ever getting Lacey back.

The second was that the pounding headache in her temples told her something she couldn't ignore. The pain of the vision was directly linked to how soon it would occur. Something this bad—almost on the level of a migraine—meant that what she had seen was imminent.

She didn't have any time to waste.

Laura grabbed a bottle of painkillers from the counter and downed two of them without stopping to get a drink of water, snatching her car keys from beside them. She needed her head to be as clear as possible, but there was no way to get rid of the pain entirely. She had to shoulder it, to move, to go. She had to get there before it happened. She had to stop it.

Laura rushed out of her apartment without even picking up a jacket, the cold of the fall day hitting her as soon as she stepped outside. It didn't matter. She half-ran to her car, fumbling with the keys, her phone. By the time she slid into the driver's seat, she had the call ready to dial. She stuck it on the dashboard and let it ring as she started the engine.

"Come on," she muttered. He couldn't ignore her now. Not today. Not today of all days.

If what she had seen was true, Amy was about to die. Someone else, too, given the amount of blood on the Governor's shirt. And if she was wrong, this was going to cost her her career. She'd been told time and again not to go near him. And not just her career; if she was caught going up there and nothing happened, she would probably end up doing jail time.

It didn't matter. None of it mattered. Only saving Amy's life.

"Come on!" Laura said again, half-shouting it as she pulled out into the street, willing the dial tone to turn into something more concrete.

"Laura?"

Her breath caught in her throat at the sound of Nate's voice. "Nate, I need you," she said, her voice coming out strained and rushed, brimming with tension and urgency.

"What's going on?"

For a brief moment, Laura's heart clenched in her chest with gratitude. Even though things between her and Nate had not been amazing lately, he was there for her. When she said she needed him, he stepped up. She knew she could count on him.

That was part of the reason why she couldn't bear to even contemplate the possibility of losing him.

"I need you to meet me at Governor Fallow's place," she said, checking her mirrors desperately and making a dangerous turn in front of oncoming traffic, not willing to wait for it to pass by. A horn honked loudly at her as she sped away.

"What?" Nate's voice was instantly on edge. "Laura, you can't go there. You've been told—"

"*Please*, Nate!" Laura said, putting everything into it. "I don't have time to explain. I just need you to be there, now!"

"This is serious," Nate said. "Division Chief Rondelle—"

Whatever he could say to her, it wouldn't matter. Laura knew the situation. She knew what she was risking. She knew, too, what she was asking him to risk.

But it wasn't so much of a risk when you knew what you were walking into. Laura and Nate would be vindicated when it emerged they'd prevented serious violence. Nate didn't know that. Couldn't know that. And she didn't have time to go through all of this.

"This *is* serious!" Laura half-screamed at him, feeling her throat strain. "Nate, I need you to trust me. Please. If you've ever trusted me in your life, trust me now—I need you at the Governor's house!"

There was a short pause. Laura was too busy changing lanes, passing on the wrong side, dodging around the cars of the city as much as she could to feel that pause too much. But she registered it. For a moment, she thought he'd gone, that he'd just hung up and refused to help her.

"You're asking me to risk everything," he said. "And you won't even tell me why."

"Nate, please…!" Laura said. It was all she had. The minutes were ticking by so fast, she could swear that time had conspired against her to speed up. They were losing time. Losing the chance to save Amy. Laura hadn't seen a clock in her vision, had no idea of the exact time when it would be too late. But she knew that every minute took her a step closer, and she couldn't bear it.

"I'm already on my way," Nate said, making Laura wanted to cry with relief. "But, Laura, I can just as easily turn around and go back home. I'll meet you there, but you have to come clean."

"I'll tell you when we arrive," Laura agreed easily. Anything. Anything, so long as he helped her save Amy's life.

"About everything," Nate pressed. His voice faded out a second, as though he was turning away from the phone, looking around. He must have been in his car already. "I mean it, Laura. Everything you know and how you know it before anyone else does. You have to promise me you'll tell me."

"I promise," Laura said, gasping the words out, because it was all she could do. She couldn't say no. She needed backup. She needed him.

It didn't matter what she needed to say.

"I'll be there in five," Nate said, and ended the call.

# CHAPTER THREE

Laura's car screeched to a stop half on the sidewalk outside the Governor's mansion, her head whipping around in search of Nate. She saw him, his own car, coming in from the other direction and parking in front of her as she jerked her seatbelt away and sprang out. He lived closer. She'd hoped he might be here before her, but—

"What's going on?" Nate asked, approaching her at a light jog. His tall and muscular frame was already encased in his standard black suit, as though he'd been on his way to work when she called him. Laura half-ignored him. There was a constant whine in the back of her head, a noise that was getting louder by the moment, telling her what she needed to do. A scream. Amy was in danger. Amy couldn't wait.

"We have to go inside," Laura said, pushing right by him and walking toward the gate. It was set a little back from the road, blocked, but for now unguarded. She drew her gun out of the holster, feeling the familiar weight of it in her hands.

"Whoa! Laura!" Nate barked, rushing to keep up with her. "Slow down! What the hell is going on?"

"In there," she said, keeping single-minded focus on the gate. She pushed it open. It was unlocked. Whenever she'd been here, it was always unlocked. She guessed that with guards in place now, Fallow didn't feel the need to keep the gate shut—but where were they?

Every time she'd been past here before, there was one stationed outside, if not two. Where had they gone? Were they—

"Laura, stop!" Nate said, moving around in front of her and blocking her way. His arms were spread out to either side, like he was trying to catch her, and his face was flooded with panic. "What's happening? Why do you need your gun?"

"He's dangerous," Laura hissed, moving to go around him. They were only a short walk from the front door of the mansion. There was no one there, either. She couldn't stop to explain everything now, not yet. She'd promised him, but there was too much to unpack. And Amy needed them. She needed them *now*.

"I'm not disputing that, but a gun?" Nate said. "We don't know if he's armed. We can't just barge in here. He's the Governor. What's going on? Do you have a tip?"

"I heard something," Laura said, her attention snapping to the house. "A scream. Just now. Didn't you?"

"What? No," Nate said, turning his head to the side all the same, trying to catch any noise from the building.

Laura hadn't heard anything. Not just now. But it didn't matter. If they waited outside here for too long, there would be a scream. The scream of a little girl being hurt in ways that she couldn't come back from. Laura wasn't going to wait for that.

"I heard it," Laura said grimly. "And the bodyguards are gone. Something's happening, Nate."

Nate hesitated, his arms dropping by his side. It was all Laura needed. She pushed past him, rushing forward. She kept her gun low but in front of her, clasped in both hands, ready to pull it up and aim if she needed to. She heard Nate swear under his breath, then follow her, making it back to her side just as she reached the door.

"Dammit, Laura," he said, under his breath. "You better be right." He reached out before she had a chance to, yanking the door open.

They both held their breath. Laura couldn't hear anything from inside. There was no sign of anyone. No housekeeper. No guards. No maids. When she'd been here in the past, she hadn't been able to get far without running into someone. Now it was so deadly quiet, it made her hair stand on end.

She moved forward swiftly and silently. She didn't call out a warning. She knew she was breaking protocol, but it didn't even enter her mind. She didn't want Governor Fallow to have a chance to run, or to stop whatever he was doing so he could look innocent. She wanted to find him, about to commit the act. When Nate saw it too, there would be no way for the Governor to deny it.

They turned a corner into a wide, open sitting room, and Laura nearly dropped her gun at the sight of what it had been transformed into.

The comfortable, plush sofa was spattered with blood spray. There were gluts of it on the floor, and a fine mist across a glass coffee table in the center of the room. But the sight that really arrested Laura's attention was the woman at the center of all the blood.

Mrs. Fallow.

She was lying there, her face a bloody mess, her clothes torn and stained with so much blood it seemed impossible. One arm was flung out, the hand stretched across the once-beige carpet as if she were still trying to get away.

A noise caught Laura's attention and she swung the gun up in front of herself, her heart pounding in her ears. But in the next instant, she realized that the sound had come from Mrs. Fallow herself. A gurgle. A kind of rattling breath.

She wasn't yet dead.

"Nate," Laura said, her voice quiet but urgent, prompting her partner forward. He fell to his knees beside Mrs. Fallow, disregarding the blood, while Laura stood watch. She kept her gun up, her eyes darting in all directions. Where was he? Was he upstairs already, or still down here? Was he waiting for them?

"Mrs. Fallow," she heard Nate say, as she turned in a full circle to check all directions. "Can you hear me?"

"I tr…"

Laura's attention snapped back to Mrs. Fallow as she spoke. The words died in her throat. Even the movement of her mouth seemed to cause her so much pain.

"What is it?" Nate asked, leaning down closer.

"I tried," Mrs. Fallow said again, loud enough for Laura to hear, and then something else that Laura was too far away to catch.

Nate looked up, catching her cye. "She said she tried to stop him. Amy. He was going after Amy!"

"Upstairs," Laura shot back, immediately on the move again. She shouldn't have delayed. She shouldn't have waited. She knew what was going to happen. Why had she held back?

She took the stairs two at a time, a pounding in her ears that threatened to drown out everything else. Up there, as she got closer, she could hear him.

"Amy," he said, his voice half muffled by the distance. "Amy, come here."

She knew what would happen next. She knew.

Nate's feet were hammering up the stairs after her, and Laura was diving down the corridor, making for the room where she knew Amy slept. The room she had already barged into to rescue her once before. She had to do it again. She couldn't hesitate. Not even for her own safety.

The door was open. Laura hit the doorframe with her shoulder, pain radiating from that spot, but she still managed to get her gun up. She pointed it at his broad back, his hands still dripping red from what he had done to his wife. Amy was curled up on the bed, behind her toys.

"Freeze!" Laura yelled, a desperation in her voice. He had to stop. He had to stop now. "FBI!"

14

Nate was behind her—she felt him there. Amy in front. Laura's eyes darted between her shaking form and the Governor, watching him turn around slowly. She watched him register who she was. He was swaying slightly, his face red underneath the blood, with anger or with something else. Black eyes fixed on her, eyes so full of hate it made her shiver.

"You," he snarled.

"Get down on your knees and put your hands behind your head," Nate ordered him. Laura was glad. She was having a hard time finding her voice. "Do it! Now!"

The Governor stood there, his hands curled into fists, his wife's blood soaking through his shirt. He stared at her with so much hatred and fury that Laura felt herself shriveling inside, as though he had the power to reduce her to nothing. He wanted to kill her. He wanted to kill them all.

"You're not going to shoot me," he sneered. "You won't risk it. Not with her behind me."

Laura froze, her hands shaking on the gun. He was right. Amy was right there. She could get hurt, caught in the crossfire. Even if she wasn't, the sight of her father being shot to death right in front of her would be awful. The kind of thing you didn't recover from. And she'd already seen so many things that would take so much recovery.

Laura couldn't shoot.

Nate holstered his gun, a strangely violent movement that was more of a threat than holding it was. He flexed his muscles, bringing his arms up into a fighting stance.

"Get down!" Nate yelled again, and something got through the Governor's single-minded focus. He fixed on Nate then and his lips opened up into a snarl, and before Laura could think of what to do or how to react he was rushing forward.

He tackled Nate, slamming into him with full force. Laura could only stand there helplessly, trying to point her gun but not knowing exactly where, as they fell to the floor together and began to grapple. She could barely keep track of what was happening, who was on top, Nate's strength a good match for Fallow's rage and recklessness. They were both snarling, making animal noises of pain and effort as they fought to get a punch in, to get the other one subdued. Laura's heart pounded painfully in her chest, her hands shaking. If the Governor got his hands on Nate's gun…

Could this be the moment he lost his life? The moment the aura of death she'd seen hanging over him came true?

But Nate was strong, so strong, and he hadn't already beaten anyone to death. He was fresh in the fight. He grappled the Governor, got himself arranged a different way on the floor, and even as the Governor fought back Laura saw what he'd done. How he'd put the Governor on his knees. Put himself to the side. How he'd given her what she needed.

"Stop!" Laura yelled, and the shouted word gave her enough of Governor Fallow's attention for him to notice.

To notice the fact that she had her gun pointed right at his head, and there was no one behind him now, not at this angle. Nate and Amy were both safely out of line. If she pulled the trigger, only he would die.

"Stop," Laura said, the words coming out breathy and strained. "I have a clean shot."

Governor Fallow stared at her with so much hate, it felt like he was trying to kill her with a stare.

But her words did the job. He froze on his knees, lifting his hands loosely out to the sides like that was a compromise, instead of putting them all the way in the air. He didn't take his eyes off Laura.

Nate rolled to his own knees behind Fallow, pulled his handcuffs off his belt, grabbed Fallow's hands, forced them behind his back. Fallow didn't take his eyes away from Laura as Nate cuffed him. He didn't take his eyes off her as Nate read him his rights, told him he was under arrest for murder. And if he carried on watching her when she stepped into the room at last, Laura no longer saw.

Because she was holstering her gun, rushing over to the bed, and taking Amy in her arms—holding the crying little girl and breathing hard in relief, clasping her so tightly, because she knew now she was safe.

# CHAPTER FOUR

Laura got up at the sound of the knock at the dining room door. It was the only place she had been able to think of to take Amy. The front of the house was impossible, because she would have to go past her mother—and out there, Laura knew from experience, the press would gather quickly. The back of the house, the open land of the backyard, was not an option because the helicopters would soon be flying over.

The only place Laura could keep her safe, and away from the press, and stop her from seeing more than she needed to, was the dining room. So she'd hidden the two of them away in there, leaving everything else to Nate.

"Don't worry, sweetie," she told Amy, when the little girl grasped tight hold of her hand to try to stop her from walking away. "I'll just see who it is, and what they want. No one's going to hurt you."

She crossed to the door and opened it, holding it only a crack to her shoulder so that Amy couldn't see out. Nate was there, but behind him the house was already a hive of activity. Cops were swarming the place, dodging white-suited forensics experts who were already analyzing the scene. A pair of EMTs were standing near the door, which made Laura's eyes dart toward the door of the lounge. It was open, and she could see law enforcement going in and out—but not the EMTs. They were chatting with a cop as though they had all the time in the world.

"Mrs. Fallow?" Laura asked softly, trying to pitch her voice so that it wouldn't carry through to Amy.

Nate only shook his head.

Laura's voice caught in her throat. They had saved Amy's life, but what now? Her father was a violent killer. Her mother was dead. Functionally, she was an orphan. Both of her parents taken away from her in the space of one traumatic morning. That meant she would need somewhere to go. She couldn't stay here alone.

Laura's hand flew to her chest, covering her aching heart as she considered the possibilities. If there was another relative, Amy could be taken in. But there was no way of knowing how that relative would treat her. They might be just as bad as the governor was, or even worse. They might blame the girl for what had happened here.

And the other option was for her to be taken in by strangers, put into the foster care system and hopefully adopted. That, too, had its pitfalls. Even though there was so much time and attention taken to avoid any harm coming to children within the care system, it happened. Laura knew it happened. She had been an agent for too long to have any misconceptions about that.

And even if Amy found a loving home with a family who supported her and looked after her, the trauma of what had happened here today, the treatment she had endured at the hands of her father, the way she had been rescued once and then abandoned again... It would be a whole lifetime of psychological damage. Amy would need therapy, specialist care, love, and attention to get through this. Would she get that in the care system? Would she get that from the adoption of a relative? Would she ever find her way to being a normal child, a balanced adult?

At that moment, Laura would have given anything to have a vision of Amy as a young adult, safe and happy and well. But her visions didn't work like that. They didn't come to reassure her, or even to scare her. They came when they came, following their own rules, and she had no way to trigger them if they did not want to come. She could touch Amy, touch her belongings, try to take deep breaths and meditate, use all of her potential triggers—but in the end it did not necessarily mean anything. The vision might not come, and if it did, she might only see some inconsequential thing that really told her nothing of what was happening in Amy's future.

"Rondelle is asking for you," Nate said, breaking Laura's spiraling thoughts. She was grateful for the interruption, even though it did not make her doubts any less real.

"Will you stay with Amy?" Laura asked. "I can't leave her on her own."

"That's why I'm here," Nate said, flashing her what was probably supposed to have been a reassuring smile. Instead, it only showed how strained, tense, and anxious he was himself.

Laura allowed him into the room, opening the door wide enough to let him through but no wider, and then closed it so that she could turn to Amy. She squatted down in front of the little girl, who was sitting propped up on one of the dining room chairs, hugging her rabbit tightly to her chest. Laura found herself wishing she had brought the one from home, the gift she had been thinking of giving her. It might have been some kind of comfort right now.

"Amy," she said, keeping her voice gentle and soft. "I have to go and talk to someone outside. But Nate is here, and he will look after you. Do you remember Nate?"

Amy nodded silently, her eyes wide in her tear-streaked face. She looked at Nate with a combination of awe and wonder, no doubt because of how huge he was. She must have remembered how he had pulled her out of what should have been her coffin, buried under the house of her kidnapper back when this had all begun. How they had seen her at the hospital, making sure she was alright. Still, she was nowhere near as comfortable with him as she was with Laura. Or even Agent Jones, who had been able to sit with her the last time Laura had pulled her out of this house.

"I'm going to look after you while Laura is outside," he said. "But don't worry, she'll be right back in."

Amy nodded silently again, which both of them took to be a sign of agreement. She looked back at her rabbit, using her small hands to push back the fur on his forehead as if tidying it. Laura straightened, standing up, and nodded at Nate. He nodded back, telling her it was all right to leave.

Every bone in her body wanted her to stay, but Laura walked to the door again with reluctance. If Rondelle wanted to speak to her, she had to comply. She couldn't have him coming into the room where Amy was sitting, upsetting her. She needed quiet and stability right now, the attention of only the people she knew she could trust. Laura trusted Nate, too, but no one else here.

Even if leaving Amy felt like a betrayal, she had to do it. She told herself it wasn't as big a deal as she was making it out to be. She turned for one last look as she put her hand on the door handle, taking a deep breath. Amy would be fine without her.

She just had to keep telling herself that.

*** 

Laura slipped outside, into the hubbub of the house. So much of it was shielded by the door of the dining room, but out here, it was chaos. Laura found herself ducked into a side room by a group of agents who gestured her out of the way, so they could clear a path. Laura was opening her mouth to ask what was going on when the answer appeared before her: the Governor, handcuffed and closely guarded by a group of agents and local law enforcement, who were leading him down the hall and out of the house.

He caught sight of Laura and snarled again, a kind of morbid smirk lifting the corner of his mouth. He had recovered enough of himself, it seemed, to not let it last for long. Instead of fixating on her like he had before, he let her know she'd been seen and then looked away, plastering on a more respectable expression as they approached the door.

Outside, Laura heard a scrambling, the sound of several voices reacting to the Governor's appearance. The tell-tale clattering of camera lenses opening and shutting. When the convoy had passed her by she stepped back out into the hall, looking down through the open front doors to watch him passing. The press was gathered outside, reporters and cameramen yelling out questions at the Governor, trying to get his attention for a good shot. Some of his media training seemed to kick in, making him lift his head and look in the direction of the camera when they shouted his name.

Laura realized that the live camera feed would show her framed in the doorway and stepped aside, self-consciously ducking back into the kitchen. Where was Rondelle? In here? Out there? She would have to wait for the media circus to clear a little before she went out there. She hated being caught on camera. The scrutiny that came with it. Especially with her custody case coming up, she didn't want to make waves of any kind.

Laura looked toward the hall again, hearing the sound of footsteps. When a familiar figure rushed past, she lunged for the doorway after him, leaning out to catch his attention. "Chief Rondelle?"

"Ah, Laura," he said, turning on his heel. The chief, a small and wiry man with plenty of gray hair in amongst the dark strands, beckoned her closer. "I was looking for you."

"Nate told me," Laura replied. "Do you need me to debrief?"

"Not yet." Rondelle paused, his mouth moving slightly as if trying to dislodge the taste of what he had to say next. "The social workers are here."

Laura looked at him without understanding for a moment, before it clicked in. "Oh."

"Yes." Rondelle clasped both hands in front of him. "I know you've taken on a kind of personal responsibility for this young girl, Laura, but we have to follow the correct protocol. She's going to have to be taken away."

"Until when?" Laura asked, her heart in her mouth. Her words arrested Rondelle's movement—he looked as though he wanted to walk away.

"Well, at this stage that isn't clear," Rondelle said. His tone was apologetic, but still direct. He looked her in the eye, making sure she was understanding every word. "I don't believe they have yet been able to figure out the next of kin. Once they do, someone will contact that person and ask them to care for her, or find an alternative."

"What if that person refuses?" Laura asked. A dozen questions seemed suddenly ready to spring out of her. "What if no one can be found to take her in?"

Rondelle raised a hand to ward her off, as if sensing that this was only the tip of the iceberg. "I can't answer those questions, Laura. First things first. We need to hand her over to the social worker and then let them handle the case. They'll do all their due diligence and update us when they can."

"I'll take her in," Laura said, desperately. "I can do it. I know how to care for a little girl. I can take her home, at least until they find her something permanent."

"You know you can't," Rondelle said. His tone was not unkind, but it was firm. "That would be a conflict of interest, and illegal. We need to do this by the book, Laura. No loopholes. No way for him to get his hands back on her later. We weren't thorough enough last time. This time, we have to be. The media are watching. Even if I wanted to let you, you know I can't."

Laura set her jaw. She wanted very badly to cry, but she knew what was expected of her. What was needed of her. She had to be an FBI agent now, not a mother. Not a woman who cared about a child and wanted to keep her safe. She had to follow the rules.

That didn't make it any easier to do, but at least she could put on a show.

She squared her shoulders. "Where's the social worker?" she asked.

Rondelle nodded, acknowledging the fact that she was pulling it together. "Just outside. I'll bring her in now."

# CHAPTER FIVE

Laura turned her back to the door for a long moment, trying to breathe. When she turned back, Rondelle was reentering the house with an older woman at his side. She was short and dumpy, with the kind of haircut that looked as though it had been cut at home with some kind of bowl as a guideline. Her frumpy, old and faded floral dress did not inspire Laura's imagination, either.

"Is she just ahead, through here?" the woman asked, gesturing toward the dining room. There was an authority in her voice that set Laura on edge. But there was also a gentle tone that offered some reassurance. Whatever Laura thought of her, it didn't matter. This was what had to be done. It was the only way for Amy to move toward security and stability in the long run, even if Laura didn't want to let her go now.

Laura led the way back inside, keeping her movements quiet and calm as she opened the door. Nate and Amy both looked up—they were sitting on the floor, Nate evidently engaged in some kind of game with the rabbit. Amy, though, was instantly on guard, cowering back at the sight of the stranger.

"Amy," Laura said, trying to look and sound as though she really believed what she was saying. "This lady here is someone who is going to help you."

"Hello, dear," the social worker said, not unkindly. Laura forced herself to stay still, near the door, when the woman took a step forward.

"I have to go again?" Amy said, looking not at anyone else but Laura.

Laura could feel the hot tears building behind her eyes and fought to push them down. "I'm afraid so, sweetie. You need to be safe."

"Like last time?" Amy asked, and her voice was so small and so scared that Laura's dam almost broke.

"Not like last time," she promised fiercely. "You're going to be safe now. I mean it."

She stopped short of saying "I promise." She couldn't.

Things had gone from bad to worse for poor Amy from the moment they met. Back then, Laura had thought being kidnapped was the worst

22

thing that would ever happen to the child. Her father's violence had topped that. And now this—the murder of one parent by another.

Laura would have liked to say that she couldn't imagine it getting any worse, but she had seen enough in her career. It had been nearly a decade since she first picked up the badge. Laura knew just how things might get worse for a young, vulnerable girl like Amy. She didn't want to think about it.

"All right, Amy," the social worker said. "Do you want to bring your bunny with you?"

Amy nodded solemnly. She got up on her own, without having to be told. The social worker held out a hand to her, but Amy hugged the rabbit tighter instead. Taking it in her stride, the social worker gestured for Amy to come closer, and then guided her with a hand on the back of her shoulder.

Talking quietly to her all the while, the social worker led Amy out of the room. Rondelle gave Laura and then Nate a meaningful glance, one that Laura was unable to interpret. She was struggling too hard to control her emotions, to breathe, to not cry while Amy could still turn back and see her.

The door closed behind both of them, and she gulped in a mouthful of air, covering her hand with her mouth as if to stop it from spilling out again.

"Are you all right?" Nate asked, his voice low. "I mean, I know you're not."

Laura shook her head wordlessly, sinking down into one of the dining chairs. She took a long moment, carefully laying her hand down flat on the surface of the table and staring at it. Trying to think of absolutely nothing at all. That was the only way she was going to get through this. Nothing at all.

Nate sat down beside her, waiting. She knew he wouldn't wait forever. At last, he cleared his throat slightly, watching her. "How did you know something was going to go down tonight?" he asked.

"I didn't," Laura said, her voice barely more than a hoarse whisper.

Nate gave a disappointed groan. "Laura, you promised me. If I came to help you, you would tell me everything. You have to answer me."

Laura's mouthed moved soundlessly for a moment. He was right. She had promised. But that was in the heat of the moment. She had been desperate. And yes, she would promise it a thousand times over in order to save Amy's life.

But Amy's life had been saved.

And now?

"I've thought something awful was going to happen every single day since we found out she was sent back here," she said, which was at least the truth. "I knew it in my bones. You must have seen it, too. There was no way she was going to be safe here."

"That's not the point," Nate said. He spread his big hand across the table, his dark skin matching the wood. "Look, Laura, we've been going around in circles for too long. I'm not going to play this game anymore. You need to tell me what's up with you. How you know the things you do."

Laura bit her lip, staying silent. What was she going to say? That it was just luck? That it was all a coincidence? That she had a feeling? Maybe make something up, say Amy had somehow been in contact with her? That she'd been driving by the place every day and knew something was up when she saw the guards weren't there?

That could have worked, if Nate hadn't seen her pull up just a moment before he did.

"Laura, I've seen too much," Nate said, tapping his fingers lightly on the table to underline his point. "Not just today. Other cases. You always know where to be to stop things from happening. And it's gotten beyond a point where you can convince me that it's just luck. If you keep lying to me, hiding this from me, I just don't know how I'm going to be able to trust you."

Laura turned her head, looking at him. She had expected that he might be looking at her with anger, cold and heavy, or disappointment. But what she saw cracked her heart open instead. His face was open, raw. He wanted her trust. He was begging her to let him in. To stop shutting him out. This wasn't so much an intervention as a last desperate plea.

In that moment, she wanted so badly to tell him. To have everything off her shoulders at last. It would be such a weight to unload. To have someone else know, someone else whom she could talk to.

If it would work out that way.

Because it might not. He might think she was crazy. Worse, he might believe her but start avoiding her as much as possible, wanting to get away from her. Her ability—she wouldn't call it a gift—might be unnerving. Knowing that someone might see your future every time you touched them.

24

And if she told him about the visions, she would have to tell him all of it. About the shadow of death she saw hanging over him whenever they touched. She would have to give him a death sentence.

She'd seen what that could do to a man. Her father, being told his cancer was inoperable, that the end was coming. Convicts on death row that she'd helped put there. The way it could destroy someone. She couldn't even give him answers to all of the questions he would want to ask—how, why, when, where.

Laura swallowed hard. This was a pivotal moment—she could feel it in the air. She could take the leap now. Trust in Nate. Trust in his strength, his fairness, the way he had always treated her with respect. He was a good man. She could take the decision to trust in that, and tell him everything, believing that he wouldn't shut her out. That he would become the rock she needed, not the hard place.

Or she could keep quiet, and shut him out instead before he had the chance to do it back, and lose him anyway.

Put like that, the choice didn't seem like much of a choice at all.

Laura looked at him, trying to preserve this moment in her mind. The last moment before he knew. The last moment before it came undone, maybe.

"Nate," she started, and he shifted his weight toward her, making her pause. It was only a split second, and she didn't react in time. He moved his hand toward her, and she should have pulled away, shouldn't have let him touch her. But he did. His hand covered her wrist, a gesture of support and comfort.

But it wasn't support and comfort that she drew from it. It was terror—sheer and unbridled. The specter of death that hung over him clouded her view, turning the whole room to black smoke immediately. When she tried to breathe, she felt the aura of darkness flooding into her lungs, filling her, choking her. It was stronger than ever, so thick she could barely see him looking back at her, barely fight her way out of it.

Laura yanked her hand away and stood up, stumbling backwards.

"Laura?" Nate said.

The shadow of death had dissipated as soon as they lost physical contact, but it didn't matter. She had felt it. Breathed it in. Absorbed it and all of the little ways in which it meant she was losing him.

He was dying. She couldn't tell him that. She couldn't make him face it, the same way that she had to. Her nerve was gone. The hope she'd clung to a moment ago was lost, leaving only fear behind.

"I've told you everything I can," she said, fighting for control of her breathing, to look as though nothing was wrong. Her head was pounding still from the earlier vision, the adrenaline of getting here, the heartache of watching Amy go. She couldn't do this. Couldn't look him in the eye.

Nate didn't say anything. He didn't need to. She could feel his disappointment radiating from him in waves. He rapped his knuckles lightly on the table once, as if closing the subject, and stood up. He didn't look back at her as he walked away.

Laura watched his broad back moving down the hall, leaving her behind, and for a moment she was the most alone she had ever been in her life.

But there was still a faint sliver of hope. She was going to meet someone tonight, and maybe, just maybe, after this, she wouldn't be alone.

She just had to keep hold of that thought, because at the moment, it felt far too slim a hope to be real.

# CHAPTER SIX

Jade Patrickson picked up her cell phone from the table, scrolling through the list of her contacts to her sister. Ruby's familiar and smiling face beamed out from the screen as the connection began to ring, and Jade left it on the dresser in front of her while she studied her face in the mirror.

The long, auburn hair that she ran her hands over was a trait she shared with her sibling. Still, Jade liked to think she could put her own individual spin on things. When they were kids, they had always copied each other—the same haircut, the same clothes off the rack, the same colors of makeup. Now that she was twenty-five, Jade felt the impulse to be the same less and less. No, she wanted to be different. She was thinking about cutting the hair, getting a cute bob or even a pixie.

She just wasn't going to get it done without talking to her sister first.

She sighed as the call rang out. "Ruby, what are you even doing?" she groaned out loud. Was she out on another date? That girl was insatiable. No, surely not after a long day at work. Jade knew Ruby had been getting tired during the week, struggling to keep up with the workload. She wouldn't be out on a date now.

Jade frowned at herself in the mirror, pulling her hair up into her hands and then holding it behind her head, trying to see how it would look shorter. She needed another pair of hands—another pair of eyes. Her sister's eyes.

Jade slumped, pouting at her own reflection. It was no use. She needed Ruby.

She dialed the number again, listening to it ringing out. Once again, no answer. Ruby's cheerful voice told her to leave a message, but Jade ended the call instead. There was no point leaving a message. As soon as Ruby saw the missed call, she'd call back right away. That was their rule.

But what if Ruby didn't see it until the morning? Jade twisted her mouth, thinking. She was probably asleep if she wasn't answering the call. She played with her hair absentmindedly. It wasn't far from here to Ruby's house—maybe she could drive over. But then if she was already asleep, she wouldn't let Jade in when she knocked.

Jade sighed. She was just going to have to wait until the morning, as annoying as it was. She got up from her vanity table and made for the wardrobe, thinking about getting changed and ready for bed herself. Might as well get to sleep early. Especially if she was going to be up late tomorrow night talking makeovers with her sister.

Jade crossed the room and then stopped, frowning. From here, she could see the door to the bathroom, and the window beyond it. It was open. Had she left it open? She didn't normally. It wasn't safe. Someone might see it as an open invitation to break in.

Jade walked the short distance across the hall to the window, still frowning. She was trying to rack her brains, to remember. When had she last opened it? After her shower in the morning? She didn't remember. It was cold at this time of year. She didn't usually open it unless she absolutely needed to, because it drove her heating bill up, and she was trying to save money.

It couldn't have been earlier than that. She'd have noticed. She must have left it open all day.

She reached out to close it, but froze when she heard a noise in the hall. Jade's head whipped round, seeking out the source of the sound. There was no one in the house but her. Or at least, there shouldn't have been. Her roommate was out of town, wasn't due back until late. She, too, would have called if she was getting back early.

A noise in the hall. An open window. Jade was starting to put together a picture, and it was one that made her heart race.

Was there someone else in the house?

She held her breath, listening, still stretched out with her hand on the window latch. She could only see such a small sliver of the hallway from here. Everything beyond that was a mystery.

She heard a creak, and she knew.

Someone was here.

Panic flashed through her mind, and the absolute certainty that it wouldn't be good. If someone had broken in, at the very least they wanted to steal from her. Maybe more. She had to get out—right now. And if someone had come in through the window...

Jade wrapped her hands around the windowsill, letting out a small whimper of fear as she grabbed on and pulled herself up as best as she could. There was nothing beyond this window—just the brick wall of the building next door, which had no windows, above an alley—but she was only one floor up, and there was a garbage can below her that she could land on. She saw all this with her head out the window, her feet scrabbling for purchase on the bathroom wall, and then glanced back—

And she saw him, framed in the bathroom doorway.

He looked like… like someone off the street. Someone normal. It was absurd, but in that moment she thought about how he didn't look like a criminal. Nothing about him looked dangerous except for the fact that he was not supposed to be in her house—

And the knife that flashed cold steel under the bathroom light.

Jade felt the breath being sucked from her body as she realized his intent was to harm her, like she'd been punched in the gut. Her feet slipped on the smooth wall as she kicked and pushed, trying to pull herself up through the window with the strength of her arms alone. She could do it, but she was out of control—going too fast. She grabbed at the windowsill for support, gasping in terror, trying to steady herself. The ground below suddenly looked further away—too far to tumble out of the window uncontrolled, to fall right on her head.

And then the window and the ground and all of it was gone, and Jade registered too late his arm around her waist pulling her back, and the bathroom floor hit her too hard for her to scream out or make a sound. She could only look up as he towered over her, going to his knees, raising the knife in his hand.

Jade's whole body was paralyzed, stiff with fear and numb with the pain of hitting the tile floor so hard, nothing responding when she tried desperately to move out of his reach. He was trapping her, straddling her legs, and she managed to put up one of her hands toward him—

And the knife flashed down, plunging into her stomach.

Jade's senses registered the ripping of cloth, her shirt giving way beneath the blade, and she stupidly thought about work and how pissed they would be that she had ruined a uniform. At the same time, she managed to draw a breath, and strangely there was no pain. "No," she managed to say, the beginning of something else, the start of a plea for her life that he would have to listen to.

But the knife ripped its way back out of her stomach, and then the pain flooded in, and then the knife came down again and even her raised hand was not enough to stop it hitting her again.

And again.

And again.

And when Jade tried to breathe there was nothing in her chest that would inflate, only darkness waiting for her, crowding the edges of her vision, sending her down and away into the sleep she had been planning for—but a more permanent and deeper one than she had imagined.

# CHAPTER SEVEN

Laura walked into the crowded bar, almost immediately assaulted by the cacophony of noise in the warm, dimly lit space. The music and the conversation conspired to make her pause, trying to adjust. She hated coming here. She'd hated it last time she was here, with its cheap tiki decorations and the crowd of young parties who didn't seem like her people at all.

But this was where she had met VirginiaMan383—the mysterious poster on a message board who had claimed to be psychic. He had been intriguing enough for her to arrange to meet with him in person, part of her desperate search for someone like her. Someone who would understand. Who would maybe be able to answer some of the questions that had been plaguing her for the last thirty-three years.

She walked right up to the bar, taking a deep breath to steady herself. This was the last place she wanted to be, but it was the place he'd chosen. The smiling faces all around her, the cheap laughter and the easy drinking, it all sickened her. All she could think of was Amy's little body, the way she had shaken with sobs. The way Mrs. Fallow had looked, lying there beaten to death's door. The smell of the blood was still in her nose.

The barman noticed her and turned her way, leaning his hands on the counter and raising an eyebrow at her. It was too loud for him to talk to her properly, to ask her what she wanted.

"Lemonade?" she shouted. He nodded and turned away to get the drink, leaving Laura staring at the space he had just vacated. The bottles of liquor on display behind him.

Laura couldn't tear her eyes away from them. She didn't want a lemonade. It wasn't exactly the right season for a cold drink, if you weren't going to be getting a buzz from it. It was just something to order. The bottles, their shapes and colors, their elaborate brand logos and markings, called to her like old friends. Each of them held their own temptation. Each of them could have been the one to break her. She wet her lips, finding her mouth gone dry.

But she couldn't do it. She couldn't break her sobriety now. She'd been doing so well for so long, and now—now it was only a few days before Lacey's custody hearing. She had to turn up there still sober, still on the wagon. She had to show up for her daughter. It was the only way she was going to get her back.

Laura took the unnecessary lemonade from the bartender and left him a pile of change in return, counted out correctly. She retreated in search of a table, grimacing at the fact that all of them seemed to be occupied.

Until her eyes landed on one of them, and she realized that the man sitting at it was Nolan Perry—alias VirginiaMan383—also known as the man she was here to meet.

His face brightened as soon as they made eye contact, and he waved her over. He even stood up to beckon her, as though she hadn't seen him well enough already. She took a breath. She wasn't sure that this was going to be any fun.

Last time they'd met, Nolan had been annoyingly flirtatious, and absolutely insistent that she learn the "truth" about him, whatever that meant. As Laura crossed the crowded dancefloor toward him, trying not to let anyone jostle her lemonade out of her hand, she wondered if she'd made a mistake by agreeing to meet him again. She'd already decided for herself that there was nothing to his claims of being psychic. He was just a fake like the rest of them, or maybe an idiot.

But he'd been so insistent, sending her message after message. Finally, Laura had caved and agreed to meet him. Today had been a low point. Even though she'd saved Amy, she'd disappointed Nate so much, maybe ruined their relationship for good. She'd failed to save Mrs. Fallow. And Amy was still far from safe. What good was the ability to save people, if you didn't end up being able to save the people you really cared about from getting hurt in the end?

She could have cancelled, given everything that had happened. But then what? Sit at home alone? Wallow in the darkness?

No. She'd thought it would be better to go somewhere, meet someone, surround herself with life.

Now, she was hoping that she wasn't going to regret it, but the way he was looking at her made her unsure.

He was looking at her with this gleam in his eyes, like they were on a date and he was onto a sure thing.

He pushed back his red hair, which was already flawlessly in place, as she approached. "Laura," he said, flashing her a smile full of white teeth. "You should have told me you were here. I would have picked up your drink for you."

"Well," Laura said, sitting down opposite him in a chair that backed onto the dance floor. She didn't want to give him hope, but she didn't want to be rude either. "Maybe if I get another drink later, you can get that one."

Actually, even as she said it, she knew it wasn't going to happen. Not that she wouldn't stay for another drink—that much was somewhat possible, though only remotely. She wouldn't ever let him order her a drink. Because if he did, she wouldn't put it past him to be the kind of guy who would order it with a shot of vodka just to liven up the night.

"That sounds great." Nolan beamed, immediately taking her words more to heart than she had intended. Laura suppressed an internal groan. Nolan was dressed much the same as last time, in a preppy blazer with the sleeves rolled up in the warmth of the bar, a plain V-necked top underneath. But his manner was different. He wasn't so nonchalant. Like he was done trying to impress her by being cool and now wanted to convince her to stay instead. "I'm so glad you decided to meet me. It's really important that you get to know the truth about me. After last time…"

Laura held up a hand, making his voice trail off. This wasn't the point of her coming here. She was sure he had a lot to say to her—he seemed like the kind of guy who always had a lot to say. But she was here to talk to him, and she wanted him to listen.

"Look," she said. "I have something to say first. I know you're not a psychic."

Nolan's forehead creased slightly, the beginning of a frown, and he opened his mouth—but she held up her hand again to stop him. Miraculously, he obeyed, staying quiet.

"Or maybe you think you are, and I accept that," Laura continued, mercilessly. She needed to do this. She needed to say it. It was like a trial run. A test. She hadn't been able to say this to Nate. But here, with this stranger, in this crowded and noisy club where she could pretend he had heard her wrong—here, maybe she could do it. She could be brave enough. "But you aren't a psychic. And I know that, because I am."

A smile curved Nolan's lips. An amused grin. Like he thought this was all part of some kind of trick, some joke that she was leading up to. Maybe even a performance. He just wanted to see where it was going, to get in on the punchline. "Prove it, then," he said, toying with his glass on the table. Like this was all just a big flirtation, a lead-up to her asking him back to her place or something equally stupid.

"I don't need to prove it," Laura said impatiently. "Besides, it doesn't work like that. If you had the visions too, you'd know already. I see things, Nolan. They come at random, and I can't control them, and sometimes they don't have any real consequences. But sometimes I see really serious things from the future, like the fact that someone is going to die. I see their deaths."

That crease had appeared in the middle of Nolan's forehead again. He was puzzled, waiting for the other shoe to drop. "What do you mean, you see their deaths?" he asked, his voice uncertain.

"It's like I'm there," Laura said. She gestured wide, her lemonade all but forgotten on the table. Now that she could say it, it was spilling out of her like it had all just been waiting to come out. "I see everything. I watch them as they die. Victims, usually. That's why I'm in law enforcement. I use my visions to catch serial killers, to stop them so they can't hurt anyone else."

Nolan stared at her for a moment, unblinking. She met his gaze levelly in return. "You think you're able to see dead people?" he said, at length. His tone had changed. From playful to straight. From light to somehow harsher.

"I don't think it," she said. "I know it. If I touched you, there's a chance I could see your death. I would know how you were going to die, and when. I would be right there watching it. But sometimes I don't see anything at all. Sometimes I just see something stupid, like the fact that you might trip on your way to the bar or walk into something carrying a drink. But mostly, because I look for it, I see death. I've seen hundreds of people die. Some of them over and over again. Some of them, I managed to save."

Nolan shook his head at her. "That's not funny," he said, swigging his drink down and finishing the glass.

"I'm not laughing," Laura told him, keeping her steely eyes on his. "I see people die. That's my power. I see the future."

There was what felt like a long pause. He stared at her, like he was trying to work out whether this was all a joke. But then, apparently deciding that it wasn't, Nolan's face twisted into a disbelieving sneer. "I don't know what you think your game is, but it isn't working," he said. "You're crazy. I don't have to sit here and listen to this."

"You contacted me because I said I was psychic," Laura pointed out.

"Yeah, but not for real," Nolan said, getting up. "You know what? You could have just said you weren't interested. This is a waste of my time." He pushed his way around the table and walked away angrily, until he was lost in the crowd of people between Laura and the door.

Laura wet her lips, hesitating. She could see his glass on the table. It was empty. That was probably a good thing, or she might have reached out to finish it off for him.

He hadn't believed a word she'd said. She was right all along. He was just using the forum as a place to pick up women who were simple-minded enough to giggle and sigh when he claimed to be a psychic. He probably thought they were all the same—just indulging in fantasies, pretending. Claiming that they dreamed something once that came true, or that they knew when someone was about to say their name. The kind of thing that could happen to anyone.

He hadn't been expecting someone who really believed it.

Laura took a gulp of her lemonade, trying to pretend to herself that it was something stronger. When she'd refused to tell Nate about her abilities, he had walked away and left her.

When she told Nolan everything, he had walked away and left her.

She was damned if she did. Damned if she didn't. And the only thing she knew for sure was that she was still absolutely alone, because there was never going to be anyone she could talk to about this without looking like a freak who needed medication.

And no one she could keep this secret from who wouldn't, sooner or later, get suspicious and ask for the truth.

Laura put her lemonade down on the table and stood, sweeping out of the club. It was the only way she could be sure that she wasn't going to get drunk.

Not that leaving guaranteed it either.

# CHAPTER EIGHT

Laura sat up in bed, rubbing a hand over her eyes. It was useless. No matter how much she tossed and turned, she couldn't sleep.

It had been a long day. A lot had happened. Amy and her father, the social worker, Nate, Nolan. She should have been exhausted. Add a vision on top of that, and the sensation of Nate's shadow of death, and Laura should have been sleeping like a baby.

Instead she was wired, unable to sit still. Sleep wasn't going to come to her when she was like this. She could already feel it.

She got up, pacing restlessly through into the kitchen. She knew why she was going in there, even though she told herself that wasn't it.

It was standing on the counter. Alone, incongruous. Everything else—not that she had much—was neatly put away. But this bottle was standing there, alone and proud, as if it had appeared there of its own free will.

Of course, it hadn't. It was there because she had bought it on the way home from the club. It had been easy enough to pop into a late-night liquor store, pick out this small bottle, and carry it all the way home. She'd set it on the counter, and then the doubts had crept in.

She hadn't been able to bring herself to open it. That was a good sign, really. It mean that her willpower was getting stronger. That the urge to stay sober was starting to be stronger than the urge to drink. That was good.

But it didn't mean the question was solved. After all, the bottle was still sitting here on the counter. She hadn't poured it away.

She shouldn't have bought it in the first place. And, having bought it, she ought to have poured it all down the sink and thrown the bottle in the trash outside where she couldn't even smell it.

But she hadn't.

And that was another kind of sign.

Laura contemplated it, the amber liquid inside. It would be so easy. All she had to do was reach out and take it, and then unscrew the top. She didn't need a glass. She could drink it right from the bottle. Measure out a shot with her own mouth. Maybe two shots. Maybe three.

Laura was leaning on the counter, her weight resting on her folded arms. She straightened up slightly, freeing one of her arms from the weight. That meant she could reach for it. She stretched out her fingers, feeling them make contact with the cool glass—

Her phone rang from the bedroom where she had left it, and Laura jumped guiltily, startled as if she had been caught by someone watching her. She snatched her fingers away from the bottle like they were burned, and raced into the bedroom to grab the phone before it stopped ringing.

"Hello?"

"Agent Frost," came the cool tones of Division Chief Rondelle. By this point, Laura was unsure if the man ever slept. "Sorry to call so late, but it's an emergency. We have a case, and we need you to go now. I know things have been hard for you today, but I'm hoping you can handle it. It's a bit of a complex one, according to what I'm hearing from the men on the ground."

Laura caught her breath, closing her eyes for a moment. Did she have enough time before the custody hearing at the end of the week?

What was she going to do otherwise? Sit here, stare at this bottle, and try to think of reasons not to drink it while remembering every failure she'd been the architect of these past few months?

"Right. I'll head in now," she said, a snap decision. Anything to stop her from picking up that bottle.

"Be quick," Rondelle warned. "And bring your bags with you. You'll need to head straight from here to the airport. I managed to get you both on a red-eye—and it's not going to wait."

"Yes, sir," Laura said, seeing the need for haste rather than continuing the conversation. She ended the call and spun to pick up her travel bags, already packed and ready to go as she tried to keep them. All she had to do was add a few daily necessities, things she had been using at home, and it was done.

*Both*, Rondelle had said. That meant Laura wasn't going alone. Which, in turn, meant that it was almost certainly Nate going with her. He must not have had time to request a new partner. Even if he did, it might take a couple of weeks to go through.

She was going to have to face him, and she had no idea how he was going to react. Would he just say right to Rondelle's face that he didn't want to work with Laura, and request they bring in someone else? Would he ignore her? Cut her off?

He was a professional. Laura knew that. She hoped he would remain true to form, that he would be able to work with her. But how fun it would be to work alongside him when they were at odds, she had no idea.

She grabbed her jacket from the peg by the door and shrugged it on, preparing to leave. There was one thing she knew. It didn't look as though she was going to get much sleep tonight, after all.

*** 

Laura stepped into Division Chief Rondelle's office hesitantly, looking up to see that she wasn't the first one to arrive. Nate was already standing there, leaning against the wall on the other side of the room. His hands were hooked loosely into his belt loops, probably because he thought it was rude to shove his hands in his pockets in front of his superior. His jacket was draped over a chair in front of Rondelle's desk, and the shoulder holster he wore over his broad shoulders was visible.

Laura gathered he had probably already been there for a while. In other words, she was late. She stepped in and closed the door behind her, trying not to let her cheeks burn at the knowledge that Nate had not even glanced at her.

"Good, you're here," Rondelle said. He was behind his desk, seemingly absorbed in paperwork as normal. "We can get started. I'm sending you to Wisconsin."

Laura moved to stand in front of the desk, slightly to the left side. Nate moved sinuously, pushing himself off the wall and standing beside her. Beside her, but apart. There was a little more space between them than Laura ever remembered there being. On one hand, it was welcome: no chance of him brushing against her and triggering that sickening shadow of death.

On the other, it was sickening enough in itself, feeling the distance and tension he was putting between them.

"What's the case?" he asked, his voice low and deferent.

Rondelle skimmed a few pages into a folder and held it out, letting Laura take it from him. "We've got a pair of twins murdered in Milwaukee. Two young women in their mid-twenties, both of them found earlier tonight."

"What's the catch?" Laura asked, opening the file to give it a cursory glance. She knew it couldn't be as simple as Rondelle had laid it out. If it was simple, the FBI wouldn't be so badly needed. And Rondelle trusted them enough to send them on the complicated cases—just like he had said on the phone.

37

Rondelle smiled just slightly. "They weren't together at the time. They were each in their own respective homes, and they were found within an hour of each other."

Laura frowned at that, but Nate spoke up before she had the chance to ask. "What are the circumstances?" he said.

"We have a roommate who got home and found the first twin dead in her apartment," Rondelle said. "Looks like a home invasion through an open window, and the local police immediately thought it was a burglary gone wrong. But then the second twin was called and contacted in order to inform her of her sister's death, and when they got no response, they busted into her home and found her dead as well. Both of them showed signs of having been killed within the same evening."

Laura nodded. "So we're dealing with someone breaking and entering both homes and killing the sisters, without much of a gap in between. Must have been premeditated."

"And that's why they want us to investigate," Rondelle confirmed. "This isn't a straightforward case. You need to figure out whether we're dealing with one killer or two, and what the motive might have been to wipe out both twins in rapid succession on different sides of the city. If this is two people, it shows planning, forethought. Maybe organized crime. And if it's just one... well. He's fast. Precise. Left no obvious evidence behind. He's capable—enough to put the local police out of their element completely. You'd better get moving. The rest of the information is in the file, and your flight is leaving soon enough that I don't want you to risk missing it."

They had been dismissed. Laura tensed slightly, waiting for Nate to refuse, to say that he couldn't work with her or that he would handle it alone.

"After you, Agent Frost," Nate said, his tone as cool and polite as before.

Laura's heart sank into the bottom of her shoes as she turned to lead the way. She had been right about Nate's character—that he would keep things professional. But to her dismay, she found she wished she had never been more wrong about anything.

She missed him already, and he was walking right beside her down the hall.

# CHAPTER NINE

Nate shuffled onto the plane behind an elderly woman who kept having to pause and lean on the seats, trying not to grind his teeth. He just wanted to sit down. It was going to be an uncomfortable enough flight as it was, and he needed to get some rest.

It had been a long day, and it had carried on into a long evening. Now it was shaping up to be a long night. Finally catching sight of their aisle number, Nate sighed in relief and half threw his carry-on into the overhead locker, not particularly caring how it landed. There was nothing valuable enough in it to worry about.

He slumped down into the window seat, immediately regretting it. They usually sat the other way around. Mostly because Nate's broad shoulders left him feeling cramped when he was against the window, and having the aisle seat was a lot more freeing. But he'd sat down so he could avoid having to stand and wait for Laura to stow her bag, because they weren't technically talking right now.

Which made him both sound and feel a bit like a teenage girl, but it couldn't be avoided right now. He wasn't even angry. Not really. He was just exhausted from the day they'd had, and wanted to sit down and be quiet and think about this new case.

"Um," Laura said, standing in the aisle and blocking an annoyed-looking banker type from getting through. "Did you want to swap?"

Nate sighed, getting up again. It was worth it, not to feel like he was being squashed into a tin can for the whole of the journey. He stepped out of the row of seats to allow her in and then sat again, this time in the aisle seat.

"Thank you," he said, because he wasn't going to stop being polite over this. But that was all he said. He didn't want to initiate any further conversation.

They settled into their seats, buckling up, adjusting the arm rests, all the usual busywork that came with getting on a flight. People around them were just filing into the last seats, and the flight attendants were emerging to start the safety demonstration. A demonstration Nate could recite, moves and all, with his eyes closed and headphones in and one hand tied behind his back. It was one of the perks of being an agent, if it could be considered a perk: frequent travel.

Nate slid his eyes closed for a moment, wishing he'd had more than a short nap before his phone woke him up. There had been so much to process today. Laura being right about the girl being in danger was one thing. Another to add to a whole list of times when she had somehow mysteriously known that something was going to happen. Try as he might, Nate couldn't make all the pieces fit. Every time there was a new clue, it felt like it only confused him more. He couldn't work out how she did it.

And she didn't feel like she could open up to him, which was a punch in the gut itself. After all this time. All they had been through together. And she still couldn't tell him.

He wasn't some random agent she passed in the corridor from time to time. He could have understood her cageyness if it was that. People had leads, resources, and they didn't like to share them. That was fine. That was the process.

But this was more. They were partners. They had been partners for years. If she could trust anyone in the entire agency, it would be him.

The whole thing just made him feel even more exhausted. He wished this flight was long enough for a sleep, but it wasn't. Only a couple of hours in the air. By the time they landed, they would need to be ready to go. He would just have to preserve his energy as much as possible, and hit the coffee hard when they got to the local precinct.

"We should look at the case notes," Laura said, her voice tentative.

It almost hurt to hear it. Nate's instinctive response was to comfort her, but he pushed it down. He couldn't keep doing this. Letting her get away with hiding whatever it was she was hiding. She couldn't keep promising to tell him her secrets and then going back on her word. Every time he let things just go right on back to normal, it was like he was endorsing it, telling her it was all right to behave that way. It wasn't. A promise had to mean something.

"Yeah," Nate said, cracking his eyes open and looking down at the file she was holding. She'd folded down the tray on the seat in front of her so she could spread the pages out, but there wasn't much. There wouldn't be. Not if the murders had only just happened in the last few hours.

"This is an information sheet about the two victims," Laura said, glancing it over. "Not much to go on, just a few personal details. Identical twins Ruby and Jade Patrickson, both twenty-five. Their home addresses, which is also the location of the two crime scenes. The name of the witness who found them, and at what time both bodies were reported. Rondelle was right—there's not even an hour between them."

"Anything as to the MO?" Nate asked. The words felt stiff on his tongue. Laura's were stiff on the air, too. Like there was a barrier between them, all of a sudden. As if they didn't even know each other and had to stick to formalities.

"Both victims were stabbed multiple times," Laura read. "No weapon found at the scenes, and of course the coroner's report is pending. We'll have to find out most of it on the ground, looks like."

Nate nodded. "Then we'll wait until then."

Laura looked at him, but he wasn't looking back. He only saw the movement out of the corner of his eye. He set his head back against the headrest, keeping his eyes right ahead on the map displayed on the in-flight screen. Watching their progress across the sky. He pretended not to pay attention as Laura closed the file, shuffling the pages back inside, and then tucked it away in the bag she'd kept at her feet. She closed up her flight tray, as if it was something for her hands to do, and then sat.

The two of them remained silent then. It was a stiff and awkward silence, a physical thing sitting between them that just kept growing and getting larger. A thing that wanted to grow. The longer it carried on for, the harder it was to break.

Nate adjusted his seatbelt slightly, settling into the chair more comfortably. He hoped it wasn't going to be like this for the whole case. Or, at least, that it wasn't going to affect the case. He couldn't take more than formalities and politeness with Laura right now. He wasn't ready for it. But they still had a job to do, a very serious job, and he didn't want that to be affected by their personal relationship.

It was like everything had changed. Even though they were still talking to one another, and even though they were still discussing the case in the level that it needed, that was all. The banter, the friendly conversation, it was all gone. The dynamic between them had shifted. Maybe forever.

Nate wasn't going to let it get between them in such a way that the case went unsolved. Justice still needed to be done.

He just didn't know how long they could last like this before something was going to have to give—and if something had to, it was going to be their partnership.

\*\*\*

Laura looked up with relief at a man bearing a sign with their names. It was makeshift, a bit of card drawn on with marker, but it was

41

still an incredibly welcome sight. The man holding it was wearing a police officer's uniform, which meant he was their contact, and he would have something to say to them in the drive over to the precinct.

Right then, Laura would have taken an escort from just about anyone—anything to break the awkward silence between her and Nate.

It was just before dawn, the inside of the airport too brightly lit and filled with bleary-eyed passengers all looking like they needed more sleep. The joys of the red-eye. Laura stepped quickly over to the young, dark-haired officer, wanting to get started as soon as they could.

"Special Agent Laura Frost," she said, by way of introduction. She didn't add anything for Nate. She didn't know if he would appreciate it right now.

"Special Agent Nathaniel Lavoie," he said, sticking out a hand for the officer to shake.

He dropped the card into one hand, letting it slip to the side now it was no longer needed. "I'm Detective Gareth Frome," he said, his Wisconsin accent lilting his words. "Captain Gausse sent me to pick you guys up."

"Great," Laura said, squaring her shoulders a little as she prepared to take the weight of her bag again. "We can get right to the first crime scene, unless your captain is waiting for us at the precinct."

"No," Frome said, looking between them with a little doubt. "She said you might want to go to a motel first?"

"No, we should get right to it," Nate said, nodding sharply. Laura was glad he agreed. She couldn't see any point to getting themselves settled in when they could just hit the ground running. They'd only been together again for a few hours, and already she was wishing she was sitting alone in her apartment instead.

"Okay there," Frome agreed, turning to gesture at the exit. "If you'll follow me, then."

They moved behind him silently. Laura had no idea what he must have thought of them: surly agents from the capitol, not used to their friendlier Midwest ways. But it was irrelevant, so long as they got their jobs done. They weren't here to make friends.

Which was good, because if that was part of the job description, Laura would probably have been fired by now.

"Um," Frome said, hesitating as he stopped beside an unmarked car. There was a circular impression in the dirt on the outside of the roof. A place where he must have recently stuck up a temporary light on a chase. "Maybe I should talk to the captain, see if she wants to meet us there, eh?"

"Give her a call," Laura gestured. "We'll get our bags into the trunk." She moved away, hoping that Frome would pick up on their efficiency and start to practice it himself. So long as he made the call quickly enough that she and Nate didn't have to sit around alone together, everything would be fine.

She was more than aware of what she was doing. Distracting herself so she didn't have to think about the problem. It was just another method of avoidance, like drinking always had been. At least this one was less self-destructive. So long as she kept busy, kept moving, they could just slip right by all those awkward moments and get back home again.

It wasn't just how excruciatingly unbearable it was. It wasn't just that it hurt because it was Nate, whom she had considered until now to be a good friend. It was how badly every single second of it made her want to tell him the truth, even though she was still too afraid—and more sure than ever, now, that it would only make him shun her faster.

Laura shoved her bag into the trunk and then walked around to the passenger side door, not waiting for Nate to put his bag in alongside hers. She took the seat in the front, so that Nate would have to be in the back. That way they wouldn't have to sit next to each other. She looked up at the sky, at the sun breaching the horizon. The weather forecast was for a mild day, overcast but not cold.

Fine weather for exploring murder scenes.

"All right," Frome said cheerfully, climbing into the driver's seat. Laura looked around, happy to have him breaking the silence that had already begun to settle into the car. In her side mirror, she caught a glimpse of Nate sitting right behind her, his face pensive. She tried to put it out of her mind. "Captain Gausse will meet us there, so we're all good."

"Great," Laura said encouragingly. "What can you tell us about the case on the way there?"

Frome started the engine, checking his mirrors as he pulled out of the waiting spot, right in front of the airport. "Well, there's not much we know so far," he said. "We've got a pair of twins. Such a shame, too. They were each killed in their own houses."

Laura got the feeling that she was about to hear the entire contents of the briefing document that they'd been given, slim as it was. "We know about the identity of the victims. Have there been any developments overnight?"

"I don't know about that," Frome said doubtfully. "We're waiting on the coroner's report. Should be coming in later. As far as I know, the captain was waiting for you guys to come in for the interviews, eh. Said it was better than doing them twice."

Laura nodded, resisting the urge to sigh heavily. They had a lot of ground to cover, and she hoped that time hadn't been unnecessarily lost. But in fairness, it had been nighttime. She supposed that was a good enough excuse not to have made a lot of progress on talking to potential suspects or family members.

She just kept hope that the lost time wouldn't hinder the investigation—and that they could get in and out again as quickly as possible. Because the less time she could spend with Nate right now, and the more time prepping for her custody hearing or checking up on Amy, the better.

She needed to get home—and she needed to go as fast as possible.

# CHAPTER TEN

Laura got out of the car and studied the building in front of them, squinting her eyes slightly against the brightening sky. It was an apartment block, without much to set it apart from any other in Milwaukee—except perhaps that it looked a little newer, a little cleaner, like there might have been a recent refurbishment.

Laura stretched out her back, placing both hands on the base of her spine and shooting her elbows backwards. She felt cramped, sore, from the plane flight and the lack of sleep. She didn't have time to think about that, though. She followed Detective Frome inside, past the officer guarding the door to the complex, and into the eerily quiet halls of the complex.

There were a few residents on the first floor, standing hushed in the small area at the top of the stairs. One man had his arm around a woman, who was pressing a tissue to her face. They looked shell-shocked, all of them pale and wide-eyed. They moved aside to let the Frome, Laura, and then Nate through, going past in single file.

"Is there any word...?" the man with his arm around the woman asked, his tone hushed, like it would have disturbed the dead to speak louder.

"I'm afraid not," Frome said, in an equally quiet tone. "We're in the early stages of the investigation."

The three residents seemed to collectively accept this response, none of them saying anything else as they passed by. They went up another flight of stairs and then walked a short way down the hall, to the obvious door: the one marked with a yellow cone outside and an officer next to it, protecting the integrity of the crime scene.

Frome nodded silently at the man on the door and led them through, the eerie hush that always seemed to settle on these places continuing to lay heavy on Laura's shoulders. She could tell already, without going inside, that the body was gone. When the body was still present, there was a different feeling at these places. More urgency, more hustle and bustle of different personnel moving in and out. Detectives, crime scene photographers, forensics, doctors, everyone focused on the job of collecting evidence and checking the body.

When the body was gone, carted out in a black bag on a rolling gurney, the atmosphere changed. A quiet respect settled over those present, as if it would be wrong to speak loudly. Even those who weren't law enforcement professionals felt it. This was a place where a Very Tragic Thing had happened, and that feeling would hang around like a bad smell for some time to come.

"You must be our FBI agents," a female voice declared, a little louder than expected, as Laura and Nate followed Frome to stand in front of an open door inside the apartment. Within the room was a petite but wiry blonde woman, her eyes creased with age, her hair pinned up just so above a crisp captain's uniform. "Captain Renee Gausse."

"Agent Laura Frost." Laura nodded, hearing Nate repeat his own name immediately afterwards.

The introductions done, Gausse apparently saw no further reason to stand on formality. "The body has been taken to the coroner's office," she said. "I have the crime scene photographs here for you to take a look at, hot off the press."

"Thank you," Laura said, stretching out her hand for them. It wasn't quite as good as looking at and touching the body, but you never knew. Maybe she'd get something out of touching the images that would be used in an eventual trial. A flash of the culprit sitting in the dock, even.

To her disappointment, no headache burned to signal the arrival of the vision. All she had in her hands was a series of images of one of the twins she'd seen in their case notes. Instead of full of life, as she had been in a shot pulled from her social media account for the briefing, here she was lifeless. Wide eyes stared white-frosted into nowhere above a bloody mess of a body, the stab wounds visible through tears in her clothing.

The cause of death was unmistakable. So, too, was the fury with which the murder had been committed.

"This looks personal," she said right away, handing them to Nate with deliberate care that their hands wouldn't touch. "There's anger here. So many wounds—and inflicted across a short space of time, I would guess. A frenzy."

Nate nodded in agreement as Gausse replied, "The initial count from the coroner is fifteen stab wounds, though we'll need to verify that after the full examination has been carried out."

"Any idea on if he broke in, or was let in?" Nate asked.

"There's no sign of anything broken," Gausse said. "The door doesn't appear to have been forced. No damage to the windows, and with the weather turning cooler, they were all closed. As far as we've been able to piece together from the timeline, this happened not long after Ruby Patrickson returned home from work in the evening."

"So, maybe we can assume that she let the killer inside," Laura said. "But the attack happened suddenly. I'm not seeing defensive wounds."

"If she was caught off-guard, I'd imagine she wouldn't have time to react," Gausse said. She took the pictures back from Nate and gestured at a few of them. "The wounds are clustered closely together and there would have been an immediate amount of heavy blood loss. From my experience, I'd suggest she fell back after the first wound. He knelt over her and continued to stab her as she lay on the floor."

"He?" Nate said. It was an assumption. Their job as investigators was to challenge assumptions, especially any that might cloud their view of the evidence.

Gausse shrugged. "I don't know many women would have the fury and the strength to plunge a blade deep like that so many times. But it's possible. For now, I'm calling the suspect he until we prove otherwise."

Laura looked down at their feet, at the blood soaked into the carpet. A grisly spill that almost could have been wine, if it wasn't for the sickly-sweet smell that hung in the air and gave the game away. It covered a wide area, soaked into the fibers, with no gap or outline where the body might have lain. A long knife, then. Deep enough to stab right through. Enough blood to soak everything and spread, far more than a human could stand to lose and survive.

"This is a good start," Laura said, nodding as she already began to form a picture in her head of who they were looking for. "But I think we need to head to the second scene and take a look. It's far away?"

Gausse shook her head. "Not far at all. Frome can drive us. Let's head out."

*** 

The second apartment block was a little older, a little shabbier around the edges. Maybe this was the less successful of the sisters, at least in their lives so far.

Gausse led them to an apartment on the first floor, larger and with more rooms than the first crime scene. It was well-kept, and Laura remembered the detail about the roommate in the case notes. This, then, must have been the twin that was found first.

"Which was struck first?" Laura asked.

"Ruby, where I met you, was the first to die," Gausse said. "But Jade, here, was the first to be discovered. There wasn't long in it. Maybe just enough time for someone to drive over here, make their way inside, and attack. In this case, the window in the bathroom was open—looking at the garbage can out in the alley there, we believe someone would have been able to climb up. They weren't able to find any prints on the sill except what looked like Jade's own."

Laura nodded, taking this all in. She had a critical eye on everything: the floors, the walls, looking for any small thing that might have been missed so far. Gausse led them to the bathroom, where another pool of blood lay slick over the tiles. Another missing body, another stack of grisly photographs for them to look through.

Laura tore her eyes away from the slippery pool of the floor to study them. It was strange, looking at these. Jade and Ruby had been identical, enough so that it gave Laura the odd feeling of seeing the same woman die twice. The killer might as well have simply moved the body to a different scene, if it wasn't for the fact that their clothing was different—although the original color was now so soaked with blood it was hard to distinguish.

"Any estimate on the number of wounds?" Laura asked.

"Seventeen." Gausse shook her head grimly. "This one suffered defensive wounds to her hands, and there was also some scraping to her palms which corresponded with skin fragments lifted from the windowsill. Of course, they still need to undergo testing, but we believe she may have tried to escape out the window. He would have dragged her back, thrown her down, and commenced the knife attack."

"This is almost exactly the same," Nate said, voicing Laura's own thoughts. "We're dealing with someone who carried a lot of anger and vented it here on the women. But why them?"

"It could be a personal vendetta," Laura said, picking up on what he was saying. "That's the most obvious option. Both of them being twins means they would have had a lot in common. They grew up together, shared the same family, probably a lot of overlap in their circle of friends. Someone who was angry with one of them could just as easily be angry with both."

"Which means we have to determine what reason anyone would have had to dislike them," Nate said, then corrected himself. "More than dislike—hate. This kind of frenzied attack combined with the premeditated action of tracking them down one by one is not just something that happened in the heat of the moment. There's the drive over here, the scouting of a way to break in, the climbing through the window. All of that is time in which someone who acted on the spur of the moment with Ruby could calm down—but they continued to attack Jade anyway. I think this has to be triggered by some kind of event, something that happened between the attacker and the twins."

"Agreed," Laura said. "Which means, Captain Gausse, we'd be grateful if you could show us to where we can interview their parents and family. Right now, they're our best guess for finding some answers. We need to figure out if this is a one-time thing and the killer's rage is spent, or whether we should be on the lookout for others."

Gausse nodded smartly, a look of satisfaction gleaming in her eyes. "I have them waiting for you at the precinct already," she said.

# CHAPTER ELEVEN

Laura allowed Nate to step into the room ahead of her, hanging back just a little. She hated this part. Talking to the parents of murder victims. It was horrible to see their distress, to understand what they had lost. She had already lost Lacey once, and not even permanently. It was hard to even imagine how much worse death would be, because if she tried, it was like her whole body and mind choked up, frozen and terrified. And they had lost not one daughter, but two, within an hour of each other.

True to form, a cacophony of questions met them as they stepped into the space, a kind of private waiting area reserved for these more informal talks. It was comfortably furnished and brightly lit, unlike the interview rooms where suspects would be led.

"Have you heard any leads?"

"Do you know who did this to our girls?"

Nate raised both hands in a gesture of surrender as he stepped inside. Gausse took the initial lead, letting Nate and Laura seat themselves on a sofa opposite the family as she spoke. "Please, I know this is incredibly difficult. We have the FBI working the case now. This is Agents Frost and Lavoie, and they'd like to ask you some questions to help with the investigation. Do you feel able to speak with them right now?"

The parents, both of them, slowly sank back onto the sofa from where they had sprung up. They were middle-aged, both of them fraying slightly at the edges—gray hairs here, wrinkles there. Their faces were pale, eyes glassy and red-rimmed from a night of shock and grief. She was red-haired like her daughters, still slim and pretty. He was taller, broader, with dark hair and a short beard. They clasped each other's hands like they were life preservers, knuckles white where they gripped hard.

"We're very sorry for your loss," Laura said in a soft tone, hoping that would help to focus their attention. "At the moment, we're in the early stages, but we think you might be able to help us shine a light on some possible leads."

"Anything you need," the father said, his jaw clenched tight and his voice hoarse.

"All right, Mr. Patrickson," Nate said. "If you could tell us about your daughters, about their relationship with other people. Could you imagine anyone who might be angry with them, or carry a grudge?"

The man blinked, glancing at his wife and shaking his head. "No," he said. "No, not our girls. They were... they were liked. Popular. Everyone loved them."

"He's right," the mother spoke up, her voice dry as though she had cried all the moisture out of it. "They were good girls. It's not just something parents say. I really mean it. People liked them. They had a lot of friends. Even after leaving school—they made friends quickly."

Laura made a mental note, and an internal groan. The more friends they had, the more potential suspects were out there. All of them would have to be interviewed and checked out in case of any potential suspicions. At least they had the local PD to help them out with getting through it all. "Even so," she said. "Can you think of anyone who wasn't happy with them? Someone they had a falling out with, maybe—even if it was a while ago?"

The parents looked at each other, searching one another's faces for answers. But in turn, they both shook their heads.

"Ex-boyfriends?" Laura tried.

"There have been a few." The mother nodded. "Especially for Ruby. But I don't think any of them parted on bad terms. Most of them broke up with her, not the other way around. She was always getting her heart broken, poor thing."

"She loved too quickly," the father said, his voice a rumble of regret. "Always jumping in too fast. That was how she was. Ready to trust."

Laura nodded. There was potential for that to mean something. If she trusted quickly, maybe she had trusted the wrong person. Gotten herself in too deep with someone who didn't want to let go. An ex-lover she was convinced away from by her sister, someone whose jealous rage could take hold of him... but Laura was getting ahead of herself. Evidence first, wild theories later.

"You can't think of anyone who might have had a reason to want to harm or punish them?" Nate asked, his voice even but firm. "Even if you don't believe it could have gone as far as this—anyone at all?"

The Patricksons shook their heads. "We have no idea," the mother said tearfully. "It's just come out of the blue. I can't imagine why anyone would want to harm them at all."

51

"Did either of the girls have any problems?" Laura asked. "I know it's hard to think about these things at a time like this, but… excessive drinking? Drug use? Gambling? Anything like that in their pasts?"

"No." Mrs. Patrickson sniffed. "They were good girls. They even took jobs on split shifts so they could always be there for us if we needed them. Ruby worked the late shift and Jade worked earlier in the day. They would come by with groceries if we needed them—my hip needed surgery last year and they waited on me hand and foot. Can you imagine that?" Her last words were muffled by a tissue, pressed against her face.

"Did they work in the same place?" Nate asked, noting that down.

"No," Mr. Patrickson said, taking over from his wife—she'd resumed crying again too forcefully to talk. "No, they were both working at different places. The last few years, they'd grown up, moved apart. Got different friends from their workplaces. But they always came back to us."

"Last question, sir," Laura said, keeping her tone as respectful as she could, as gentle. "Did you talk to either of them in the last day or days? Did you sense anything off?"

"No," he said, shaking his head. "I mean, yes. I saw them both this week. But they didn't seem bothered by anything. They were… they were normal. Happy. Like they always are."

"All right," Laura said. "Thank you. Please—if you think of something else, don't hesitate to call us. Any little thing could help." She took a business card from her pocket and held it out, letting the father take it from her hands.

It felt so stiff and strange, like she and Nate were conducting this interview separately. Normally, she would have glanced at him now to check if he was done. He would have looked back, and from their eyes both of them would know it was time to leave. But when she looked at him this time, he didn't return her gaze. He just stood, nodding his thanks to the parents.

"We'll leave you in peace, now," he said. "Captain Gausse?"

"Yes," she said, stepping toward the distraught parents. "I'm going to leave you in the capable hands of one of my officers. He'll escort you back home and make sure you have everything you need for now. Just wait here a short while, and I'll send him along."

With those words, all three of them—Laura, Nate, and Gausse—left the room. Outside in the hall, Frome was waiting for them, leaning against the wall with his hands in his pockets. He straightened up as soon as they emerged, like he was snapping to attention.

52

"I thought you'd want to see this as soon as possible," he said, holding out an object wrapped in an evidence bag. "The techs have managed to unlock Ruby Patrickson's phone, eh."

"And?" Gausse asked, all business.

"She's on a dating app," Frome reported. "Exchanging messages with a number of men all week."

"Let me see?" Laura asked, holding out her hand. Frome opened the evidence bag and slid the phone out right into her palm.

Laura opened up the app, which was positioned centrally on the home screen for easy access, and started looking through Ruby's message history. As she did, she felt a familiar pain spike into the center of her forehead, sharp and strong. She tried desperately to figure out if it had been triggered by one of the messages in particular, or—

*She was walking along a street. She was inside him—inside the man. She knew she was. She could see things in her peripheral vision— his hand as it brought a cup of takeout coffee to his lips. Definitely a man's hand.*

*She was seeing things from his point of view. He walked at a good pace, a deliberate pace. He walked to a nook in the side of the road, the doorway of a store that was closed. He stood there and sipped his coffee, watching people going by.*

*Laura started to feel impatient. What was this? Just a vision of nothing? One of the men that Ruby had been talking to on the app, going about his day? Why was she being shown this?*

*It didn't make any sense. They never came with any sense. She was trapped here, unable to leave until the vision was over, just standing and watching people walk by for no reason...*

*The man stiffened, his eyes jerking up and latching onto one passerby in particular. Another man. A young one. He was in his twenties, no more. He had an easy smile as he talked to someone on the cell phone pressed to his ear, the other hand stuffed into the pocket of his jeans. He was blond-haired, tanned, dressed casually in a loose jacket over a tee. He had a look on his face while he spoke, like he was flirting with whoever was on the line.*

*The man who was carrying Laura's vision stepped forward, throwing his coffee cup into a nearby garbage can and setting off after the young blond man. He kept him in his sights, letting him get far enough ahead that there were others between them but not far enough to lose him. He watched his every move, paused when he paused, looked away whenever he turned to look over his shoulder.*

*He was following him.*

*A growing fear rose inside Laura as she watched. This was not just any daytime stroll. She was following that man—and she could feel how wrong it was, how carefully her host was avoiding being caught. This was something he was doing for a reason. He was stalking him.*

*The way that a killer might stalk his intended victim, in order to get him on his own.*

Laura surfaced with her eyes still on the list of messages, and only paused a moment before continuing to scroll through them. She was no longer really reading them. She was thinking about what she had seen, about what it meant.

And what she was afraid of was that it meant there was going to be another murder.

"We'd better start contacting everyone they knew," she said, looking up at Gausse. "Including the men on this list. One of them has to know something."

One of them, she hoped, would be the man in her vision—and even though all she had to go on right now was a hand, it would have to be a start.

# CHAPTER TWELVE

"We should start going through everything we can find on social media."

Laura looked up at Nate's words, only to find he wasn't even looking at her. He was moving the mouse to wake up a computer they'd been assigned, out in the bullpen. Not exactly as nice as having their own office, but it would have to do. Gausse had led them to a pair of adjacent desks and told them to make themselves at home.

Laura's jaw tensed slightly, hearing the formality in Nate's voice. He was talking to her the same way that he would talk to any other member of the investigation. Like she was no one. Around them, she noticed a few of the other cops watching them curiously. They were no doubt interested in the FBI agents who had turned up in their midst. Laura wished they wouldn't look, wouldn't see how stiff Nate was with her.

"Right," she agreed, because the investigation needed to continue. "We can use the list of names that Gausse's team has already whipped up. Start looking for people with known records, anyone behaving suspiciously. Messages in their accounts that flag up any arguments or grudges."

Nate was already sitting, adjusting the keyboard to the right position for his long arms. "I'll take social media and dating apps. You go through the records."

Laura sat down silently, doing as she was told. There didn't seem much point in arguing with him, or even voicing her agreement. He had decided who was doing what so that they didn't have to talk about it any further.

Laura blinked a few times to try and clear her bleary eyes, looking at the computer screen and clicking around to bring up the national database where she would find any necessary records. It was useful, having a whole team of detectives working around you. They'd already combed social media for the names, and Gausse now had them out there working their way through interviews. There were far too many for Nate and Laura to handle themselves, but until one of them found something that was worth looking into or the coroner's report came back with something interesting, they didn't have a lot to do. This kind of admin could have been handed off to another detective as well, but Laura preferred sitting here to being out there.

Out there, there was more chance that someone would touch her, whether by accident or deliberately. That would mean the possibility of more visions. Laura wanted to save those for the important moments—the moments that might affect the outcome of the case. If she had too many unnecessary encounters, the headache would build into a migraine until she couldn't handle it anymore. And then the case would go unsolved for another day while she recovered, and it would be one more day of sitting next to her partner and feeling like she was a stranger. And thinking about two little girls who needed her help back home, who were waiting for her to return.

Laura typed the first name into the database and waited a moment for the results to load up. There was no match. She deleted her query and concentrated on the next name on the list, waiting for a hit.

This time there was one, but it was for a man who was now deceased, as of several years ago. She doubted it was the same one that the twins had been in contact with. Even if it was, it was irrelevant. He couldn't have been the one to kill them now.

She moved steadily down the list. When there was a need to cross-check, to be sure she had the right person, she used her phone to look up the person on social media, going through friends lists the same way that the cops had when putting the list together. Almost every person she looked up was friends with both Ruby and Jade. They had remained close, it seemed, through the whole of their lives. So many shared connections. Their pages were already flooded with memoriam messages, people posting about how much they would miss each of the women.

Going by this, what the Patricksons had said was correct. Both of the twins were popular, well-liked. They knew a lot of people, and those people thought highly of them. But, of course, that was how it was when someone died. People would post good memories, good thoughts and wishes—not bad ones.

Laura sighed, finding herself looking up the last name on the list. When that returned no hits either, she was at a dead end. She'd gone through what looked like the full branch of the Patrickson family, given how many there were in the list with the same surname, as well as dozens of friends, colleagues, and acquaintances. It wasn't that none of them had a record—that would have been unrealistic. No, it was that the records they had were unrelated: parking fines, possession of minor recreational drugs, drunk driving. Nothing related in any way to violence or theft, nothing that suggested a reason to break into a house and stab someone.

She was getting nowhere. Laura glanced across the aisle at Nate. He was sitting parallel to her, engrossed in his screen. He didn't glance back at her or show any signs of stopping. The task he'd chosen was the larger one—he'd probably be doing it for a long time.

Laura hesitated. She didn't want to interrupt him or try to get his attention. The atmosphere was so frosty, she was almost afraid of what his reaction would be. She turned back to her own screen, trying to think of what else she could do with the information they had. Her thoughts strayed back home, to Amy.

It had been a long night for Laura, and now that the morning was in full swing she couldn't help but think it must have been long for Amy, too. Where had the little girl slept? Not in her own bed, that was certain. Had she been able to get any rest? Had she been huddled up under unfamiliar covers, scared and alone? It sent a lump into Laura's throat, and before she even realized it, she was dialing Rondelle's number to check in.

"Division Chief Rondelle," he said, giving his customary greeting—but he must have checked the caller display before answering. "Is there a problem in Milwaukee, Agent Frost?"

"No," she said, wondering again at the fact that he was still on duty at his desk this early—even after last night. The man didn't seem to sleep. Not that they had, either. "I was just wanting to check in, see if you'd heard anything…"

"About Amy Fallow." Rondelle sighed. "No, Laura, I'm afraid we don't have any updates yet. Like I told you, we have to wait for Child Protective Services to find her next of kin and discuss things with them. It could be days, or even weeks, before we hear any update."

"Right," Laura said. She knew that, of course. It was just hard to hear. She wanted to be there, making sure that Amy was all right. The last time she'd trusted in the state to get it done, Amy had ended up right back in the lion's den.

"Please focus on your investigation," Rondelle said, a hint of harshness coming into his voice. "You've got a job to do, Agent. Don't mess it up because you're too distracted."

The call ended, leaving Laura listening to the hiss of nothing with the phone pressed against her ear. She sighed and put it down on the desk, rubbing her eyes. No news was good news. That was what she had to tell herself.

She just wished she could be there.

"I've got a hit," Nate said, drawing her attention. His voice was still stiff, but it had dropped, becoming a little more gentle. He must have overheard her conversation, knew that she was worried. "A rejected ex-boyfriend."

"For which twin?" Laura asked, trying to push herself back into investigation mode. If this was the guy, they could be home sooner than they'd even expected.

"Both," Nate said. "He's connected to both of them on social media, but it looks like he met Ruby first through the dating app. They talked a lot around six months ago. Then it died down to only the occasional message, mostly one-sided from him. Looks like she was ignoring him there."

"And Jade?" Laura asked. She turned toward him in her chair, wishing she felt comfortable enough to wheel herself over there and sit close to him while he showed her the messages.

"Well, that's where it gets interesting," Nate said. "I can't see when he connected with both twins exactly on social media, but I went back to the time in their message history when he first agreed to meet with Ruby. About six months ago, she posted an image of herself in a slinky dress holding a glass of wine, with the location tagged as a restaurant. He commented saying that it had been a great night. They did it again, a few times, but the relationship seems to have petered out."

"Any indication of why?" Laura asked.

Nate shook his head. "If they did have a specific reason for not seeing each other again, it must have been discussed in person. There's no hint in the messages. But, like I said, he was connected with Jade as well. I went back in her history to the same time, and about a month after that first date with Ruby, he pops up commenting on her posts as well."

"That's extremely interesting," Laura said, frowning. The phone was sitting in front of Nate—Ruby's phone, now unlocked for them to use. "Have you been able to check her private messages?"

Nate tapped a few times on the screen and handed it to her without a word. Laura took it from the very tip of the phone to avoid his fingers, and studied what he had brought up. It was a message thread with what Laura assumed had to be the man in question—his username was PeteyBarton1996. Her eyes flicked over the most recent messages, all of which had gone unanswered by Ruby.

- *Aren't you going to talk to me now, just because I asked your sister out?*

- *I'll give you another chance if you're jealous.*

58

*- Come on, why do you have to be such a bitch? Just give it a try. I'm not dating Jade anyway. We can go out next Saturday.*

*- Don't fucking ignore me. This is why people say you're a cold bitch.*

*- You're screening my calls too? Pick up or I'm coming around there to see you.*

*- You can't hide from me forever. I'm going to find you. You better rethink and start talking. I'm not letting you get away with treating me like this.*

*- Fine, you fucking bitch! See if I give a fuck. You'll get what's coming to you. You'll wish you had another chance with me. When you come begging I'm going to throw you out in the street like the stray bitch you are.*

"Wow," Laura said, raising an eyebrow. She almost expected another vision to come after reading how violent his words were, how clearly threatening. He was obviously a man with a lot of issues. If he could flip that quickly—across a matter of days—from flirting to rabid anger, he might have been capable of anything. Laura flipped to the call log, checking the dates—and as she had suspected, there were a number of missed calls from a man labeled as Pete in Ruby's contact list. At some point, she had blocked the number, leaving an abrupt cutoff in the calls.

"It sounds like he asked Jade out, but she most likely turned him down," Nate said. "Would you agree?"

Laura nodded, internally wincing at his too-polite words. He was acting like he did with inter-departmental investigations. Checking that all parties were on the same page, to avoid any etiquette snafus and prevent anyone from feeling like he was taking over. But he didn't need to do that with her. He must have known he didn't need to.

"I guess we know who to talk to first," she said, grabbing her jacket from the back of her chair. "Do we have an address for him?"

Nate nodded. "I would have looked it up, but thankfully he's the kind of idiot who posted a selfie in front of his new home to brag about moving in."

"Good," Laura said, moving through the bullpen already and looking back over her shoulder. "Then maybe he's also the kind of idiot who would kill someone and then leave evidence lying around."

She made for the double doors at the end of the room, ready to sink her teeth into an interrogation—because at least with a murder suspect, she could throw some of her internal frustration into making him confess to it all.

# CHAPTER THIRTEEN

Laura squinted at the sun, her back to the door. Behind her, Nate was still waiting patiently for the homeowner, their suspect, to answer his knock.

It was getting late in the morning, and the hubbub of people going to work for rush hour was long since over. The sky was clear, which was good as far as their prospects for schlepping around all day tracking people down. But the weather was still cool, and Laura couldn't help but shiver. There was something about waiting for a potential murderer to open the door that would send one of those down your spine.

"I don't think anyone's home," Nate said, calling her attention. She turned to regard the silent house, a small building set in a moderately nice suburb. No one's windows were boarded over, but then again, no one's lawns were tended to perfection either.

Laura nodded. "You could be right. Any idea where he works?" she asked, remaining out on the sidewalk. She'd chosen not to step up close when Nate knocked, not wanting to share the small step in front of the door with him. It was too cramped. Maybe a week ago she would have stood up there with him without a thought, except for keeping their bare skin from touching so she wouldn't feel that dark aura rolling off him. But now it just looked too uncomfortable.

"He's at a construction site by the waterfront," Nate said, nodding. "I called them before we set off. They would only confirm that he was employed there, not when he was working, so I guess he must be working. Should only take us a short while to get over there."

Laura said nothing in response. She'd had to dig for the information, rather than him offering it. It felt like silence was the expected norm between them now. They both lapsed into it quickly, and for the whole of the ride neither of them said a word. Laura bit her lip, staring out the window miserably. None of this felt right. She guessed that this was just how it was now.

The construction site loomed welcomingly, at least offering a respite from the heavy silence. Laura jumped out of the car even before Nate had finished putting it in park, desperate to be out of the tiny tin box that kept them both so close and yet so distant. It was unbearable.

The site was a hive of activity. Two cranes sat dormant to the side, glinting slightly in the pale sun, but below them the ground was alive with workers. There were a number of buildings going up alongside one another at the same time, or perhaps it was all part of the same complex. One at the far side already had concrete walls going up, with marked-off spaces for windows. Another beside it was only a framework, and beside that was a framework still being put together. The rest of the lot was bare ground, dug and smoothed flat in preparation for the foundations.

A few cabins sat off to one side, temporary structures that bore signposts designating them as the site offices. Laura headed in that direction immediately, not waiting for Nate to follow her.

Maybe he could give her the silent treatment. But she could give as good as she got. If they were all about work now, then she would just work.

And maybe that was only going to end up driving an even bigger wedge between them, but Laura was too wrapped up in the emotional blow of his standoffishness to even think about whether her reaction was the right one. She only knew that it hurt, and the first impulse she had was to throw herself even further away from him so that the hurt would stop.

She knocked on the side of an open door before stepping up a couple of short steps into the first cabin, glancing around. There was a desk on one side occupied by a young woman in a pantsuit, and three more desks across the rest of the cabin scattered with plans and documents and loose hard hats. More hats and hi-vis vests hung on the wall, and the only other person inside was a man in a vest frowning in what seemed like deep concentration over a document.

"Hi," Laura said, pulling her badge out of her pocket. "I'm with the FBI. I'm looking for a specific member of staff that we're told is working at this site."

"Of course," the young woman said immediately, giving Laura a brittle smile. It was the kind of smile she saw often. Politeness, a willingness to help, but under it a fear that something was terribly wrong. "Can you give me their name?"

"It's Peter Barton," Laura said. Nate caught up with her, standing in the doorway of the cabin while she edged further out in front of the reception desk. "We'll need somewhere private to speak with him. Can you suggest a good place on the site?"

"You can use the cabin next door." Laura looked around to see that it was the man behind them who had spoken. "I'm the foreman here—

it's all right, Candy, I know where Pete is right now. I can bring him to you, if you'd like."

Laura nodded. "That would be most appreciated. The cabin next door is empty?"

The foreman grunted, shrugging his shoulders and swiping a hard hat off the desk to set it on top of his head. He had a weathered, beaten look to him, his skin creased and sun-spotted, a telltale sign of a life worked outside. "If it isn't, I'll clear them out. Follow me."

Even though Laura had done all of the talking, Nate was the one who slipped into stride with the foreman as they walked across to the other cabin. It was exhausting, all of this, already. Like they had to fight for control of the investigation between them, instead of operating as equal partners—as they always had.

True to the man's word, there was no one in the second cabin. It had a set-up much like the first: safety equipment hung on the walls, desks scattered with papers and filing cabinets pushed against the walls. Laura figured that the people who worked in here were out on the site right now, supervising other workers in their roles. She leaned against one of the desks, letting herself rest slightly, but the feeling of unease only deepened when the foreman disappeared back outside to leave her alone with Nate.

She wondered what she could say. The thought of discussing their interview technique flashed through her mind. It wouldn't normally. She and Nate were often so in sync that they didn't need to. They would fall into the same roles time and time again, the ones that had proven the most effective in getting the truth out of people.

When she stood next to him, Laura normally felt confident. Powerful. The only question was whether they had the right man, and if he would break. But now, today, she felt nervous for the first time in a long time. Her mouth was dry, her palms damp.

She didn't know how long she could take this for.

Nate lounged against another desk, as far away from her as he could get in the cramped space without making it look like they weren't even together. The two of them face forward silently, just waiting for the suspect to appear. But when he did, with the gruff voice of the foreman sending him inside, Laura couldn't help but jump slightly. She'd become so nervous, she wasn't even prepared to see him.

He was taller than she had expected—almost as tall as Nate. He had a wide frame, probably enhanced by the physical labor of the site, and his skin held a deep tan. When he swept off his hat to step inside, he revealed a short crop of blond hair stuck to his head with sweat. He had evidently been in the middle of a job when the foreman found him.

"You're the FBI?" he asked, frowning.

"Peter Barton?" Laura asked.

"Yeah, what?"

Laura showed him her badge. "I'm Special Agent Laura Frost."

"Special Agent Nathaniel Lavoie," Nate said, quickly, as if trying to get in before she continued and cut him off. "We need to ask you a few questions."

Barton scowled, looking between the two of them with clear annoyance. It was not the usual reaction of someone who had just been told the FBI wanted to speak with them. "Why did you have to come here?"

"Excuse me?" Laura said, taken aback.

"This is where I work," Barton said, practically growling it. "It's embarrassing. Couldn't you have called first, or seen me at home?"

"We visited your home this morning," Laura said, plowing on as though she was undeterred, not wanting him to sense any weakness. "You weren't there, as you surely realize."

"What's so urgent you couldn't wait?" Barton asked, his eyes flashing anger at her. "It looks bad. If I get fired, I want your badge numbers so I can report you!"

"This is extremely urgent, Mr. Barton," Nate said evenly, using the power of his low, rumbling voice to impress on the suspect exactly who was in charge of the room. "We're investigating a double homicide."

"Homicide?" Barton said, frowning. "What's that got to do with me?"

"Do you know a pair of twins? Ruby and Jade Patrickson?" Laura asked, watching his face closely.

"Yes," he said, his frown deepening. "How are they caught up in this?"

"They're the victims," Laura said quietly, waiting for the penny to drop.

It did, and it did so visibly. Barton stared at her, the anger and any other trace of emotion dropping off his face like a slate being wiped clean. There was only shock remaining behind, a particular kind of blankness behind the eyes as he struggled to process what she was telling him. A blankness that looked, to her expert eyes, real enough.

"The victims of what?" he said, as if he couldn't understand it.

"They're dead," Laura said. "They were murdered last night. You haven't seen it on social media?" Both of the twins had already received plenty of in memoriam messages from their friends commenting on their last ever posts. Anyone who followed them had to have seen it, unless they hadn't been on social media at all today.

"I…" Barton stopped, putting a hand to his mouth. He turned half away, then back, then away again, as if he couldn't figure out what to do with himself.

"Take a seat," Nate suggested.

Barton turned and found one behind him, then sank into it. The wheels of the office chair squeaked as he rolled back slightly, a stunned expression on his face.

He wasn't bluffing. Laura had seen real shock and fake shock. She'd seen psychopaths playing pretend, even ones that were really good at it. This wasn't that. He hadn't known until they'd told him.

Or he had known, but he was shocked beyond measure at the fact that they'd managed to connect the dots to him so soon. It was hard to tell.

"You didn't know about it?" Nate asked, when Barton seemed to be regaining a little color.

He looked up as if he'd forgotten that Nate and Laura were in the room. "No," he said. There was a pause. "No, I'm not on social media anymore."

Laura frowned. He'd been prolific in his messages, and his account clearly hadn't been banned—the messages were still visible when she and Nate had looked at them. "Why not?"

"I quit," he said. "I just quit and deleted everything off my phone."

"Why would you do that?" Laura asked, pressing him. She had a feeling this was connected somehow. It had to be.

"They…" Barton stopped, his jaw tensing and his face blanching again. "Aw, man. No—it wasn't me, okay? I didn't have anything to do with this. I swear!"

"Why did you quit social media, Mr. Barton?" Nate asked. "You know we're going to find out sooner or later. You may as well tell us."

Barton swallowed, looking at the ground. "They posted my messages on their feeds," he said. "Ruby and Jade. And then I had to quit because people kept sending me… things."

"Things?" Laura prompted.

Barton shrugged his shoulders, more of an expression of hopelessness than an answer. "Threats. Insults. Telling me how wrong I was."

Laura folded her arms across her chest, eyeing him closely. "We read those messages," she said. "They weren't pretty."

Barton swallowed hard again. "I know how it looks," he said. "I've been known to shoot my mouth. But that's all it was. Just venting."

"You told Jade she was going to get what was coming to her," Laura said.

"I didn't mean I was going to be the one," Barton said, his voice taking on a pleading whine. "I just meant… like someone was going to break her heart someday, and she'd know what it felt like."

Laura wasn't buying a single word he said. This innocence act—it had to be just that. An act. There was no way he was all butter-wouldn't-melt in person and spewing hate like that online. Especially given that he already had an in-person relationship with the twins. It didn't track.

"Enough," Nate said, standing up from where he leaned on the desk as though he was tired of all of this. "Where were you last night?"

"I was…" Barton looked up, hope flaring in his eyes. "I was with my new girlfriend. I took her out on a date, to a restaurant, and we were there until late. Then I went back to her place. You can ask her!"

"Name and contact details," Nate grunted, taking out a notebook. "We'll need to talk to her."

"Yeah, of course," Barton said, almost stumbling over himself in his rush to jump out of the chair and dig his phone out of his pocket to recite her number.

It was almost certain, Laura thought, that his alibi would check out. He was far too confident about it. And his hands—they were wrong, the wrong color. She'd seen the man in her vision that they were after. Just because he was going after a man, didn't mean it wasn't the same killer. There were killers who had crossed gender lines. They tended to be rare—most of them went after one type of person and one type only—but they existed.

Laura reached into her pocket and found Ruby's cell phone nestled in there. She opened the screen absentmindedly while Nate took down the woman's details, scrolling onto the dating app. He was in there somewhere, she could feel it. Somewhere in this code, in all these matches…

A headache stabbed her in the temple, and her eyes shot over the screen quickly, trying to see what had triggered it. The messages she was looking at were different from the ones that had triggered the last vision. Different men. Maybe she could—

*She was walking behind him again, studying him closely. He went into a café ahead, and Laura watched him—no, the man she was* carried along by watched him—as he walked up to the counter, keeping an eye on him through the window.

He moved comfortably alongside the café, staring inside. Laura stared hard at the one they were following, trying to make out his features. He shared a laugh with the barista, throwing his head back, glancing outside and then flashing her a wide grin. A charming grin.

The same grin she'd seen in the vision earlier.

Bu, wait—this was all wrong. It was the same man, yes, but he was different. Different location. Different clothes. Even his hair was styled slightly differently, as if he'd been for a shower and then dried it off and put it back in not quite the same place.

Was that what had happened? He'd been for a shower? Changed his clothes? Maybe after finishing work? Laura tried to make sense of what she was seeing, running through the possibilities even as the vision played on. He was picking up his coffee now, moving toward the door.

It might have been later on in the same day. The killer had stalked him all day long, even as he returned home to change his clothes, before coming back outside dressed differently.

It could have been a different day. The headaches were strong, but Laura had no precise way of timing things out. Maybe it was happening a few hours from now. Maybe it was happening tomorrow and her headaches were just getting worse, or compounding on top of one another from the vision earlier.

It could have been that the future had changed. Laura had seen it plenty of times before. Had made it happen herself. The visions showed only a possible future. If something happened to affect the outcome, then everything could change. Had the guy woken up differently than expected? Bumped into someone who spilled something on his shirt and made him need to go home and change?

Or...

He moved outside, and Laura noticed there was something subtly different in the way he moved as he began to walk down the street again. Something off from the rhythm she'd observed before. It was so slight, but it was there.

It hit her like a slap in the face.

Twins.

She was watching the killer stalk another pair of identical twins.

Laura blinked her eyes, closing them on a crowded street where a young man walked with a coffee in his hands and opening them on Ruby Patrickson's cell phone in her hand. Nate was just taking down the last digit of the phone number. No time at all had passed here, no matter how long the vision had felt.

Laura straightened up, her mind racing.

Another set of twins was going to die. Male twins.

How the hell was she going to convince Nate to follow her gut and investigate that?

# CHAPTER FOURTEEN

He walked along behind him, studying the way he drank from his coffee cup. Such a little thing, but that was where we gave ourselves away: in the little things. Those tiny mannerisms we couldn't quite control. They were the things that pointed to the heart inside.

He'd spent a lot of time studying this. He'd had to. It was the only way to know what he was dealing with. He had to get to know a person, understand who they were, just from observing them. Sure, people made broad strokes sometimes. They would torment a homeless man, or pass him by blindly, or stop to give him their spare change. But a lot of that could be down to social pressure, to wanting to appear good, not to actually being good.

And it was important to know whether someone was good or bad. It really was. If you were going to remove them from this world, he thought, you ought to first do the due diligence of knowing as much about them as you could.

It had been a long day, tailing first one and then the other. Making notes and comparisons. Seeing the differences between them that only those close to them would notice. That one of them walked *this* way, the other slightly more *this* way. The way they interacted with strangers, with friends and colleagues. The speed of their movements, the toss of their heads, the way their eyes squinted to catch something in the distance.

He'd been reading up a bit about things like micro-expressions. Supposedly, the tiniest movements of the facial muscles could give away the whole story about what someone was thinking inside. Of course, you had to be pretty much a savant to read them all. Not even then. You'd need specialist equipment that could slow down someone's movements in your vision, like playing video footage real slow. And real close up, too.

He didn't have the luxury of those things, which was a shame. A huge shame. Because he had to observe them as closely as he could and figure out what kind of a person they were, and it would have been easy as hell if he'd been able to read their minds.

He ducked into a store, sensing that he'd been almost caught a couple times too many on this trip. The target kept looking around as if he felt that he was being watched. That was different, too. The other one hadn't had any idea. It was one of the things that made him so certain now that he was right.

That he had the right one. This was the one he had to focus on next. The one he would strike first.

But it was early in the day still, frustratingly so. As he walked down the street, the man wove between other pedestrians, and cars flashed by them all the time. There were faces in windows, eyes in all the stores. There was no way he could do anything now.

He was going to have to wait. As much as it irked him, knowing that this man was alive and walking around, he couldn't exactly go right up to him now and attack. Aside from anything else, he was sure to be caught right afterwards, and that was a risk he didn't want to take.

If he was caught now, it would all be over. And then there would be no one left to do what needed to be done. No one else would take up the burden that he had to carry.

But still, he had the right one. He squared his shoulders, formulating a plan. He couldn't strike now, but he could spend the time putting things into place. Making sure that he was ready when the time did come.

He let the man disappear out of his sight, knowing that it was unwise to push things too far. To get caught watching him. He knew enough now, had seen enough. There was nothing more to do.

Nothing but to wait, and plan, and prepare for the coming darkness that would shield him while he did what he knew was right.

# CHAPTER FIFTEEN

Laura snatched up her ringing phone, putting it to her ear as she answered. The loud noise had snapped her out of her thoughts, which was welcome. All she was doing was spiraling, trying to think of ways to work on this case quickly without pushing Nate even further away— or making things even more uncomfortable. Since lunch, all she'd been doing was going over the same ground over and over, trying to look for something she might have missed in the crime scene notes or the dating app messages or the friend and family connections. Any clue that would lead her to another pair of twins, another set of victims.

"Hello?" she said, her eyes drifting over the computer screen and the last record she'd been idly looking up.

"Am I speaking to FBI Agent Laura Frost?"

Laura sat up straighter, realizing that this wasn't the kind of call she had been expecting. It wasn't Detective Frome or Chief Gausse calling, and she didn't recognize the voice as one of the parents of the twins. "Yes, this is she."

"My name is Maria Greene, I'm calling from Child Protective Services," she said, her voice professional and steady. She spoke at a fair clip, obviously running through a script that she had to use every time she made a phone call. "I understand that you were recently closely involved in a case which required a minor to be taken from her home."

"Amy Fallow," Laura said, sitting on the edge of her chair anxiously. "Yes, that's right." From the corner of her eye she noticed Nate looking at her, but he didn't say anything out loud.

"All right. I have it on my notes here to make sure to notify you of updates in her case file, and we have managed to make a breakthrough today."

Laura's heart was beating hard in her chest. A breakthrough? What did that mean? Her words were so clinical, like she could have been talking about anyone—or anything. A piece of evidence that was being filed. "Is she all right?" Laura asked, which was all she really wanted to know.

"Yes, I believe the child is in good hands as we speak," Maria replied. She remained even, calm, as though there was nothing in the world that could hurry her or make her panic. "We wanted to let you know that we have been able to track down a next-of-kin for her, and that person has agreed to take on her care. She won't be entering the care or foster system."

"Okay," Laura said. She felt unsteady, like the wind was blowing in two directions at once and she didn't know which way to let it drive her. Was this good news or not? She didn't know how to tell. "Who is the new guardian?"

"Ma'am, I'm afraid I can't divulge that information," Maria said, again just like she was reading from a script. "All we are required to tell you is that the child's case is now being moved on to the next stage, and that she does have a guardian confirmed. Further information can only be obtained if it is relevant to a court case or an ongoing crime."

"What if it is relevant?" Laura asked, beginning to panic. Amy was going to live with someone else. What if that someone was just like her father? Someone who would beat her, terrorize her? Someone worse?

"You would need to speak with a judge in order to get the information," Maria said.

"Well, where is she going? Is she at least staying in the state?" Laura asked. How was she supposed to check up on Amy, make sure that she was all right, if she had no idea where to find her?

"Ma'am, I'm not authorized to divulge that information," Maria repeated. "I would advise you to speak with a judge if you have reason to believe that a crime is being committed. If there is a pending court case, which I'm seeing there is on file, you will most likely hear the information in court."

The trial of Governor Fallow—ex-Governor Fallow, now—would be a long way away. If he even went to a full trial. He'd been caught quite literally red-handed. There were two FBI agents ready to testify against him, plus a wealth of physical evidence. The most likely thing for him to do would be to just plead guilty and get his sentence. In that case, Laura wouldn't be able to hear anything about Amy at all.

And even if he was stubborn and insisted on pleading guilty, citing something like not being in his right mind, it would be months until anything happened.

"That will take too long," Laura said, desperately. "How can I find out if she's all right now?"

The social worker paused, as if weighing her words. "I'm afraid the only way for you to have further contact with her at this stage would be if the guardian was to reach out to you directly," she said, sounding for the first time like she was a real human. Something in Laura's voice must have spoken to her, explained how important this was.

"Then, can you give him my details?" Laura asked. "Tell him—or her—I want to speak with them?"

"I can try," Maria said. "I can't promise anything. It will be up to the guardian to decide whether they want to speak with you, given there's no current legal concern."

"Thank you," Laura said, because it was better than nothing. "You can give them this number. Please tell them I'm concerned about Amy and I just want to help."

"I will ask for that message to be passed along," Maria said, her tone turning more businesslike again. "You have a good day now, ma'am."

She hung up, and Laura bit her lip for a long moment. It was better than nothing, but not by much. All it would take would be for this new guardian to decide they didn't want anything to do with law enforcement—which an abuser normally wouldn't—and Amy was essentially on her own again.

The only comfort Laura had was that the girl was smart enough, for her age. She'd been through enough. Maybe, just maybe, if she was in trouble, she would have enough knowledge now to try and find a cop or look for some way to get to the FBI headquarters. To look for Laura.

"She's being taken into care?" Nate asked.

Laura looked at him. He was still watching his computer screen, still doing his own research task. As if she wasn't there. But he was asking, which meant he cared on some level.

At least he still had that.

"No," Laura said. "They've been able to find her a new guardian. Apparently, her new next-of-kin was willing to take her on."

"Great," Nate said, nodding. "I guess that case is all wrapped up for now, then."

Laura's mouth dried around her tongue. She wanted to tell him that it wasn't wrapped up at all. It might as well only just be beginning. There was a whole world of bad things that might happen to Amy with a new guardian. She needed someone looking out for her.

She needed Laura.

Or Laura needed her—needed to know that she was safe.

"Did you find anything?" Nate asked, nodding his head sideways towards her desk, and Laura realized he'd moved on already. Back to the case at hand.

And as much as she hated to admit it, he was right. There was nothing else she could do right now—not from here. She could wait until the new guardian contacted her, if they ever would. Or she could try to talk to someone on the ground, go to the agency, see if someone would slip up and give away any clues she could follow. But neither of those things were things she could make happen right now, so focusing on the case would be better.

Focusing on getting it solved, and getting back home.

"No," she admitted. "I was thinking about looking for other potential victim profiles."

Nate stopped typing and looked at her with a frown. "What do you mean, other victims?"

"Well, I don't want to be pessimistic, but I'm not seeing a lot of reasons for someone to want to kill both girls," Laura said. "I could understand a home invasion or a theft gone wrong, or even something personal that spilled over and ended up in violence. But twice, on the same night, targeting both twins one after another? It doesn't make a lot of sense to me as a random crime."

"That doesn't necessarily follow that it's some kind of serial killer targeting twins," Nate replied. "We only have two deaths. That's all. Why assume there would be more? I thought we agreed that the frenzied nature of the attack made this more likely to be personal."

"Personal is relative," Laura said. She might almost have enjoyed this conversation, in another context. Talking over the theory of crime, of criminal behavior. What made people tick. If it wasn't that the stakes were high, because she already know another set of twins were at risk. If it wasn't for the argument she and Nate were having. As it was, she just needed to convince him—and fast. "Jack the Ripper was probably not intimately acquainted with and angry at each of the sex workers he killed. He just had anger towards sex workers in general. And those attacks were the very definition of brutal."

Nate twisted his face in a doubtful expression. "It's a little hard to prove anything using the example of a case that was never solved," he said. "We can't speak to his motive at all."

"All right, but you know what I'm talking about," Laura said impatiently. "Some of the most vicious killers in history have targeted seemingly random people, who reminded them of the person or people they were truly angry at."

"You don't have to put me back through basic training," Nate grunted. Laura almost flinched at his tone. "We should be paying more attention to the links to the twins we know are victims, before we start looking for more that might never happen."

"I've done everything I can here." Laura shrugged. "The detectives are already out there, interviewing all of the contacts Ruby recently made on that dating app. What more can we do? I might as well take a look."

Nate sighed. He rubbed the bridge of his nose, as though he was developing a headache. "If you feel that's the best use of your time, Agent Frost."

It was like a dagger in her chest—an image that made Laura shudder all the more given what they were working on right now. His formal use of her name was a clear message. That they were partners only, colleagues, no longer friends. Even if she'd felt the chill from him all this time and knew where they stood, it was still awful to hear it.

She turned back to her computer. It was all she could do. Bury herself in work and stop thinking about it.

At least he was no longer arguing with her or trying to stop her from going down the path she wanted to follow.

Laura idled a moment, trying to think where she could even start. She figured she could look for people with the same surname first, using the local law enforcement records to see if anyone in the area had ever been arrested or questioned for something. She would then be able to narrow it down by age. Anyone who was the same age and had the same surname could provide a source of inspiration.

And within moments of even beginning to try, she quickly saw the flaw in her plan. How could you search for a surname if you didn't know which ones to go for? She couldn't just scroll alphabetically through the whole list of all of the people who'd been put into the system in Milwaukee. That would take weeks—maybe even longer. It wouldn't get her anywhere.

She experimentally ran a search for people born later than a date that would make them thirty years old, remembering the men in her vision had seemed fairly young. But as the results loaded onto her screen, she suppressed a groan. It was still dozens upon dozens of pages long, each page holding scores of results. Still too wide a net.

Laura chewed on one of her fingernails, a habit she'd gotten out of when she was a teenager. Apparently, it was coming back. She had to think. How could she find out who was a twin? Just limiting it to people with criminal records would probably only give her a fraction of the population anyway. How likely was it that every single twin out there was in the police system? Ruby and Jade Patrickson hadn't been, before they were logged as murder victims.

Laura hit the internet, trying the simplest solution she could think of: a search for *Milwaukee twins*.

And almost immediately, she stumbled upon a hit.

There was a charity catering to twins in the local area, helping their families to deal with the unexpectedly doubled load of two babies instead of one. It was a resource center and a social club, too, the kind of place parents came for help with infants and stayed to let their teens connect with people who were like them. And then hung around to help when they became adults.

The kind of organization that would have a lot of records, and a lot of names, related to twins in the city.

Laura held her breath as she clicked around on the charity's official site, looking for a way that she could access the records quickly and without having to get a warrant. She found a news page with updates about fundraising events the charity had recently done, and—

And her heart almost stopped.

She clicked on the news article that had caught her eye, desperate for the page to load the larger image quicker. She needed to see it in higher resolution. She needed to be sure…

And, yes. There he was.

The man from her vision.

He was standing behind a stall, grinning at the camera with his arm around an older woman. A few others were gathered around, either twins or individuals all ranging in age, all of them posing for the camera. The caption told of a successful bake sale, the proceeds of which were going to a local hospital to include the equipment and specialist units required for premature babies—which twins often were.

Laura stared at him, almost disbelieving the fact that she had found him by chance. She scrolled down the article, searching, until she found a quote from a young man who was listed as being twenty-four years old. A male twin who'd helped at the sale. It had to be him. Kevin Wurz.

Kevin Wurz. Born twenty-four years ago, or perhaps between twenty-three and twenty-five if the article was outdated or incorrect. Laura switched back to the system and searched the records: surname Wurz, date of birth within the ranges she had identified.

And one result came back.

Not Kevin Wurz, but Kenneth. Twenty-four years old. He'd had a misdemeanor charge about six months ago, for vandalism of a local business. The name, the age. It fit. It had to be one of the twins she was looking for. It had to be.

And there, right there in the notes attached to his arrest record, was a statement from a Kevin Wurz, same birthdate. Different address. But she'd found them—both of them.

She had their home addresses.

She could save them.

# CHAPTER SIXTEEN

Laura glanced sideways at Nate. He was concentrating, but a frown of frustration had developed in the middle of his forehead, which meant he was probably getting toward the end of his list.

Laura changed her mind about speaking to him right away, getting a sense that it wouldn't lead her anywhere. They still had a little time. If she had more evidence, something more concrete to go on, she could persuade him to help. But firing it at him out of the blue wouldn't do a thing.

Instead, she started combing the database again, this time looking for murder victims. Victims who were twins. That, at least, should be in the searchable data. If she had precedent, she could demonstrate that it was going to happen again. That the danger was imminent. And then he'd have to listen—and they could protect the Wurz twins at their home addresses before it was too late.

Unbelievable as it was, there was only one set of twins listed as victims in the past thirty years. Sure, there were the odd single twin here and there, but the other one always survived. And the one case Laura did find had been a hit and run, the victims just children in a buggy. Nothing at all similar to this MO.

Which meant that her job of persuading him to listen just got that much harder.

Detective Frome appeared at the end of the bullpen, coming through double doors that led out to the street. Spotting them, he headed over quickly, ducking his head slightly as he walked. Not good, Laura thought. He looked faintly guilty. Like he was about to give them bad news.

"Hi, Agents," he said, stuffing his hands into his pockets. "I just spoke to the other guys who were out talking to the dating app people. We've managed to cover them all. No one suspicious without any alibi, eh."

"Anyone without an alibi at all?" Nate asked, squinting his eyes slightly.

"Only a couple." Frome shrugged helplessly. "I can give you their names, but they're not at all suspicious according to the guys who talked to them. We'll have full written reports for you by the end of the day."

For a moment Laura thought Nate was going to insist, to ask to speak to the two without alibis immediately. But he seemed to deflate. "I'm at a dead end with this myself," he said. "Doesn't look like we're getting anywhere right now."

"Sorry we couldn't be more help, eh," Frome said. He seemed dejected, like a kid having to let down a parent.

"We'll get there," Laura said, trying to sound brighter. "I think we should go down this twin route."

"Twin route?" Frome said, raising his eyebrows hopefully.

Nate only sighed.

This was her chance, Laura could see. Nate was on the ropes, having used up all of their resources so far and got nowhere. Short of waiting for the coroner's report and some kind of miracle, like a fiber from a one of a kind glove left in one of the wounds, there wasn't likely to be any advancement then. They might find out what kind of knife was used to kill the girls, but what help would that be without an actual weapon to pick up and analyze for prints?

Not only that, but with Frome here, she had a more captive audience. And Frome was clearly impressionable, a young detective who wanted to be better at his job. He might listen to something an FBI agent said just because they were an agent. He might believe her, back her up.

"I think we're striking out on finding a personal connection to the killer because there is none," she said. "I think, whoever this is, he isn't connected to Ruby and Jade. He's killing them for another reason."

"What reason?" Frome asked, practically rushing forward to hear more. She had to suppress a smile. He was the perfect audience, just like she'd thought.

"I don't know that yet," Laura said. "And besides, just because he has a reason, doesn't mean it will make sense to us. But any profiler worth their salt would look at this case and immediately pick out the fact that they were twins as being an obviously defining characteristic."

"I don't see any basis for suspecting that anyone else is going to die," Nate said, although this time it was a lot more half-hearted than his previous objection.

"I hope they won't," Laura countered. "But if they do, I'd rather be ready for it. And from what I've seen in my research this afternoon, if this is a killer going after twins, I have a pretty good idea of where they might strike next."

That was more than enough to pique Frome's attention. Nate shifted in his seat, looking at her openly now. "Where?" Frome asked, his eyes gleaming, like he was watching the masters at work and couldn't get enough of it.

Laura leaned forward, playing into it. Addressing both of them as if she'd spent the whole afternoon coming up with some theory and narrowing it down, instead of finding the twins she knew all along were next in line. "I searched for twins in the Milwaukee area, right? And I came up with this charity, which works with families who have twins to make sure they have the support they need. That gave me some names to start with." She paused, tucking her blonde hair behind her ears. "I checked some of them out—the ones who were adults, but not too old. And I came up with something really interesting. A pair of twins who match Ruby and Jade's situation pretty closely."

"Two girls?" Nate asked. At least he was beginning to sound slightly interested, even if he was still frowning.

"Boys," Laura said, shrugging. "That's the only thing that doesn't match up closely. But they're identical twins, twenty-four years old— less than a year younger than Ruby and Jade. They both still live in Milwaukee, but, crucially, they live separately. That means the killer could strike and take them both out in different locations, the same way he did with Ruby and Jade."

"You think he might attack them tonight?" Frome asked.

Laura hesitated. She hadn't seen deadly intent in her vision. She hadn't seen him actually follow them inside or take out a knife. But she'd felt it. You didn't stalk someone just because you wanted to know what they were getting up to. You stalked them because you were planning to take them out, and soon. At least, you did if you were the kind of killer who needed to get access to people's homes.

"Yes," she said. "I think that's a very real possibility."

"Then we should do something!" Frome said fiercely. "We could get there ahead of him, stop it from happening."

"I agree," Laura said. "Speak to your captain about getting us some men. We need to cover two different locations at once tonight. The quicker we can get down there, the better."

Frome turned smartly and rushed away, clearly excited to be taking part in what was now a bona fide FBI investigation.

"Laura," Nate began, his tone warning. "This is a long shot."

"I know it looks like a long shot," Laura said. She sighed, took a breath. Why not? He was already not talking to her properly anyway.

"Nate, you know how you think I'm not telling you something because I always seem to know what's going to happen?"

"Yes," he said, his gaze snapping to her in the same way a guard dog zeroed in on a noise. He thought she was about to tell him something. She tried not to let her heart sink at that.

"Well, that means you know, at least on some level, that my hunches usually turn out to be right," Laura said. "Doesn't it?"

Nate frowned. "We disagree on calling them hunches. But, yes, fundamentally speaking."

"Then trust me on this one," Laura said. "Even if you don't want to trust me as a person, as a friend. Even if you don't like the way I do things. For the sake of the case and the possibility of saving someone's life, trust me that I might be onto something here."

Nate waited a long moment. She watched him, her heart in her mouth. But at last, reluctantly, he nodded. "We go to check out one of the twins, make sure they're safe, and send Frome with backup to the other?" he asked.

Laura nodded sharply. "Exactly what I was thinking."

\*\*\*

Nate watched Laura from the side of his eye as they drove to the address she had picked out. She'd seemed to hesitate when deciding which one they should go after, and which one to send Frome to. Like she didn't understand which of them would be the best to prioritize. Nate didn't see why it made a difference, if she was so sure they were both going to be attacked anyway.

And that was why he was watching her. Trying to catch some kind of sign. It wasn't as though this was the first case they'd worked together where she'd had one of her weird hunches, but in the beginning he'd thought it was just a quirk. Then, as he began to think it might be something more, he'd thought she would tell him.

Now, he was realizing that if he wanted to know anything, he was going to have to figure it out himself.

She seemed to be concentrating only on the road, giving him no outward sign of anything out of the ordinary. Out of the ordinary for Laura, anyway. Her pretty, delicate face was marred by a frown that pulled down the corners of her lips. Worry. She was worried that they weren't going to get there in time, he thought.

She was always worried. She always seemed to take on every case as a huge personal responsibility. Yes, as federal agents, it was their job to solve tough cases, sometimes in a race against time. But the responsibility was never shouldered by one person alone. She had a partner. They often had locals on the ground to back up the investigation. They worked as a team.

For Laura, it always seemed different. Like she thought she was the only person alive who could stop something bad from happening.

And Nate had to wonder why that was.

"I think this is it, up ahead," Laura said, ducking her head to peer through the top of the windshield at an apartment block that was looming in the near distance, just down the street. It was tall and modern, shiny glass marking floor-length windows in each apartment. Most likely a sight more expensive than the ones they had visited earlier, where Ruby and Jade had met their ends.

Nate adjusted his position in his seat, gearing himself up mentally. They would have to go up there and talk to this guy, try to explain everything. If Laura was right, he would be in danger. There might even be a chance that the killer was around somewhere. It was still late afternoon, the evening some time away yet, but with the year getting later it was getting dark earlier. There could be danger here.

If Laura was right.

But what unsettled Nate so much was that she so often was.

He watched her as she parked in a private lot under the apartment building, flashing her badge at a camera until the gate buzzed open for them. Behind them, a marked police car followed, their own backup. The closer they got to the apartment, the more and more anxious she seemed to be. Everything about her tightening, tensing. She was getting ready for a fight.

It was her certainty that troubled him the most. She *knew*. Or, at least, she was convinced she knew. And where did that conviction come from, if it really was just a hunch like she kept pretending?

They traveled up to the main building in an elevator, not saying a word. Nate noticed how Laura's hand strayed to her gun, checking it, while they waited to arrive at the correct floor. When the doors pinged open she was through them first, practically charging down the hall. The cops were still far behind them, maybe still walking to the elevator, she'd moved so fast. She knocked on the apartment that was marked with the right number without waiting for him to catch him, practically thrumming with nervous energy.

An energy that, clearly, set the young man who opened the door instantly on edge.

"Hello?" he said, raising a questioning eyebrow as he looked at the two strangers standing in his doorway. He was blond and blue-eyed, looking more like he should be an aspiring movie star in LA than here in Milwaukee.

"My name is FBI Special Agent Laura Frost, and this is my colleague, Special Agent Nathaniel Lavoie," Laura rattled out quickly, giving him no chance to jump in and speak for himself. "We need you to come with us. We have reason to believe you may be in danger. There's no need to panic just now, we're going to look after you. But you do have to come away from here into our protection."

The man blinked a couple of times, looking between the two of them as if expecting this to be some kind of prank. When he peered at their badges and apparently found them authentic enough, his tanned face paled slightly.

"What?" was all he managed to respond.

Laura made an impatient movement with her head. "Kevin Wurz," she said. "I need you to come with us into protective custody. Your life may be in danger if you don't. We're here to protect you."

Kevin blinked again, shaking his head. "Why?"

Laura forced herself to take a breath. Nate saw it, how she was trying desperately to hold herself together and explain it to this man. She wanted him to just comply so she could do her job. She was frustrated. "We believe someone—a killer—may be targeting identical twins. Now, it's not certain that he'll strike here, but we want to get you to safety in case he does."

"My brother," Kevin said immediately. "Kenneth. Have you—"

"A team is on its way to his home right as we speak," Laura replied. Behind them down the hall, the elevator doors were opening, the cops walking out. Nate spared them a glance. They looked pissed at having been left behind. "This is a precautionary measure, and we can't force you to come with us, but I really do recommend that you come along. It's for your own safety."

"Yeah," Kevin said, still blinking, totally bemused and baffled by what she was saying. He scratched the back of his head, turning to look into his apartment and then turning back. "Um. Should I bring anything with me?"

"You're permitted to." Laura nodded. "You're not under arrest. If you want to bring something to make yourself comfortable, or entertain yourself tonight, you're welcome to."

"Tonight," Kevin repeated, as if trying to work out the meaning of the word. "How long do you think I'll need to stay?"

Nate glanced at Laura. She didn't seem to have an answer. "We aren't sure yet," he said, speaking up for her. "We hope not long. With any luck, this guy will come along and we'll catch him. But we'll need to make sure it's safe before we send you back home."

"Right." Kevin hesitated again before walking back into the apartment—and Laura followed, glancing around to make sure that there was no one lying in wait for him.

"We should stay here," she told Nate in a low voice. "Let the cops take him back. I want to see if this guy shows up."

Nate nodded grimly. He didn't see the need to disagree. Right now, he wanted to keep watching Laura—and above all, to see if she was right. Because if she was, then his questions were only going to get more urgent, and he wanted them answered as soon as possible.

If not by her directly, then he was just going to have to be a cop and get to the bottom of it himself.

# CHAPTER SEVENTEEN

He settled behind the door, waiting.

This was the worst part of the whole thing. The waiting. He never knew for sure how long it was going to take for them to arrive, even though he did his best to study their routine. People were late for all kinds of reasons. Traffic. Delays on the subway. Stopping to take a phone call. Doing errands on the way home.

They could be early, too, which was why the waiting took so long. He had to be there in good time, get himself situated and hidden in the house. It was hard to work out where to go. That was part of the research, too: spending time figuring out how to get up to their windows, or how he would be able to pick the lock on the front door. He'd spent hours watching videos to try and get it right.

And then there was the time spent looking through the windows before he actually broke in, trying to find the best place to hide, where the shadows would be falling by the time the target got home from work. He wasn't used to this kind of thing. It didn't come naturally to him. It just had to be done. So, he took the time, learned, figured out what he had to do to stay hidden for as long as possible.

He'd been inside for so long already tonight. He felt himself almost drifting off, lost in the monotony of it all, when a key finally scraped in the lock. It startled him upright again, making his heart race, adrenaline bursting through his body. He grabbed the knife, set down on a side table so that it wouldn't get sweaty in his palm, and gripped it hard.

The door opened, and he heard someone come inside and shut it. Just one person, from what he could tell. Excellent. The guy was alone. No need to make this more complicated than it already was.

He tensed his whole body, hearing the sound of someone coming down the hall toward him. He'd chosen the bedroom this time. The best place to wait. Almost everyone ended up coming into their bedrooms after getting home from work—to get changed, to freshen up, or just to lie down on the bed for a moment with exhaustion. Even if they stopped by the kitchen first, they had to come and get ready for the night eventually.

And the footsteps in the hall were coming right this way.

He raised the knife just slightly, steadying his grip, rocking a little on his heels. Ready to spring out and strike. Ready to take him down. It wasn't a girl this time. It wasn't going to be as easy. He needed to get in some good hits with the knife before this twin had the chance to fight back. Right into his back, maybe—he'd been trying to study the location of the kidneys, understood that it was a good place to strike...

There was a knock on the front door, resounding loudly through the small apartment, and he almost gasped in despair as the footsteps started to move away again.

No, no, no—this was all wrong. A guest? He couldn't have a guest! For all the time he'd been watching, this man had never had a guest on a weekday. He just didn't do it. Now everything was going to be ruined. If there was someone else in the house, how was he going to do what he needed to do?

There was a conversation at the door, muffled somewhat by the intervening space and the walls. Whoever it was spoke in a low voice, but he strained to hear. He thought he could pick out some key phrases: *reason to believe... danger... come with us...*

He wanted to hiss, but he didn't dare move or make a noise now for fear of being discovered. It was the police. It had to be. But how had they known? He had thought that at some point, inevitably, someone would figure out what he was doing. But choosing this twin, out of all the twins in Milwaukee? Had they realized already that he was the one behind it and simply followed him here?

Wouldn't they have been raiding the place if so, not just asking the twin to leave?

"Okay," he heard the twin say. His voice was louder, carrying more clearly. Like maybe he was projecting into the apartment instead of out into the hall. It held a note of shock. "Um. Should I bring anything with me?"

There was a murmur of something that might have been agreement, and then he heard the door close. The same footsteps came back down the hall, quicker this time. He gripped the knife tighter again, seized by a sudden rush of realization. The twin had come back inside alone. This was his chance. He could strike now before the police came inside to check up on him.

But, no, wait. The police! They were right outside. Could they be out the back, too? Waiting for him? Could he get caught if he tried to flee?

Staying put, staying hidden—maybe that was the smart thing to do. But the footsteps...

The twin was coming into the room where he was hiding. He was coming right for him. It wasn't a big enough room to hide in. He would be seen. And then the twin would raise the alarm, and he wouldn't get away anyway…

He couldn't do nothing.

Even if he went down today, he was going to have to go down swinging.

This was the only shot he was going to get.

He couldn't waste it.

He was pouncing forward the moment the footsteps strayed into the room, and for a moment he even had the horrifying thought that he'd moved too fast. But the twin was there, just a fraction of a step ahead of him, his back to him. He didn't see him coming. Didn't see the knife.

He plunged it into that spot on his lower back that he'd been reading about, angling the knife up, twisting before pulling it out as fast as he could.

It was surprisingly easy. The first two had been, too. It turned out that with a sharp enough knife you could slice anything. He hadn't expected that. It still threw him just a little. So, too, did the twin's reaction—just a grunt, a small noise of surprise—and then he was spinning him around to plunge the knife into him again, this time into his throat.

It had to be the throat. He had to cut off any shout or scream that he might make. That was necessary. But it also had another effect: the blood pouring down, over his hand, splattering what seemed like everywhere as he withdrew the knife to stab again and again.

The twin slumped to the floor, and he leaned over him, finishing his work. Making sure. But then he registered the noise of the body falling, the fact that it might have been audible out in the hall. That the police might be concerned.

He looked down at himself and panted for breath, seeing how he was dark with it. The blood. His black clothing was soaked, the front of his shirt and his jeans saturated with it. So much blood. Until now it had only been spatters, but this had gushed right out, and—

It didn't matter. He had to get out of here either way. The worst thing would be to get caught here, standing over the body with the knife in his hand. He could stick to the shadows out there, try to avoid being seen. The first thing was to get out.

There was a heavy knock at the door. "Are you all right in there?" someone shouted, loudly enough that he could hear it. He couldn't hesitate any longer.

Not daring to reply in case his voice might be recognized, he found the bathroom window he'd climbed in through and slipped out that same way, jumping most of the way to the ground, jolting his ankle. Not badly enough to delay himself. He shoved the knife away into a sheath and then his waistband, running forward as quickly as he could, keeping low to the ground and against the wall.

Out front, there was a cop car parked up against the side of the road. There was no one in it. He gave it a last glance and then ran in the opposite direction, trusting the gathering darkness to hide him well enough.

# CHAPTER EIGHTEEN

Laura paced through the living room nervously, unable to stay still any longer. It was fully dark outside now, a pale sliver of moon rising through the apartment's windows. It was getting later. She couldn't tell how long it had been since they'd packed Wurz off to the precinct. Maybe ten minutes. Maybe longer. She checked her phone, but there was no message from Frome yet. The other apartment had been further from the precinct. Maybe they hadn't gotten there yet.

She had no idea what time he would come, she realized. Maybe later. Maybe he wouldn't strike until the early hours. They only had two data points to go off. And if his plan was to strike the other twin first, maybe he wouldn't get here until after that was done.

Or he wouldn't get here at all, because the local cops would catch him there, and it would all be over.

She could only hope.

Except that she'd gotten to a point where she only trusted herself to get the job done, and she fervently wanted it to be here the killer struck—so she could take him down without the risk of him killing anyone else or getting away.

She stuck out the fingers of her left hand in the darkness, brushing them lightly against the wall of the living room. Nothing happened. She trailed around the room, letting her hand settle on the side of the sofa, a cushion, a bookcase. Trying to see if something would trigger. A vision of something that would happen in this apartment in the near future.

Nothing.

Maybe that was good. Maybe it meant nothing bad was going to happen here.

Or maybe it just meant that she had no control over her visions, and once again, they were proving to be frustratingly spotty.

"Do you really think someone's coming tonight?" Nate asked, the first thing he'd said since the other officers left with Wurz in tow.

Laura looked at him, almost startled by hearing his voice. It was beginning to feel like she didn't hear it often, especially when they were alone. "I don't know," she said, keeping her voice low and quiet. She didn't want to be overheard, not if the killer was making his way inside even now.

"You said to trust you that the killer would go after these twins," Nate said. It was almost an accusation, but not quite. Just far enough on the other side to be deniable.

"I stand by that," Laura said, trying not to snap. She wanted to, but it wasn't going to help the situation. They were already at each other's throats as it was. "I just don't know if he'll show up now that we're here. He might have seen the police car outside, seen them taking his victim away. He might have overheard us coming in or even managed to catch sight of us before breaking in, and run off instead. Or maybe he went to the other twin's place first and they're arresting him now. I don't know."

Nate gave a grunt that could have been an agreement, or could have been scorn, or could have meant nothing at all. They lapsed back into uncomfortable silence again, waiting for a man who might not even show up.

\*\*\*

"He's been gone a while," Frome said, looking at his watch. Not to check the time. In all honesty, he hadn't clocked what time it was when they arrived, so knowing what time it was now was useless. But it was a gesture of frustration, because he knew he was right: Kenneth Wurz had been gone a long while.

Too long, if he was only picking up a bag and coming back out. And there had been that clatter earlier. One of the officers Frome had brought along had muttered something about him probably knocking things over in his haste, but now Frome was starting to feel more and more uneasy.

"Mr. Wurz?" he said, calling out loudly, knocking on the door for good measure. He listened then, holding up a hand to silence one of the officers when he opened his mouth to speak. There was no sound from inside. Not even the creak of a floorboard.

"What should we do?"

Frome glanced at the man who had asked. "We're going in," he said, drawing his gun. He didn't like to use it. In fact, he'd never had to discharge it on duty. He had this horrible, horrible feeling like this could be the first time. But it wasn't like they could just stand outside. Frome was in charge here, the senior of the three of them, and he had to do something.

He reached out for the door handle, nodding to each of his colleagues to check they were ready, and then flung it open. He peered inside, searching for any sign of anything off. The house was still silent, despite his intrusion.

He inched down the hallway, holding his gun up in his hands like he'd been told to in training. Should he call out? He didn't know whether it was better to give the killer, if there was one, enough time to get away, or to avoid accidentally shooting the homeowner when he emerged unexpectedly from one of the rooms. In the end, he stayed silent. He wouldn't fire, he told himself. Not without looking.

There wasn't a single sound anywhere in the house except from behind him, his backup following him along the hall. He could barely breathe. He felt like he was holding his entire body tense, trying to stop even the sounds of his own heartbeat, straining to catch any little bit of noise.

He moved toward the bedroom door, the most obvious choice, and signaled the other two officers to peel off to either side. One to the bathroom, one to the kitchen and living room area.

He stepped a few places closer, and the sight of something gleaming darkly underneath the door made him pause.

Whatever it was, it was a liquid. A liquid reflecting back the lights of the hallway, so dark it was almost black...

Blood.

He couldn't be sure, but something in his gut told him it was. His heart was in his mouth, beating so hard he felt he might throw up. He moved closer slowly, pace by pace, heading for the half-closed door. He walked right past the opening, throwing himself against the opposite wall so that he could peer around without staying in the line of fire. He pushed the door open tentatively, reaching out with just his fingertips.

It hit something on the floor and rebounded back.

There was nothing for it. Detective Frome stepped forward, throwing out his gun in front of him at the same time as he pushed open the door. This time, whatever it caught on made it stop dead, but he was able to see the whole of the room beyond. There was no one in it, no one standing looking at him. Just an open window.

And on the floor, the body of the man he had been sent here to save.

"He's here!" he roared, turning and yelling it in the direction of the hall, letting the sound carry to the other officers. "Don't let him get away!"

He swung in all directions himself, searching for the killer. Now it felt like every shadow could hide a sinister secret, someone lunging out to kill them. He checked the shower behind the curtain, looked behind the door. There was no point in trying to check on Kenneth Wurz. It was already beyond clear that he was dead.

Frome stuck his head out of the open window, looking down. There was a smear of blood on the windowsill, a print left in the rough shape of a large hand but with a texture that was not fingerprints. Gloves, instead. Then below, a drop that wasn't so far he could imagine a human male wouldn't make it.

He swore under his breath. The killer was gone. This right here was the only piece of evidence he'd left behind, and it was probably useless. Frome scanned the alleyway behind the apartment block rapidly, looking for any sign of a camera, but there was none. Maybe they'd get lucky and find one out the front.

He grabbed his cell phone. Time to call it in.

That FBI agent had been right. The killer had struck right where she'd expected.

And he'd failed.

# CHAPTER NINETEEN

Laura's cell phone buzzed quietly in her pocket, the only setting she'd allowed it to stay on. As quiet as possible in case they ended up having to silently stalk the killer. But she'd known she might need to hear it ring—and it was ringing now.

"Hello?" she said, casting her voice low. Her eyes strayed to the windows again, making sure there was no shadow leaning into view that might disappear when her voice was heard.

"Agent, this is Detective Frome." The dejected sound of his voice brought Laura crashing down into despair as well. She knew what he was going to say next even before he said it. "We're with Kenneth Wurz. Uh... what was Kenneth Wurz. The killer got to him."

Laura's hand flew to her head, her eyes closing. "How long ago?" she asked. She needed to know, now, when he was coming. When he would be here.

"In the last five minutes," Frome said. "We... we were here. We told him to get his things and bring them to the station. When he went back inside—the killer must have... must have already been waiting. He left out the back window, eh."

"All right," Laura said. The time for recriminations would be later. He should have gone inside with Kenneth like they had, checked the home for any signs of an intruder. In any case, it was too late now. Now, she had to focus on catching the guy when he came here. "Call it in, get everyone on scene to begin investigating. We'll wait here to see if he comes by next."

She hung up, not wanting to make any more noise than was necessary. They'd missed him once. She wasn't going to miss him a second time.

She pulled her gun from its holster, checking the safety, and held it in both hands ready.

"What was that?" Nate asked, his voice a low rumble in the silence of the room. He sounded annoyed. She hadn't intentionally meant to shut him out of the update. She just had other things on her mind.

"Kenneth Wurz is dead," she said, turning her head toward him and whispering it in the gathering darkness of the room. "They didn't protect him enough. Let him go back into the apartment alone. Five, probably going on ten minutes ago."

Nate inhaled sharply. "We have to get over there."

"No, we don't," Laura said. "We need to wait." She turned her head away, expecting that to be the last of it.

"How far away is Kenneth's apartment?" Nate asked instead, making her turn back in exasperation. They were supposed to stay quiet. If the killer came up and heard someone else's voice, or even just a whisper in the dark, he wasn't going to hang around.

"Fifteen minutes on foot," Laura whispered back. "It's not far. He'll be here soon."

They lapsed into silence again, waiting. Laura couldn't allow the tension in her body to go down. Her heart rate remained high, fluttering in her chest with nerves. He could be here any minute. If he drove, it would take him no time at all to arrive. Factor in a little time to scout the place—or maybe he didn't need it. Maybe he already knew his entrance point so well that he would just smoothly come inside without waiting.

Or try to lure Kevin Wurz out, not knowing he wasn't here.

No, the other three had been home invasions. He would be here. Laura tightened her grip on the handle of her gun, flexing her trigger finger just to test it. Any second now.

"We should go."

Laura almost spun and pointed her gun at him, Nate's voice was so unexpectedly loud. She turned her head instead, glaring at him. "Quiet!" she hissed, as angrily as she was able to without making herself louder. He was going to ruin their stakeout.

"Laura, I'm serious," Nate said, although he conceded a little by whispering back. "There's no point in staying here any longer. It's been half an hour, double the time he'd need to get here. And that's not even including the time it took them to find the body after he was gone."

Laura looked down at her watch, checking. He was right. It hadn't seemed like that long, with the adrenaline rushing through her veins. It had felt like no time at all, one long suspended moment of waiting. "It's too early," she whispered back. "He might still be checking the place out, waiting to come inside."

"Laura, this is pointless," Nate insisted. His repeated use of her name ground on her nerves, how he sounded so annoyed when he said it. "We don't have to be here. We have no idea if he's even coming."

"But if he does, and we miss him, then we miss the chance to stop him from killing again," Laura countered. "He's just taken his third victim. You think he's going to stop?"

"I don't know what he's going to do. That's my point," Nate said. "We're investigators. We have to investigate facts and clues, not sit around waiting for something to happen. We need to be at that crime scene while it's still fresh. We might pick up on something that the locals haven't."

Laura bit her lip. "You go, then. I'll stay."

Nate let out a sharp, frustrated breath. "You know that's not safe."

"But I still think he might show," Laura said. "I'm not leaving this place unguarded."

"Fine," Nate snapped, then seemed to take a long and calming breath. "I'll send Frome a message to assign some officers over here. They can take over from us and keep watch, while we go to the other apartment."

Laura didn't want to go. She could see, too, that activity at the apartment might easily scare the killer off. But when she looked at Nate, she saw he was serious.

He'd taken a leap of faith yet again by following her here. And she still couldn't tell him why. Maybe things would be better between them if she bent a little now and then, too.

"All right," she said. "They'd better make it quick."

*** 

Laura stepped inside the apartment with one last deep breath, knowing it might be the last one that was easy to take in. Within seconds, the smell hit her nostrils: the sharp tang of blood. The scent of death that she was all too familiar with. At least this one was fresh. The older they were, the worse it got.

"Detective Frome," she called out, bringing his attention their way. He was standing in the living room of the apartment with a loose cluster of other detectives, discussing something in serious and quiet voices, standing with arms crossed over chests or on hips.

"Agents," he said. He looked pale. Laura wondered how many homicides he'd actually attended. Even if the answer was a lot, there probably weren't too many that he felt personally responsible for. She felt bad for him, but underneath that was still a little anger. He should have known to protect the victim first. "The body is this way—in the bedroom."

Laura hadn't needed him to tell her that. Even if her nose hadn't told her, the crime scene photographer flashing his bulb through the doorway would have. "You were first on the scene," she said. "Tell me your impressions."

Frome looked to the side, then back at her, almost helplessly. Like he didn't know the answer. "It was very quick, eh. Didn't get a chance to look at him or anything. He was gone through the bathroom window before I came in."

"What did you hear through the door?" Laura pressed. Maybe Frome was too young, too inexperienced to be taking point on something like this. She should have seen that, assigned someone else to the duty. She'd just gone for him because she knew his name.

She should have handled it herself, like she did everything else. Sent Nate to one apartment and tackled the other herself. He was the only one she could trust, at least when it came to following procedure. She knew Nate would never have allowed this to happen.

And even before that, she could have acted sooner. Could have swallowed her pride and spoken up and not cared whether Nate was off with her or not. Could have rushed off herself without waiting for Frome to offer the opportunity to suggest new targets.

This was on her.

"Not much," Frome admitted. "There was a kind of thud, I suppose—I called out to ask if Kenneth was all right, and the guys suggested he probably dropped something in his hurry to get ready. It was when he didn't answer and didn't come out that I started to get suspicious."

"You didn't hear anything else?" Laura asked, trying to confirm. She tried to push the lingering guilt to the back of her mind. Not to forget it. To allow it to fuel her. To make her push harder, try more. To not make the same mistakes again.

Frome thought back, his eyes going up to the ceiling. "I don't think so."

Laura nodded. She moved to the crime scene, slipping on a pair of gloves. The photographer was just moving out of the way, leaving them alone with the body. She edged tentatively around the pool of blood, trying to neither step in it nor lean above it. The last thing they needed was to have the evidence contaminated right now, but she needed to test a theory.

She reached for the bathroom window, the one the killer had evidently left through. It was the sliding type, the kind that you needed to lift up or push down to open and close. She pulled it down

95

halfway—not all the way, so she wouldn't disturb the blood evidence on the sill—and then pushed it up. It made a squeaking, groaning sound, like most windows of this type tended to when they'd been around a while.

The apartment building was clearly a little older. There was thick paint on the frame, which probably contributed to the noise—years of being repainted rather than replaced would do that. Laura tried it a few more times at different speeds, but always producing the same loud result.

"You didn't hear anything like that?" she asked Frome.

He shook his head no. "I think we would have heard it, even from outside."

Laura nodded. "I suspect the same. Which means the killer must have come inside before you were even here, if the entry method and the exit method were the same."

She peered down out of the window, checking the route down there. It wasn't an easy one. There was a short drop to the window of the apartment below, but then a straight drop to the ground. She could see a few more bloody prints from here on the sill down below. Evidently, the killer had let himself down first by dropping to the second sill, then to the ground. Getting up, though...

It wouldn't have been easy here. But one row of windows across was a row of railings. These windows were taller, leading into a living area in each apartment, so the railing was no doubt installed to make sure they were safe to be opened. Unlike this row of windows, with its drop to the ground, those railings went down to the ground floor.

It would have been a physical feat, but possible. To start with that ground floor railing, pull yourself up to balance just on top of it, then grab the railing above and climb the brick wall, digging your toes into the mortar. Rinse and repeat, then simply reach out and step across—albeit a wide gap, and one high above the ground—to the bathroom window.

It was doable.

"There wasn't any other sign of forced entry," Frome said, reinforcing her idea even further.

Laura nodded. "Then he's extremely brazen, we can say that. He came inside and waited, risking being caught climbing up the wall or falling down in the process. When he heard the knock at the door, he must have realized that this was his only shot to get at Kenneth before he was taken into protective custody. He did... this," she paused, gesturing at the body below her. The formerly handsome Wurz twin was now staring vacant-eyed at the ceiling, strangely deflated with his throat a gaping wound and his torso riddled with stab wounds. "He didn't just stab him once and get out—he made absolutely sure the job was done, like with the other two. And then he walked out, again taking his life into his own hands by jumping, without being seen by anyone."

"This rules out any possibility of it being a crime of opportunity," Nate said. "We already suspected it, but this makes it pretty clear. He would need to stake out the place, figure out how to get in. Maybe even try it a few times to make sure the way was clear. He also knew when Kenneth would be home from work, which implies he would have been stalking him in the days, or maybe weeks, prior to now."

Laura nodded grimly. It all backed up what she already knew from her visions, which was a good workaround for having to explain them.

"Unfortunately, it also means one more thing," she said, glancing at Nate and Frome. When neither of them responded, she completed her thought. "We're dealing with a man who wants to target twins specifically, and who has already struck three times in two nights. And the only way we can stop him from adding to his victim pool now is to catch him—because I would bet my badge that he's not going to stop."

\*\*\*

Laura slumped down on the stiff, uncomfortable bed in her motel room, unwilling to settle. She hadn't wanted to come back here at all. Nate was the one who insisted they both get some sleep, after how bad yesterday had been.

They'd taken down Governor Fallow, then she'd gone to the bar, then late in the night they'd got on the plane and come straight here. And when they landed in the morning they'd jumped straight into investigating. Nate was probably right. She did need some sleep.

She just couldn't.

Laura was exhausted, if she dared to admit it to herself. But she was also still wired from yesterday, from everything that had happened since. She couldn't switch off the worry for Amy inside her head.

And even if she did, right on its heels was the fact that Lacey's custody hearing was still looming, and she hadn't had time to prepare.

That sent a sickening jolt down into her stomach, made her open up her browser on her cell phone and start searching for tips. What was she going to say? Do? How should she dress?

She barely even knew her own daughter these days. She'd been so restricted from her for the past few years, after Marcus broke things off and told her not to come home anymore. After the alcohol had sent her down a path she wasn't sure she could come back from.

Laura closed the browser, chewing her lip. It was late. Past midnight. But, just maybe…

She dialed Marcus's number, knowing it was probably a stupid thing to do, but so racked with guilt she knew she had to do it anyway.

"Laura?" His voice was a little rough around the edges, like he was tired. "What the hell?"

"I know it's late," she said, quickly. "I'm sorry. I just…"

"You can't talk to Lacey right now," Marcus snapped. "Christ, are you drinking? It's far too late. She's been in bed for hours!"

"I know, I know," Laura said, quickly, trying to cut off any more assumptions. "I don't want to talk to her. I mean, I do, obviously, I always do. But I'm calling for you."

"Me?" Marcus grunted, the anger not quite gone from his voice. "I don't think we have much to say to each other."

"We do," Laura told him. "We do. I… Marcus, I keep thinking about the custody hearing. It's so soon, and the thing is—not that I'm blaming you, but—I haven't seen her much at all lately. I just… I don't know what I've missed. What's been going on with her. I want to know."

"I can't catch you up on years of your daughter's life," Marcus said roughly. "You should have been here."

*I tried to be,* Laura thought. Marcus didn't know how hard she'd tried. What kind of demons she'd been fighting.

"I don't expect you to give me a day by day account," Laura said, trying not to snap. She needed him on-side, or he would just hang up the call. "Just, tell me. What kind of girl is she, our daughter? Who is she growing into?"

There was a short pause before Marcus spoke again. "She's growing into someone wonderful," he said, and even the anger wasn't enough to dampen the fatherly pride in his voice. How it softened him, everything about him. "She's curious, and always asking a million questions. She makes friends easily. She shares without being prompted. If she sees someone looking sad, she'll do her best to cheer them up. She likes ponies and dolls and singing. And she's beautiful."

Laura couldn't speak for a moment. It was like her breath had been taken away.

Hearing all of that—it was amazing. Learning what her daughter was like.

But it also brought with it a fresh wave of so much pain that she thought she was never going to breathe again.

She'd missed it. All of it. And if the custody hearing didn't go well, she would miss the rest, too.

"Laura?" Marcus prompted, his voice rough and suspicious again.

"Thank you," Laura choked out, because it was all she could manage. "Good night."

She hung up the call, her hand going to her chest as if she could soothe away the pain in her heart there. She closed her eyes.

And she cried.

# CHAPTER TWENTY

Laura stepped into the unwelcome clatter of the bullpen, squinting her eyes slightly at the noise. It was too early in the morning for this. She'd only managed to snatch a few hours of sleep, between getting to the motel late and not being able to get her mind off whether the killer was at the apartment at any given point of the night. She'd kept on expecting to hear from someone that he'd been apprehended, but her cell phone never rang.

"Agents," Captain Gausse said, greeting them almost at the door. "No report of any activity at the second apartment. We still have Kevin Wurz in protective custody—I assume you'll want to speak with him?"

Laura nodded, feeling her stomach drop into her feet. No activity. Somehow, they'd missed him. Or he'd never been there at all. "Yes, we'll need to ask him some questions."

"We transferred him to a safe house to keep him comfortable overnight," Gausse said, making a beckoning motion to someone behind Nate's head as they began to walk back to their desks. "I'll have him brought here for you."

"Thanks," Laura said. "Any other updates overnight?"

"Preliminary report from the crime scene, but as I understand, it doesn't tell you anything you didn't see for yourself," Gausse said. "We're expecting a more thorough coroner's report on the twins—I mean the female twins—later on today."

Laura didn't hold out a lot of hope that the report was going to tell them anything they didn't know. Unless the killer had carved a written message into some hidden bone that couldn't be seen until the autopsy was done, there wouldn't be any evidence.

All they knew about him right now was that he was tall enough to climb using those railings, that he was bold, and that he didn't like twins. It wasn't a lot to go on.

She and Nate headed over to their respective desks, temporary as they were. Nate slumped into his chair with disappointment, running a hand over his short-cropped black hair. "We went after the wrong twin," he said, at length.

Laura couldn't help but take that as a personal attack. He didn't mean "we." He meant she. She had chosen the wrong twin. She was the

100

one who had told them where to go in the first place. She was the one who had messed up.

If they'd been in the right place, they would have gone inside with Kenneth. They would have checked the apartment, found the killer. Maybe there was still a chance that someone would have gotten hurt—he could have still tried to attack. But they would have caught him, at the very least.

Right now he was in the wind. Knowing that the police were onto him, maybe he would even go to ground for a while. Those cases were the worst. Not knowing when the next attack was going to come. Having to stand down the taskforce eventually, as the leads petered out. Only for it all to begin again as soon as your guard was down.

Laura couldn't think about that—not yet. There was still a chance he had messed up somewhere.

"We should keep Kevin in protective custody after we've spoken with him," Laura said, because at least this was something that they could address right now. "We have no idea if he's still in danger."

"The killer didn't go after him," Nate pointed out. "He could be safe."

"We don't know that," Laura sighed.

"We know he wasn't at the apartment," Nate argued. She could hear the disapproval in his voice. "He might not be going after both twins at all. Maybe he changed his methodology."

"Why would he do that?" Laura asked. She knew it was more of a rhetorical question than anything else. They had no idea what was going through this killer's mind, not yet. "Killers like this don't just change."

"We haven't got any way to know," Nate said, echoing her own thoughts. It hurt, how much they were still in sync. How much they still followed the same lines of thinking, had the same conclusions. They had worked together for long enough that this was routine now. Just the way they were.

In some way, it reminded Laura of the first time she'd seen Marcus, after they split up. When she begged him to see her so they could talk about access to Lacey. He'd flat out refused. And yet all of his mannerisms, the way he spoke—it was so achingly familiar it made Laura want to cry.

And now here it was, happening all over again. Nate was the same old Nate. He just wasn't her Nate anymore.

"We need to get back into this case," Laura said, because there was no point continuing to argue over whether the killer had wanted to strike both twins or not. It was of no consequence, except in maybe understanding the methodology a little more, and they didn't have enough clues to do that. Either way, Kevin would have to stay protected. They couldn't let him go back to his home like he was live bait. Whether the killer had evolved or not, they could only work with what they knew for sure. "Figure out why someone is targeting these people in particular."

"You said that Kevin and Kenneth were involved with the charity," Nate said, rocking back slightly in his chair. "Were Ruby and Jade?"

"I haven't seen any evidence of it, but it's possible," Laura said. "That's a question for Kevin. And if he can't answer it, then maybe the charity organizers."

"That could be a connection between them," Nate pointed out. "Something gone wrong within the charity itself. Both sets of twins are around the same age, so if they grew up involved in the charity, they would have a lot of connections."

"That's a place to start," Laura said. "But nothing got flagged up in the twins' friends lists or social circles. Or the dating app, either. You'd think we would have seen it."

Nate frowned slightly. "There were no twins in the lists we had at all," he said.

"And if they were involved with the charity in any meaningful way, you'd expect some of that to spill out into their social lives," Laura said. It almost felt like she'd won a point, shooting down his theory. But then it wasn't a real win at all, because they were left with nothing again. They needed a lead. She would chase it down no matter who it came from.

For not the first time and most certainly not the last, Laura wished for a vision. Or at least that the visions she did have would be clearer. What she had seen had been next to useless. Yes, they'd managed to put themselves in the right place at the right time, but without knowing who the real target was she'd been unable to do a thing to stop it.

Nate couldn't possibly be more disappointed with her hunches than she was with herself.

Laura opened up the screen of her cell phone, opening up social media apps. She began to search around, finding profiles for both Kevin and Kenneth Wurz. "I'll check to see if they have any friends in common," she said. "I guess it's possible that they hung out, and just didn't connect directly online."

"There's a report here," Nate said. "Looks like it was dropped on my desk overnight." He passed it over to her.

102

He hadn't thought to do so earlier?

She cleared her throat, feeling like she ought to stay professional and share her findings, even if he was being quiet. "I can't see any connections in common on social media," she said. "It doesn't look as though they have mutual friends, or even knew each other at all."

"And there's no mention of the Patricksons on the charity site," Nate said, in a tone of reluctant concession. "They've contacted their webmaster for a list of names, but there's only an email form and not a phone number, so who knows when we'll get a response."

Laura opened her mouth to reply to that, but swung around at the sound of some motion at the entrance of the bullpen. She saw a couple of offices leading in Kevin Wurz, his eyes red-rimmed now and his posture slumped even as he walked. Their interview was here.

Laura only glanced at Nate to see that he was nodding and following her as she got up. They walked over to Kevin, greeting him in low voices.

"We're terribly sorry for your loss," Laura said. "As I'm sure these officers have explained to you, we need to do anything we can to catch the man who killed your brother. We have reason to believe he'll kill again, and we need to find him before that happens."

Kevin nodded, sniffing as he did so. "I know," he said. His face was pale, his clothes crumpled and unwashed. Laura couldn't imagine the kind of night he'd had, in an unfamiliar place after being told his twin brother was dead. They'd been through twenty-four years of life at each other's side. Laura didn't have that kind of close and long-lasting relationship with anyone. Even her parents—leaving home at eighteen to study had put them out of her sphere, and she'd never gone back. She couldn't imagine how hard it would be to now know you had to go through the world alone.

"Let's head upstairs," Nate said, turning from addressing one of the officers in an aside, obviously figuring out where they could talk to Kevin. They were all led up in the elevator to the next floor, where they located a comfortable enough room with a sofa and several chairs. Not an interrogation room, like the one they used for criminals. This one was clearly for victims and their families, to soothe them while they answered the questions that needed to be asked.

"All right, Kevin," Laura said, keeping her voice as gentle as she could. She always tried to think how she would want someone to talk to her if she'd lost someone special, and went from there. "We need to start by talking to you about someone you may or may not have heard

103

of. I just want you to let me know if you recognize the name. Does that make sense?"

Kevin nodded slowly.

"Have you heard of either Ruby or Jade Patrickson?" Laura asked, watching him closely.

Kevin hesitated. "No," he said. "No, sorry."

In a way, it was good that these killings were happening so close together. After being taken in last night, Kevin wouldn't have seen the media coverage that broke this morning, naming the twin women who had been reported as killed the day before. It was a genuine reaction. He'd had no chance for his memory to be tarnished by reading it in the news.

"They were twins, like you and Kenneth," Laura prompted, just to be sure. "You haven't met them through the charity you work with, for example?"

"No," Kevin insisted, then his unsteady gaze focused on her. "Were?"

Laura took a breath. There was no point in hiding it from him. "Yes," she said. "I'm afraid that both of them were killed, much in the same way as Kenneth."

"By the same person?"

"We believe so," Laura said.

Kevin's face screwed up, a mask of pain and bitterness. A sob escaped his throat before he shook his head stubbornly, wiping a hand across his eyes. He looked as though he'd been up for half the night crying already. "Do you know who?" he asked.

Laura wished she had an answer for him, but she didn't.

"We were hoping that you might help us with that," Nate said, taking over. "Any kind of lead that you can think of might come in handy. Even if you didn't know the girls, there's a chance your brother did, and we don't know what the link is between you just yet. So, ignoring the other deaths for now—is there anyone you can think of that might have wanted to hurt your brother?"

"I've been thinking about it all night," Kevin said. "Kenneth was... well. It's not like when you read in the news about how someone was loved by all and they never had any enemies. He wasn't like that."

"What was he like?" Laura asked softly.

Kevin shrugged, as if he didn't want to say it—but he did. "He was an asshole sometimes. He got into trouble a lot. But he wasn't a bad person. He was..." He broke off, covering his eyes as another sob racked through him. Laura looked at him with new eyes. He was clearly broken up, devastated by the loss. If he was willing to go so far as to use the word "asshole" even in these circumstances, then he was probably playing it down.

Kenneth was probably a lot worse than just an asshole.

"Can you tell us who came to your mind, when you were thinking about who could have done this?" Nate prompted quietly, his voice soft. An invitation to help Kevin move on, rather than berating him for pausing.

Kevin gathered himself, nodding. "There was the guy who had Kenneth brought up on charges last year. He was a real prick about it. So angry."

"What exactly happened?" Laura asked.

Kevin shook his head ruefully. "It was so dumb," he said. "He was just showing off, trying to be the big man. He smashed up this hotel room when some friends were in from out of town. He got arrested for it right away, and the police had to haul the owner of the hotel away from him. He didn't just want him arrested, he wanted to kick his head in. He tried to argue that he should be owed all these damages, above and beyond what it would actually cost. We thought he was going to sue us, but I guess he couldn't afford the legal fees anyway."

"Was this an independent hotel, or a chain?" Laura asked. She saw out of the corner of her eye that Nate was scribbling down notes, so she didn't have to. She could check what he'd written later on for her own records.

"Independent," Kevin said. "It's a local place—the Milwaukee Rest. I think the manager was called... I don't know... Wales, or something like that? Anyway, he's the one that filed the charges, so it should all be in the records. He was really angry. Said we'd cost him a few nights of business and they were barely hanging on."

Laura nodded thoughtfully. It was kind of a lead. She wasn't sure it was the kind of thing that would prompt murder. At least it was a solid thing they could look into. "Anyone else?" she asked.

Kevin nodded. "Like I said, I was up all night," he replied. "Kenneth was really popular, and people didn't like that. He had a couple of friends that always rubbed me the wrong way. I didn't hang out with them myself much. I could see they didn't really like him as much as they said they did."

"What do you mean?" Laura asked.

"When we were in school, Ken always struggled," he said. "He wasn't... I don't know. Academically minded. I was good at studying, he wasn't. People thought that meant he was stupid, but... he just couldn't take the tests well. Anyway, these friends, I think they clung onto him because he made them feel superior. Like they were better than him."

"And that changed, since school?" Laura said, picking up on the undercurrent of what he was saying.

"It changed massively," Kevin agreed. "After we got out of that whole studying thing, and Ken got a job, it was like he was on fire. He got promotion after promotion, already. He really started to come into himself. He wasn't a loser anymore. I don't think they liked that—or the fact that he had new friends."

"You mentioned some enemies?" Laura asked. "Do you mean those friends you mentioned, or someone else?"

Kevin bit his lip slightly. "I don't know. No one in particular, except that manager guy. Just... people everywhere. He would walk into a bar and end up getting into a fight. It could be someone I didn't even know. The last few years especially, you know? We have different jobs. More and more of our friends were different people. We still spent a lot of time together, but there was time apart, too."

"What were the names of those friends?" Nate asked, jotting them down as Kevin recited them and spelled them out for him. Laura was already thinking ahead, ignoring the names themselves. She could read them later. What she needed to do now was *think*. To figure out how anything he'd said—anything at all—could be a clue toward the killer himself.

"All right," Nate said. "Thank you, Kevin. Anything else, you just let us know—or ask the officers you're with to call us. We're going to work hard to bring this killer to justice."

"Catch him quick," Kevin said, looking at them both in a way that chilled Laura to the bone.

His gaze was cold, angry. Full of grief.

And without them even agreeing, it felt like they'd made a solemn vow—one they couldn't break.

\*\*\*

"I don't know about any of these leads," Laura said, shaking her head as they went over Nate's notes. "It just sounds like he's grieving. Angry. Looking for someone to blame, no matter how tenuous."

"We still have to look into them," Nate said. He glanced her way and must have caught something in her expression. "I don't mean I disagree. It's just, we have to check. That's part of the job, after all."

106

Laura nodded. "We should start tracking people down and interviewing them."

"No," Nate said. "It's a waste of our resources for us both to cover the same ground. We should split up."

Laura blinked at him. He wasn't looking at her. Did he really think that this was a good suggestion for the case, so they could work more leads between them? Or was this his way of getting rid of her, getting to spend some time alone? Normally they would do the interviews as a team so that they were both up to date on any possible clues.

Not to mention the fact that they each saw things in their own unique way, which meant they could pick up different things from the interviews when they were there in person. A lot harder to do when you were being given a biased report from another person.

"What leads am I following, while you're interviewing these people?" Laura asked carefully. She was ready to object, especially given that she didn't know they even had anything else for her to do.

"Family," Nate said, looking right at her. "You need to talk with Kenneth and Kevin's parents. See if they've got any leads they can give us."

Laura swallowed. He had it figured out already. It was almost like she'd walked into a trap, except that was a stupid way to think about an entirely logical move for the good of the case.

This was for the good of the case.

She just had to remember that, and pretend it didn't hurt that he wanted her away from him.

"I'll get right on that, then," Laura said, getting up. "Send me a message if you find anything—or if you don't. I guess we'll meet back here after."

Nate nodded silently, turning back to look over his notes again as if they were totally engrossing. Laura turned to leave, feeling something bubbling up inside her in response to his obvious dismissal.

Anger.

Which was a relief, because anger was the energy she would need to power through on this case and get the answers they so badly needed.

# CHAPTER TWENTY ONE

If dealing with grieving brothers was hard, a grieving mother was so much worse.

Laura passed frizzy-haired and red-eyed Mrs. Wurz a tissue from a box that lay open on the table, allowing her a pause so that she could blow her nose and wipe her eyes for what had to be the sixth time since Laura had arrived. Not that she could blame her. The poor woman had lost her son.

Just thinking about losing Lacey sent an ache through Laura's chest so hard she couldn't breathe. It made her want, more than ever, to solve this case. But it wasn't because she wanted to get justice for this woman's grief. No, it was more selfish than that. It was because she wanted to get back to focusing on the custody hearing, and preparing enough that she would never lose Lacey again.

"I'm sorry," Mrs. Wurz said, managing to compose herself just enough to speak again. Even her voice was watery, like she was so soaked in tears it was spilling out everywhere, and her skin was so pale without makeup she could almost be translucent. "I just…"

"It's quite all right," Laura said. "You take your time."

"I just can't think of anything," she replied, placing the used tissue delicately on the sofa cushion beside her. She was growing a pile of them. "I don't know why anyone would want to do this. My boys have lived here their whole lives, had the same friends since they were in school. I wish I had the answers, but…"

"Kevin mentioned that Kenneth had been brought up on a misdemeanor charge for vandalism," Laura said, trying to tread softly. There was so much about this that would only be more upsetting for the woman, but that was how it had to be. She couldn't skip the difficult questions to spare her feelings. She needed to know. "Do you recall anything about that? About the man who pressed charges?"

"Oh, yes," Mrs. Wurz said. "He was a very bitter man. But then Kenny did such a stupid thing. He knew it, afterwards. And the police were so helpful back then."

"They were?" Laura asked, raising an eyebrow.

"Oh, yes," Mrs. Wurz said. She dabbed one of the old tissues against her eyes. She was so upset, she probably didn't even realize it wasn't a new one. "We thought it was such a blessing at the time. He could easily have been charged with a felony, you know. The property damage—it would have amounted to enough. But they downgraded it to a misdemeanor because he had a spotless record until then, and he avoided jail time. That really straightened him out."

Laura nodded. She noted it down, even though she couldn't see that it added anything important. Nate was already on his way to interview the hotel manager; he'd know if anything was suspicious. And even though this maybe gave the man more reason to be angry at Kenneth, it didn't give him more reason to kill him. And it certainly didn't go any way toward explaining why he might want to kill Ruby and Jade.

"Thank you, Mrs. Wurz," she said, getting ready to wrap things up. "I know this has been very hard for you, so we really do appreciate your cooperation."

"Of course," the woman said, looking about ready to burst into a fresh round of sobs again. "Anything to help—to help…"

Laura paused sympathetically, not wanting to leave her on her own. "If you think of anything else, you can reach me at any time," she said. "And if for some reason you don't get through, you can count on the local police force as well. They've got detectives and officers working on this round the clock, so there will always be someone to take your call."

"Thank you," Mrs. Wurz said, brightening—or at least, pretending to brighten—enough to reassure Laura. "I'll do that."

Laura held her gaze for a moment and gave her one last nod before turning to leave. What else could she say? All the old cliches always seemed worthless in these situations. Besides, you never knew how someone would react. People got angry, sometimes, at empty platitudes.

She left the house feeling far heavier than she had when she entered it, and checked her phone. The interview had taken longer than expected with all the pauses, and she'd found out nothing at all. All she could do now was get back to the precinct and hope that Nate had had more luck.

***

Laura saw him sitting at his desk already as she entered the bullpen, and her heart sank. Nate was sitting with his hands up on top of his head, leaning back in his chair, staring blankly ahead at his screen. He looked like he was absolutely racking his brains, which in turn meant all hope she'd had of him finding something from those leads had failed.

"Nothing from the mother that we could use," Laura said. She set the car keys down on her desk, happy to let go of them for a moment. Between the isolation of tackling it alone, and the fact that Mrs. Wurz lived out on the outskirts of the city, she was done with driving for a moment.

"Nothing here, either," Nate said. "All three of them have alibis, and I don't think they're suspicious anyway. The hotel manager even had to look up the name of who I was talking about. I gather hotel room destruction is not an uncommon thing."

Laura sighed. "I think it's time to put out a media statement," she said.

"Already?" Nate frowned. "What if he goes to ground?"

"What if he kills again tonight?" Laura countered. She shook her head. She was exhausted already, and they likely had so much further to go. The thought of running against the clock again tonight, with no idea where to go next—Laura could barely face it.

Nate rubbed a hand across his eyes, reflecting the same tiredness. "Fine," he said. "It's not a bad idea. We hit the TV, radio, all major local newspapers—get them to tell any identical twins in the city to be aware."

"Not even identical," Laura said. "Just twins. We can't be sure, at this point. We should cover all possible bases."

Nate nodded in agreement, stretching his arms up above his head before tipping himself out of his chair. "Lock your doors, stay home, have a friend over," he said. "I'll go and tell Captain Gausse to start coordinating a press conference."

Laura nodded. "I'll go over my notes again," she said. "I don't know. There must be something here to go on. Something we've missed." She wanted to add, something we've missed by not working together properly. But it wouldn't help. Playing the blame game would only make things more tense between them. Besides, it probably wasn't even true.

The frustrating thing about being in law enforcement was that sometimes, criminals just didn't make mistakes. And until they did, you had about as much chance of catching them out as becoming Pope, no matter what tricks you had up your sleeve.

Laura sunk back into her own chair as Nate crossed the bullpen, leaning her head back against the seat and slumping down. She ran the conversation she'd had with Mrs. Wurz back in her mind, reanalyzing every word, every angle.

*My boys have lived here their whole lives.* That was what Mrs. Wurz had said. They were born and bred in Milwaukee. Laura wondered if the Patrickson twins were the same. It might be a link. She had no idea what it would mean, but it might be a link.

She started to search birth records on her computer, looking up Ruby Patrickson. The good thing about it being twins was that she didn't need to look up both of the women. Their records would be the same, which meant half the work. In a matter of minutes, Laura found her: date and time of birth, name of father and mother, the local hospital she'd been born in, the doctor who had delivered her.

So, they were local after all. Could that be part of it? Milwaukee twins…

If they were in Wisconsin, that could have made sense as a reference. But Milwaukee? Even Googling the term brought up nothing she could use.

Out of curiosity, and for the sake of completionism, Laura looked up Kenneth Wurz then. She was already on the right page, anyway. His record came up, and Laura looked across it without much more than vague interest: date and time of birth, name of father and mother, the local hospital…

Laura stopped. She frowned. She looked down at her notes, where she'd absentmindedly scrawled Ruby's details. Ruby and Kenneth were born a year apart, but…

Same hospital.

And the same doctor name as attending.

That had to be more than just a coincidence. It was too strange to ignore—for all three of the victims so far to have been delivered at the same place, by the same man. It was nearly a quarter of a century ago, but it had to mean something.

Praying internally that the doctor was still alive, Laura picked up the phone, hoping she'd finally found the one thread to tug that would unravel the whole thing.

# CHAPTER TWENTY TWO

"Hello?"

Laura sat upright at her desk, jolted from the hold music that had been playing in the background for the last ten minutes. "Yes, hello. This is FBI Special Agent Laura Frost."

"My colleague tells me you were looking for information on Dr. Richard Fairmont," the woman who had finally answered replied. "I'm his successor in the ob-gyn department."

"The receptionist mentioned that he no longer works at the hospital," Laura said. "She couldn't tell me much more than that. Did he retire?"

"No," the woman said, in a strange tone, and something set Laura's skin tingling. Like the feeling of an approaching storm. "He was fired."

In that instant, a burning pain shot across Laura's temples. She held herself from crying out. "What happened?" she asked, managing to get out just the two words before she was pulled—

*She was in his body again, watching through his eyes. Watching what he could see.*

*And what he could see was a woman.*

*He was sitting down this time, at some kind of café or perhaps outside a bar. The rest of the street around them was faded into darkness, frustratingly so. Laura searched for some kind of sign that would give her a location. There didn't seem to be a thing.*

*He was watching through the windows, sipping from a coffee cup in front of him. Laura only knew because of how he looked down at the cup to pick it up. The windows were reflective, but the angle was all wrong. The place where she knew he sat was shaded by an awning, rendering him all but invisible. She could see a little of the street further along, but that was all.*

*If she could see his face...*

*But he wasn't moving. Wasn't getting up. And the reflection stayed maddeningly out of reach.*

*He kept staring steadily back inside the café, and Laura realized with a jolt what he was looking at. A young woman, maybe in her mid- to late twenties. She was serving, wearing a white apron tied around her waist. A maroon T-shirt, black pants. Was it a uniform? Laura could use that if it was, try to figure out who she was...*

*But then another server passed by, another young woman in a white apron. She was wearing a blue top and beige slacks. No uniform.*

*The glass was dirty as well as reflective, and Laura couldn't quite make her out properly. She was always on the other side of the café, just too far away, always talking with customers and moving briskly. What Laura wanted was one good look, head-on, straight through the glass. But every time the young woman began to turn toward the glass, the man who was watching her looked down at his coffee. Dropping his eyes. Not giving away that he was watching her.*

*Laura wanted to scream. She needed more information. She needed to know—*

"Well," the doctor said, then hesitated. "This is a confidential conversation?"

"As far as it can be," Laura said, her interest piqued now. At the same time, she was cursing her vision. How useless could it be? She knew nothing from it—nothing at all. There wasn't even any real evidence that she'd seen a crime about to be committed. It was reasonable to assume, given the situation they were in. And it must be linked, somehow, to the hospital records, or it wouldn't have triggered while she was discussing them. But what...? "If the information is relevant to a case we're currently working, it may be used as evidence."

The woman made a humming noise, like she was unsure what to think of that.

"Look," Laura said, trying again. "This information could potentially save someone's life. We're investigating three murders. I don't know yet if it's relevant or not, and I won't until I hear it, but you need to tell me. Either now, or when I come back with a warrant for your employee records in a couple hours' time."

That did the trick, as it always seemed to. "Dr. Fairmont was formerly one of our most celebrated members of staff," the doctor said, sighing, "He specialized in delivering multiple births—twins, triplets, and so on. He had a very successful record. He was... well, a bit of a poster child for our department."

"So, what went wrong?" Laura asked. Something must have, and she braced herself for the worst: tiny newborns smothered in the ICU, mercy killings, attacks on exhausted new mothers...

"He was operating with a suspended medical license," the doctor said, which seemed like an anticlimax in comparison. "He'd been sanctioned years before and never got it back. Something happened at another hospital, and he always claimed it wasn't his fault and the suspension was unfair. But it didn't matter. He was committing fraud, opening us up to all kinds of malpractice lawsuits."

"What happened to him after that?" Laura asked. She still needed to track him down, to talk to him. To see if there was any link between the twins that he could identify—or even if he was the link himself, and potentially the killer. Though, the hand in her visions—she was sure it was the skin of a younger man.

"I'm not entirely sure," the woman admitted. "He was blacklisted from every hospital in the state. Once word of something like that goes around, there's no way back. Not even if you get your license reinstated. Your career is over."

Now, that was slightly interesting, wasn't it? A career over, a reputation in ruins. That was the kind of thing that could drive a man to madness. To turn him into the kind of violent monster that would seem to be the opposite of a kindly children's doctor. "Do you know where we might find him now?" Laura asked.

"I can look up his address in our records, but we have no way of knowing if he's still there," the doctor said.

"Good enough," Laura replied. It was a start, after all. She took down the details.

Something about this doctor had triggered a vision. That was enough to tell her exactly where she needed to go next. Maybe, just maybe, this was the path that would make her find the killer—and intersect with him before he claimed his next victim.

The vision had seemed useless. It was frustrating. Sometimes she wanted nothing more than to rip this ability out of her head, for how confusing, painful, and meaningless it could seem to be. But then again, the visions had saved Amy's life—and more people than her, besides.

Maybe this time she hadn't seen a killing because she was about to go and stop any more from happening.

Nate was coming back across the bullpen, and Laura waved her notepad at him as she leapt up from her chair. "Turn around," she said. "We've got somewhere to be."

***

"Do you think he still lives here?" Nate asked, squinting at the house. Laura could understand his doubt. It didn't look as though anyone lived there anymore.

114

The address she'd taken from the hospital had led them to a suburb where most of the houses were white picket fence dreams, with manicured lawns and rose bushes. The kind of place you'd expect a highly respected doctor with a huge salary to live.

But the property they had pulled up in front of was different. The paint on the fence—and the doors, and windows—was peeling. The lawn was overgrown in some places, and overladen with trash that had been left scattered out in others. The windows were dirty, the brickwork bore strange stains, and the curtains that blocked every window were torn in some places. It looked like it had been abandoned, maybe for some time.

Laura wouldn't put it past the place to be full of squatters, even if the bent and battered mailbox out front still read "FAIRMONT."

"I don't know," Laura said. "There's only one way to find out."

Nate grunted in response to that, getting out of the car, Laura followed him up the short path to the front door, which was overgrown with weeds splitting through the flagstones. Laura stepped forward and tapped on the door, cocking her head to listen for an answer.

There was no telling what they were about to find here. It was a nice neighborhood; that didn't rule out something nasty inside. For all they knew, it had been claimed by meth addicts who were in there right now thinking up paranoid delusions about why the cops would be standing outside. Not that they were dressed as cops. But in Laura's experience, people who were on the wrong side of the law often picked up a sixth sense for these things.

There was no sound inside. Maybe that was a good sign. Maybe not.

Nate stepped forward slightly and knocked himself this time, harder and louder. At his touch, the door slipped forward, having evidently been only just latched. It opened wide in front of them with an ominous creak, leaving the hallway empty behind.

Nate and Laura exchanged a look, their hands going to their guns.

"Maybe it is abandoned," Laura said quietly.

"Take no chances," Nate replied, his tone gruff. She figured that was his new way of telling her to be careful, while maintaining the pretense that he didn't care what happened to her either way.

She stepped inside first, cautious and light, looking in all directions. Her hand hovered near her holster, but she didn't draw the gun yet. If there was no obvious reason to do so, it was too much of a chance. You could get spooked, end up drawing down on a cat jumping out of a pile of junk. Or just some kid who was staying in the house illegally and thought it would be a good idea to jump out from a doorway and run.

Laura tried to minimize her noise as she walked forward, glancing into the first room on the right and finding nothing. She was creeping along, not wanting to give any indication of where she was just in case someone had bad intentions. She moved to the next door, caught her breath first. Then leaned around swiftly, glancing inside—

And letting out a tense breath.

"Nate," she called, her voice still low. He joined her in the doorway and she pointed. The gray-haired homeowner was asleep on the couch, or maybe passed out. He was surrounded by empty beer cans and whiskey bottles.

Passed out, then.

"Sir," Laura called out, loudly. "Sir, can you hear us?"

There was no response from the man on the couch.

Nate stepped forward, past her. He moved to the man's side, squatting down in order to take his pulse. "He's alive. Just passed out."

"Must have drunk himself into a stupor," Laura muttered, moving to join Nate. She shook the man's shoulder, then again a little rougher, raising her voice. "Sir, wake up. We need to talk to you."

At length, there was a mumbled, incoherent noise from the man, and then his eyes flickered blearily open. If he was surprised to find a couple of strangers in his home, he didn't show it. He just stared at them dully, then screwed up his eyes—perhaps in pain. If he'd drunk enough to pass out, he was probably nursing a hell of a hangover.

"Are you Dr. Richard Fairmont?" Laura asked, loudly. Partly to make sure that he understood her. Partly because she knew it would make him wince, and he was either a dangerous medical fraud or a killer.

"Not anymore," he said, brushing them aside and struggling to sit up. His hands groped for a bottle at his side and found it, pressed into the cushions. He lifted it and squinted, then sighed at finding it empty. "Go away. I don't want any dreams today."

"We're not a dream, sir," Nate said, with a patience that Laura didn't quite feel. "You're awake. We're FBI agents. We're here to ask you some questions."

Dr. Fairmont blinked at him, staring at the two of them for a few seconds. He looked down at the empty bottle in his hand, as if considering whether it was real or not. Apparently, the feel of the cool glass on his hand was enough to tell him that it was.

He moved quicker than Laura would have thought possible for a man in his state. He flung the glass bottle at the ground between Laura and Nate, making it shatter into pieces. The two of them flinched aside, away from the flying shards, and in that instant he was gone.

He lunged between them, jumping over the glass in his bare feet, and shot toward the front door—which they had left open after entering the house. By the time Laura turned around, with Nate still getting to his feet, he was outside, gone down the street.

She cursed and began to race after him, hurtling through the hall of the house and outside. She had to pause for a moment to look to either side, spotting him running off to the right. He was only dressed in a robe over a vest and boxer shorts, no shoes or socks, nothing to keep him warm below the knee. It was probably a shocking sight for the neighbors, too. He'd just shot out of there like a bat out of hell, apparently with no regard for even his own health.

Laura had several advantages. She was younger, she was fitter, and she was wearing shoes—and she was sober. A fact that she somewhat regretted at times, but now it would help. Behind her she was dimly aware of Nate's heavy boots running out of the house, but he didn't follow her. She assumed he was taking a different direction, just in case they needed to head the guy off. That was standard practice for them, after all.

Laura normally relied on her visions to help her in these situations, but nothing was coming. She hadn't had time to touch anything in the house—hadn't wanted to. It was all so grimy, and the stench of alcohol didn't help. She was almost afraid of it. Like if she touched something and found it sticky she might end up licking her fingers just to get a taste of it. But now she had no way of knowing which direction he was going to go in, and some kind of wild adrenaline was pushing him faster than she'd expected.

They flashed by house after house, until Laura was right on him. Almost caught up.

"Stop!" she shouted. She didn't want to have to tackle this guy down. He was old, and probably frail in at least some way, and the street was paved. That would mean injury for him—scrapes, cuts, and bruises that were harder to recover from for a man of his age. Maybe even a dislocated hip or a popped knee.

He ignored her, but he must have heard how close by she was. He must have, because he suddenly darted to the side, down a narrow side street, and Laura had to skid to a stop so she could turn and follow him, losing precious seconds.

But it didn't matter, because Dr. Fairmont had run right into Nate's broad chest, and was now struggling to breathe from the impact as Nate held him up.

"Dr. Fairmont," Nate said, only just out of breath. "I think you'd better come with us to the precinct."

# CHAPTER TWENTY THREE

Nate took a sip of the instant coffee from the precinct's machine, wishing that there was some kind of law for places like this to have decent coffee instead of the hot, brown water they normally served. It did almost nothing for his tiredness, tasted like garbage, and in the end only really succeeded in making him feel more weary.

But he drank it out of habit anyway.

"Maybe we should make the next one a double shot," he said, nodding at the matching cup that Dr. Fairmont was holding. He'd stopped swaying quite so much in his seat, but now he was starting to shake. Clear signs of alcohol withdrawal. Nate wasn't confident he would be useful to them for very long, but he'd rather get the guy sober enough to talk than try to get him back into action with an Irish coffee.

"If the machine does it," Laura said, sighing into her own cup. "Or maybe I ought to send someone on a run to a local place. Get something that has actually been in the vicinity of a coffee bean."

Nate wanted to chuckle at that, but then he remembered that he wasn't talking to her. Not outside of a professional capacity, anyway. He looked at Fairmont closely instead, trying to assess his level of competency.

"What do you think?" he asked. "You need another coffee to get you back with us?"

Fairmont shifted in his chair, throwing back the last of his unspectacular plastic cup. "I would rather know what this is all about," he said, and for once the slur on his words was gone.

Nate glanced at Laura, who nodded just subtly. They were on the same page. He seemed ready enough. For an alcoholic this severe, maybe this was as good as he was going to get. Once the withdrawal really set in, it could be powerful enough to stop him from being any use to them at all.

"Dr. Fairmont, what were you doing yesterday evening?"

Fairmont looked at him as though he'd asked the most stupid question in the world. "Getting drunk."

"On your own?"

"Yes. At home," he said. "I'm not stupid, you know. You're asking me for an alibi. What's this about?"

"What about the previous night?" Laura asked instead. "Were you doing the same thing?"

"Yes," he snapped. "That's what I do every single night. It's not like I have a job to sober up for anymore. Or a family. I might as well just drown my sorrows."

Nate glanced at Laura from the corner of his eye. Maybe she shouldn't be here for this. It could trigger something, end up making her drink again. And he didn't even think it was useful anymore. Sure, the guy didn't really have an alibi. But with how drunk he'd obviously been—was there really any way he would possibly be able to commit a murder? Especially one as smooth as those they'd seen, right under the noses of police?

Would he have the coordination, or even the body strength, to climb up and then down a wall to get in through a bathroom window?

"Have you been watching the news this week, Dr. Fairmont?" Nate asked, deciding to switch the conversation away from alcohol and onto the crimes at hand.

"No," he answered, sharply. He obviously held a lot of bitterness. At least that was interesting. And there was always the possibility that he was trying to bluff them. Maybe he wasn't as drunk as he claimed. Maybe he'd started drinking only once the murders were done. "I've been on a bender for months. What part of that don't you understand?"

"So, then, you haven't heard about the latest spate of murders in Milwaukee? The deaths of three people?"

"No," Fairmont said, then seemed to stiffen a little, his eyes darting between Nate and Laura in search of answers. "What's that got to do with me?"

Laura opened a folder she had sitting in front of her and pushed three sheets of paper from it toward Fairmont. He leaned over, having to put his head down closer to the table to focus on them. "These are the birth records of three people," she said. "Each of them is shown as having been delivered by you."

He squinted at each of the records in turn. "I don't necessarily remember the names of the babies, but yes, I'd say these were mine. I was working at that hospital at the time, and these are all multiple births, so I would have been the doctor on call for them."

"Each of those people was murdered over the last two nights," Laura said. Her words seemed to crack through the air, making Fairmont lift his head in what certainly looked like genuine shock.

120

"What?" he said, then looked down at them again. "But… they were so young." There was a sadness in his expression that Nate hadn't banked on.

"Murderers don't tend to consider age as a saving factor," Nate said drily. "Now, as far as we can tell, the only link between these three people is the fact that you delivered them."

Fairmont cocked his head at that, frowning. "Nearly twenty-five years ago. Surely you don't think that's still a relevant factor?"

"It is if you were the one to kill them," Laura said coolly. She was leaning back in her chair, fixing the doctor with an even stare.

She was colder since they'd stopped talking properly. More distant. Not just with Nate, but with everyone. He'd hoped it wouldn't impact their work, but it clearly was. It was probably working in this case, though, and he said nothing. For all he knew, she mystically knew something he didn't, and this was all part of a plan to lure him into telling the truth. She wouldn't confide that to Nate, even if it was. He was operating in the dark with one hand tied behind his back.

"Me?" Fairmont said, with a curve around his mouth that seemed to be about to burst into laughter. He looked between them uncertainly, and it died on his lips. "You're not serious?"

"You were practicing medicine with a suspended license," Nate said, which sounded like a change in topic but really wasn't. It was all linked. If he was the killer, then it had to be.

"And?" Fairmont asked. He looked down at the three pieces of paper in front of him almost helplessly. "Doesn't that prove I would be the last person in the world to hurt them?"

"How so?" Nate asked, narrowing his eyes.

"Because I did everything I could to carry on helping people," Fairmont said, the trace of bitterness in his voice coming back. "I just wanted to give these babies the best chance at survival. Multiple births are tricky. They can be dangerous. They need someone with steady hands, someone who knows how to make sure they all make it. I took the risk of continuing to practice because I just couldn't leave them in the hands of someone with less experience."

Nate considered him, studying his face. His eyes were open wide. His hands were spread beseechingly on the table, palms up. It made sense, what he was saying. But… there was always that "but," that doubt.

"Or perhaps losing your career made you feel bitter," Laura said, and she was obviously right about that much. "Perhaps you decided to take it out on the people you'd helped over the years. If they won't let you help anyone else, maybe they don't deserve to benefit from your work. Maybe you decided to undo your record, wipe out the babies you'd helped to birth. Show them all what they're missing, what they would have missed if you hadn't continued to practice."

Fairmont shook his head incredulously. "Why would I do that? I'd have given anything to work again. Anything. I dedicated my life to this. Why would I destroy my own legacy?"

"Yes," Laura said evenly, looking at him. "Why would you?"

The subtext was clear. His decision to carry on practicing instead of getting his license fully reinstated first had shot himself in the foot. Then he'd become a drunk. He'd ruined his own reputation, reduced himself to the mess who sat in front of them. He'd done that.

Fairmont hung his head, looking at the table. He had nothing to say.

A fact that only made Nate more convinced than ever that the man they were looking at was not their killer.

"Why did you run from us, at the house?" Nate asked. He had to clear up this one thing, and then his doubts would be taken care of. But there was still this one thing.

"I was confused," he said. "Drunk. You woke me up and told me you were the FBI. Of course I ran."

Nate raised an eyebrow. That didn't necessarily sound like a standard, expected response. Just because the FBI turned up, you didn't run. Not every person they spoke to ran.

Laura looked at her cell phone, which was silent. "We'll be back in a moment," she said. Figuring this was some kind of ruse to pretend they'd just had a new update or a new piece of evidence, Nate followed her when she got up and walked out of the interview room. He didn't like it, though. It was frustrating, having to second-guess what she was thinking—and having to follow along with tactics she'd decided on without discussing it.

Outside, once the door was closed, Laura retreated down the hall a way before turning to face Nate.

"He doesn't strike me as guilty," Nate said, deciding to take control rather than letting her dictate the conversation.

"Nor me," Laura admitted. "But we can't let him go just yet until we're sure. He did still run from us, and he's the only link we have. Plus, with no alibi…"

Nate nodded. "We can leave him to stew for a bit. Maybe send in Frome or someone else to keep talking to him every now and then, try and get him to give us the truth. If he isn't telling it already."

"Agent Frost?"

122

Nate turned at the unfamiliar voice, to see a shy-looking young officer standing behind them. Given that he'd been the one to react and look at her, she started toward him, but then Laura spoke up.

"That's me."

The officer flushed a little at her mistake, clasping her hands together in the air. "We've got a delivery just came through for you. Patient records—the note with it says that they're related to a Dr. Fairmont?"

Laura nodded sharply, walking past Nate to join the officer. "Show me," she said firmly, leaving Nate to watch them and then trail after them a moment later.

He hated the feeling of being left out. Being the last to know. It was like this was Laura's investigation, her suspect, and he was on the outside looking in.

He was self-aware enough to feel a spark of chagrin at the fact that was probably how she felt when he reverted back to professionalism only, changing their relationship completely. She was only doing to him what he'd already done to her.

That just didn't make it feel any better—or make him want to back down.

He gritted his teeth, following Laura to the documents, with the hope that they would shed some light on this whole sorry mess and get them back home to D.C. Where, if things still hadn't improved, he might just think about putting in for a partner transfer after all.

# CHAPTER TWENTY FOUR

Laura sifted through the first few documents in the box, already feeling despair settle over here. There were so many of them.

Dr. Fairmont was a specialist in multiple births only, but he also delivered single births when other opportunities didn't present themselves. The hospital hadn't taken the time to narrow things down for them. They'd just sent over everything, the whole filing cabinet worth of records. Every birth that Dr. Fairmont had been involved in.

There must have been hundreds of them.

"The first thing we should do is get someone to filter out all of the twins," Nate said. He was standing look at the daunting stack of boxes with his arms folded over his chest. They came up almost as tall as he did from the top of Laura's desk, and there were two piles of them. "It's busywork, but someone has to do it."

"Might as well be us," Laura sighed. "It's not like we have any other leads right now. We don't even have a good suspect."

"Then why are we even bothering to look through his records?" Nate ground out. "All we really know is that twins are being targeted."

Laura shrugged, almost helplessly. "It's something. Both of them being delivered by him. It's not a hell of a lot, but it's something. And it's all we have."

"What if it's just coincidence? Just the fact that he always delivers the twins in this city, so of course it was bound to be him?" Nate argued.

Laura rubbed her temples. "How many twins are there in Milwaukee?" she asked.

"I don't know." Nate shrugged. "I guess we'd need to look at census data for that, and it may not be accurate."

Laura dug out her phone, doing a quick search. "The population of Milwaukee is currently around five hundred and seventy-seven thousand people," she said. A moment later, she found the next result she was looking for. "The average percentage of people born as twins in the US is three in every one thousand. So, that's..."

Nate did the math while she was still staring off into the distance, trying to work it out. "A bit under two thousand people."

"No way we can cover them all," Laura said. "We need to narrow it down. We could at least start with this, see how many of them were both delivered by Dr. Fairmont and still live here. It could be a lead."

"And then what? Try to protect them all? There could still be hundreds."

"Or what? We just do nothing, sit on our hands and wait for him to kill someone else?" Laura snapped. She had had enough of Nate arguing with her. Not trusting her. Second-guessing every decision she made. "I'm going to do it, because it's the only thing I can think of to do. You do whatever you want."

She turned away from him, her eyes burning, and started to go through the files. She took a whole stack of them out of the box, as many as she could get at once, to dump them onto her desk and start discarding the ones that weren't relevant. She already had a stabbing headache from the stress that Nate was causing her, and…

No, that wasn't stress. That was—

*Laura found herself staring at a woman from behind, as she walked down the street. A quieter street this time. A residential area, not one surrounded by stores and cafes. She was wearing a smart uniform—a skirt suit with black heels. Like she worked in a professional, customer-facing job.*

*Not at all like the vision of the woman in the café, who was dressed casually. But Laura recognized her all the same. Her hair. The shape of her body, which was the same even if she hadn't been able to fully clearly see her face before. It could be the same person.*

*Which Laura knew, by now, meant that she wasn't.*

*She was a twin.*

*The man she saw through was hiding, ducking behind buildings, staying in doorways. Letting her get far away and then following her another short distance to a hiding spot. Doing everything he could not to be seen.*

*Where were they? Laura didn't recognize the neighborhood, wasn't familiar enough with the city. And there were no landmarks, no businesses she could track down. He was following her home. He had to be. She was alone. She walked toward a small row of houses, turning onto the path, getting her keys out of her purse as she approached the door…*

Laura jolted back into herself with force, feeling like she had whiplash with how quickly the vision had come and gone. It was frustratingly short, light on details. She'd still only seen the woman from behind or at a distance, no clear view of her face. And even if she'd seen her face, that wouldn't do her much good. Not if she didn't know where to find her, or how.

And there were two of them. Which of them was the target? Was the killer going to go after both of them? Or was this going to be like the Wurz twins, and he would only kill one?

The only thing she knew was that they had to get to them quicker than they had last time—and that the clue to who she was looking for had to be somewhere in the pile of documents that she had picked up. It was touching them that had triggered the vision.

Laura took a deep breath. "Nate," she said. "I really think the person we're looking for is in here somewhere."

She knew her tone would sound odd. That she had layered meaning under it. Stressing the point: *trust me.*

There was little point in pretending anymore, was there? Nate knew something was off with her. That she was able to know things. He didn't understand how, but there was no longer any way to put him off knowing that she did it.

She needed to save someone's life. And her secret was only a secret in the *how*, not the *what*. So, why keep the what from him anymore?

"The person?" he said, frowning. "You mean the killer, or the next victim?"

"The next victim," Laura clarified. She looked down at the files on her desk. "Or victims. I still don't know if he's killing one or two. Whether Kevin got away because we saved him, or because Kenneth was the only target all along."

"And how are we supposed to find them?"

Laura hesitated. She bit her lip. He was asking her not just a rhetorical or procedural question. She knew that. She heard the undertone in his words, too. He was asking *how*. But she could only give him *what*.

"I think we're looking for a woman next," Laura said. "It fits the pattern, doesn't it?"

"The pattern," Nate said, with a heavy dose of skepticism. "Sure."

"She would have been different as a baby, of course," Laura said. "But she has long, curly brown hair now. Messy curls. Her sister, too."

Nate frowned at her. Laura met his gaze for only a moment, then looked away, almost afraid to hold it. It wasn't just a look. It was a glare. He was furious with her, and she knew exactly why.

"How would you know that?" he asked.

Laura cleared her throat quietly, starting to look through the files. The one on top was a single birth. The next were twins, but male. She started to sort them into piles. "I just feel it," she said. "And I know you know that… that I'm going to be right."

This was dangerous territory. Never before had she even acknowledged to Nate that he was right about her knowing things. She'd always tried to play it off before. Telling him that it was coincidence. Intuition. Good detective work.

Now she was as good as admitting it openly. And still refusing to tell him the details. Yes, she'd known there was a chance it would piss him off even more. But he already wasn't talking to her, and he already knew really. What was the harm, when she could end up saving a life?

When it was her duty to do everything she could to save a life?

"You can't be serious," Nate said. She felt his gaze burning a hole in the side of her head.

"I just think the quicker we get on this, the better," Laura said, trying not to let his words get to her. She needed to get this right. She needed to save them. Why couldn't he just go along with that, and argue with her after the case was done? "Last time, we weren't quite quick enough. We let Kenneth Wurz down. This time, we need to be there—and ready to stop him from going after anyone else after this, too."

"So, how are we supposed to know who he's going after next?" Nate asked. There was barely controlled fury in his voice. He was keeping it down, but he wanted to scream at her. She could hear that. She glanced around at the nearest cops, who were all busy with their own tasks. No one seemed to be paying attention—yet. "Has he called you up and told you while I wasn't listening?"

"Nate, please," Laura said, trying to keep her voice steady. Two more files went to either side of the first: one for male twins, one for female. The single births and other multiples went back in the box. It was a system. "We need to focus on solving the case before anything else."

"Or how about you tell me how you know first, and then we can get on with the case," Nate said, his voice a low snarl.

"I really think…" Laura began, but he cut her off.

"If you want to solve the case so bad, this is how you get to do it fast," Nate said. He moved closer, leaned his hands on the desk, put his face right up at her. "Tell. Me. How. You. Know."

Laura swallowed. "Just trust me, Nate," she said. "You've known me for long enough. You know that I… that I get these things. I have a sense for them. We have to find them. There's two, and we need to cover both. If we don't, we could lose them again. We have to find them, warn them. Bring them in so they won't get hurt."

"I'm not going with your hunches anymore," Nate growled. His voice was still low, but even so, a couple of nearby detectives flicked glances in their direction. Laura wasn't surprised. The anger was practically rolling off him like a wall of heat. "I'm not putting my career, or people's lives, on the line for your hunches. Do you understand me?"

Laura looked at him. She was almost taken aback. She knew he was angry with her, but to refuse to solve a case just because she couldn't answer his questions, even though she was giving him the information? "Are you willing to put someone's life on the line because you *don't* trust my hunches?" she asked, point-blank.

Nate's face contorted with anger then, and she realized she'd said the wrong thing. Taken the wrong tactic. He was a good man, a man with integrity. She knew that better than almost anyone. Calling that into question was going too far.

"How do I know that your hunches, as you like to call them, don't put someone in danger already?" he asked. "You can't even be straight with me about them. That makes me think one thing only: you think I wouldn't approve. More than that. It has to be more than that. You think I'll be so angry it will be even worse than this. Or that I'll report you. End your career. It has to be something that bad, or you would have told me by now."

Laura flinched a little at the sound of his words. He was right, of course. Just maybe not for the reasons that he thought he was. She wasn't harming anyone, but she couldn't start telling him what she wasn't doing unless she was going to tell him what she *was* doing. That way would only lead to him eliminating things one by one. She could imagine it as clear as day in her head: him asking her in exasperation whether she was psychic or something, her not being able to deny it because they'd already started down a path of honesty. And then she would have as good as told him.

"It's not... it's not like what you're thinking," Laura said desperately. She couldn't tell him he wasn't right in some ways. He was. But not in the kind of ways he must have imagined. She didn't have mob contacts, or some serial killer insider who was giving her information Hannibal Lecter–style. She didn't go around hurting people or bribing them to get information on the sly. She just had an ability—a gift or a curse, whichever way you looked at it—and that was all.

"Then tell me what it's like, or I'm going to go on thinking that way," Nate warned her.

Laura closed her eyes for a moment, putting her hands down on either side of the pile of documents she hadn't yet gone through. Her fingers brushed the sides of the files, and there was another sharp stab of pain in her head. Not again, she thought, not right now while I'm trying to concentrate. Not when they've been so useless anyway and so vague, and Nate wants—

*Laura was sitting at the café again, drinking her coffee. She put the cup to her lips.*

*She was here again? Why? Why was she being shown the same vision twice?*

*This didn't make any sense.*

*Through the window, she could see her: the waitress. She was serving another table. Bending slightly to talk to them and then nodding, her hair moving up and down over her back. Laura tried to turn, to look around, to break out of the one specific view of the killer that she seemed to be locked into.*

*She didn't understand this. Didn't get why it was that she would see things from the perspective of a person in some visions, and yet from above while she was floating in others. Why she would see the same things twice. Why some of her visions were useful and others told her nothing at all.*

*How could she explain all of this to Nate, if she didn't even understand how it worked herself?*

*She wanted to scream, but here in the vision she had no mouth. She wanted to fight her way out, but here she was only a passenger, an observer. She had no arms, no legs, no gun. She was trapped here, watching as the waitress went through the same motions, as the killer looked down and sipped his coffee, as—*

*As the other twin walked up the street toward the café, making him duck his head quickly in surprise?*

*This wasn't...*

*This wasn't how it had been before.*

*Laura remembered. She'd been watching past this point before. She'd seen the waitress serve the table to the right—but now, instead, she turned and greeted her sister, the two of them embracing inside the café and someone else taking over the table.*

*It had changed. The vision was different this time around. They were together, not apart. And the killer wasn't expecting it, because now he was casting around, trying to figure out what was going on just*

129

*like she was. She couldn't read his thoughts, but she could read his movements, the sharp way he lifted his head to watch them and ducked it whenever they seemed to look in his direction.*

*They were discussing something with what had to be the manager, and the waitress was taking off her apron. She folded it onto the counter and disappeared for just a moment, returning with a purse slung over her shoulder. Then the sisters left the café, walking out and down the road together.*

*Laura finished—no, the killer finished his coffee, setting the empty cup down and gathering his things in a measured way, as though he'd simply finished his drink and wanted to move on. No hurry, no rush. But he was in a rush. He needed to keep up with them.*

*He moved down the street, and Laura followed too. The girls walked arm in arm, clearly taking comfort in each other's presence. They moved to a subway station and walked inside, and he followed at a short distance until he could watch them go through the ticket barriers.*

*Then he lounged back, like he was satisfied. His movements didn't speak of frustration at having lost them. He hadn't.*

*Laura realized, with a jolt, that he knew where they were going. He turned around toward the exit and—*

Laura found her eyes closed, opened them forcibly to see the pile of papers in front of her sitting on her desk.

"It changed," she breathed, just a sliver of a voice, and Nate cocked his head at her.

"What did you say?" he snapped.

Laura looked at him, blinking. She'd almost given away more than she'd meant to. She doubted he would have understood that as anything more than a cryptic statement, but still. She felt like she was spiraling out of control. His constant questions. The stress and worry about Amy, about Lacey's custody hearing, about the case itself. The feeling of frustration toward her visions that had been building more and more lately.

She needed a drink.

No. She needed to solve this case.

"We made a mistake," she said. She didn't look at Nate. She hoped he would just hear her, instead of getting angry again. "The press conference. We just made it easier for him."

"What are you talking about now?" Nate asked.

"The killer," Laura insisted, frustrated that he didn't just understand. "We told all the twins in the city to make sure they weren't alone tonight. And what are they going to do? They'll go to each other, of course. We're so stupid! Why wouldn't they rely on each other? And now all we've done is make it easier for him. Don't you get it, Nate? We've encouraged them both to put themselves into the same location—into one of their homes—the exact place that we already know he can get to them!"

Nate stared at her for a moment and then shook his head, throwing his hands up into the air. "I just can't win with you right now," he said, muttering it almost under his breath.

And to her shock—he simply walked away.

# CHAPTER TWENTY FIVE

He watched them go into the subway and then turned, feeling lighter. He knew exactly where they were going now, didn't need to follow them. All he had to see was which platform they were going to, and he'd known.

They were going to the waitress's house. How strange. They normally spent the evenings apart on weekdays. He hadn't caught sight of anything, overheard any plans. The waitress was often so talkative with her customers, telling them what she was getting up to that night.

She hadn't mentioned anything about seeing her sister.

It was almost strange, watching them together. He hadn't had the chance yet. They avoided each other, as they should. They had separate lives. One of them a bank teller, already on the rise in her career. The other one nothing but a waitress. Surviving on tips, just trying to get by.

And yet now, here they were. And they'd even embraced one another when they met! Stranger things had happened, he knew. People were nice to others, even when they hated them. It was a human thing. To pretend. To avoid conflict.

But they seemed so close now, walking down the road. How could she stand to touch her sister like that? To be so close to her? Was she doing this under duress? He hadn't heard what the banker had said when she walked into the café. Maybe she was strong-arming her sister into being like this.

The waitress was the weaker one. The one who put more stock in feelings, in people and relationships. Of course, she would be susceptible to it. He hadn't been immune to that kind of pressure himself in the past. Ending up spending time with people who were nothing but bad for you.

He turned and headed for his car, knowing he could cut them off and arrive before they did. The time of day was good—less traffic on the roads. They'd both left work early, maybe to beat the rush hour on purpose. And he knew where they were going.

The train was fast, but they'd have to walk on the other side. He could drive there, pull up a couple of streets away, and jimmy that old, rotten back door he'd spotted before they got back. He hadn't quite worked out where he would hide, but the plan had to change now, and he had to think on the move.

It was going to be harder now, of course. Both of them together. Each could defend the other, and he might be seen. But that wasn't going to be a problem, not when the waitress realized why he was there. Maybe at first she'd be shocked, horrified. He could imagine that.

But if she saw him, well, he'd just have to explain. Show her that he wasn't there for her. That he was just there to take care of the banker, because only one of them had to go. Only one of them had no place in this world.

And once he'd done that for her, once he'd relieved that burden, she would be grateful. She would probably tell the police she hadn't seen anything, or even give them a false description. Because there was no way this sisterly camaraderie, this closeness, was real.

And he was just going to have to take care of that for her, so she never had to worry about it again.

Or if she wasn't grateful, if it turned out that he'd presumed wrong and she was the spiteful one, the hateful one, all along… then he could correct his mistake and kill her, too.

So long as he could figure out a way to change his plan on the fly so that only one of them had to get hurt, he could still make this work.

# CHAPTER TWENTY SIX

Laura sat alone at her computer, the files spread out across her desk. Nate had gone. She didn't ask him where he was going, and he didn't tell her. He was too angry to get anything out. She hoped he was off investigating somewhere, putting all of that angry energy into the case, but she had no way of knowing.

She didn't want to call him or send him a message either. He had made it clear what he felt about her right now, about her methods. And if she was going to be alone in this investigation, then she needed to get it done. She couldn't let his attitude put her off. Even without his help, she needed to find the twins, figure out where they lived before the killer followed them home. She had no doubt that it was going to happen tonight. The intensity of the headache she'd felt, now soothed away by a few painkillers into just a dull ache, confirmed it. He was stalking them, maybe even right now, and he would find them tonight.

Laura couldn't bear the idea of failing again. They had missed the opportunity to predict Kenneth Wurz. She wasn't going to miss the chance to protect these women, whoever they were.

She had the files separated neatly into piles, with all of the irrelevant cases put back into the box and all of the male twins set off to one side. Maybe they would be useful in the future, if she couldn't stop him tonight. But right now, they were useless. She needed female twins, and the good news was that there were only a handful of them in the box.

But the bad news was that these files were slim, and a handful still amounted to a score of births. Add in the fact that each of those births had two babies, and she was looking at a pile of forty women. They ranged in age, but only slightly. By coincidence, the first box that she had chosen to open was the box of those born in the same span of five years as the cases they had already seen. That was why it had triggered her visions—it had to be.

Laura had already taken Ruby and Jade Patrickson, and Kenneth and Kevin Wurz, out of the files. All she had to do then was look at the ones that remained. But it was slow going. These children were now in their mid-twenties, and while that might have meant that they all had social media profiles because they were from the right generation for it, it wasn't so easy to find them. So long as she could find one twin out of the pair, she was able to set the files aside. All she had to do was confirm that they did not look in any way like the twins she had seen in her vision, and she would be able to rule them out.

It started well. The first three files were all women she could immediately find just by searching their names. But in the fourth file, the first twin was nowhere to be found. After finally locating the second twin, she realized that it was because the first twin of the couple was married and changed her name. This was a complication Laura hadn't even thought of yet.

The sixth file made her want to tell her hair out. She could not find any mention of either of the twins anywhere on social media, and they did not seem to appear when she searched their names in any kind of database. For all intents and purposes, they might as well have been ghosts. She tried searching census records to see if they still lived in Milwaukee, and it appeared as though they did. Which only made it more annoying. She needed to know what they looked like, or she couldn't rule them out.

Of course, there was a little hope. Perhaps it was just that these were the twins she was after. If she ruled out all the others, she would be able to say for sure that these were the ones she wanted.

But then when the ninth set of twins came up blank as well, she knew she was in hot water.

It was going to be hard enough to track down and protect the twins even if she only had one address to go on. She had to get there in time, had to organize backup, had to get this research done all on her own. Nate was nowhere to be found, and the detectives that Gausse had assigned them were already working on other tasks. Things that they still needed to be done, just in case Laura was unable to stop what happened tonight. And not just that—they needed to keep building a case, they all did, because if they caught this guy they would need to potentially take him to court and prove what he had done. There was no forensic evidence right now, no way to pin things on him definitively unless he was caught in the act or confessed.

This was the delicate balance of cases that the FBI always had to bear in mind: solving the case was one thing, but actually getting a result in court was another. And if no one saw justice for what had happened, and the perpetrator simply walked away to be able to kill again, what did it all matter?

Laura kept searching doggedly, working her way through the files. Another set of twins had the same kind of hair that she was looking for, but as she scrolled through their profile, she realized with a mounting sense of despair that she still had no idea what their faces really looked like. This could have been them. Could have, but was it?

Having long, dark, curly hair was not exactly a rare thing. Before she had even got all the way through the files, she had another pair of twins who fit the bill in terms of that description as well. Irritatingly, none of them posted anything that would make her able to identify them from their jobs. There was no waitress in an apron in any of the shots. There was no woman in a smart suit, not in a way that would definitely mean she was looking at the right person. They posted selfies with their friends, pictures of their special occasion dinners, vacation shots and date nights. But the mundane, the everyday, was not documented to the same extent.

In a way, Laura was glad, because it would mean it was harder for someone to track down these women the way that the killer was. But in a way, it did not help her at all. Because he had tracked someone down somehow, whichever of these twins it was, and he was going to kill them anyway. If she could not figure this out in time, their lives were over.

She finished working her way through the pile and looked down at the five files she had not been able to rule out. Two sets of twins who did not come up on social media at all. Three sets who had dark, curly, long hair. The final set she couldn't quite be sure of, because neither of them had updated their social media profiles in such a long time. One of them had shorter hair, but the post was dated two years ago. Could she have grown it out since then? Could she match her sister now?

Laura put her head in her hands, trying to think. She couldn't. She had no way to narrow this down any further, not without another vision to tell her where to find these girls. And she had no idea, still, who the killer could be. He had been as blank to her as the screen in front of her was now. All she knew was that he was a man, and that she might recognize his right hand if she saw it again up close, but that was all. And when it came down to it, what did a hand really look like? It wasn't unique enough to pick it up out of a line-up. The information was almost useless to her.

And then it hit her again, like a ton of bricks: maybe the only reason she'd triggered a vision with this particular pile of files was because Ruby, Jade, Kevin, and Kenneth were located within it. Maybe that was the link to the killer, not the new file of tonight's intended victims. The women she was looking for could still be in the other boxes.

It was enough to make her want to give up and scream.

A message alert beeped on her phone. She looked down to see that it was from Chief Rondelle. A brief, to-the-point missive: *Amy Fallow has been taken in by her next of kin. Reported safe by CPS.*

He'd obviously sent her the message because he didn't want to distract her from the case with a phone call—or, more likely, didn't want to get into a shouting match with Laura about why she couldn't go visit and see for herself.

Laura stared at the words on the screen miserably, feeling as though she was slowly sinking into a black hole of despair. She had an awful feeling about Amy, about what would happen to her now. Once before, Rondelle had reassured her that Amy was safe, that she was away from her father. Then she'd ended up right back where she started. Maybe that wasn't an option now, with Fallow in police custody, but she still wasn't sure that safe was the right word.

This person who had taken her in—she had no idea who it was. Whether it was even a man or a woman, a couple or a single person. Someone with other children, or with none of their own. Whoever it was, Laura couldn't shake the bad feeling that Amy shouldn't be with them.

She should be with someone who could really care for her. Someone like...

And Laura had to pull herself back from that thought, because it wasn't right. It wouldn't work, at any rate. She already had a little girl to be a mother to. Lacey needed her. The court case was getting closer and closer every day that they spent out here in Milwaukee. Laura hadn't even had a chance to prepare, and if she wasn't prepared, it could go badly.

And there was the possibility she didn't want to face: what if she was still out here when the custody hearing was due to start? Could she get back there in time, handle the hearing, and then return to solve the case? What if she was right on the killer's heels? Could she be selfish enough to let people die so that she could get a formal visitation agreement for her daughter?

Could she take the risk that Marcus would still allow her to see Lacey if she didn't show up, even if it meant letting people die?

Laura closed her eyes, trying hard to think. It was so noisy here, in the bullpen. On top of that, she felt like everyone was watching her. Not only was she the highest authority in the room, and an out-of-towner for them to gawk at, but there had also been the argument with Nate. They were probably all talking about her behind their hands.

She had to get out of here, go somewhere she could try to find some kind of center, focus down again.

She got up, leaving the files and her phone behind. She just needed a minute. Just a minute. She'd come back for it all later.

Laura headed right for the interview rooms, where she had taken Dr. Fairmont before. She knew there was a whole row of them. She found one that was unoccupied, stepped inside, and closed the door firmly behind her. No one would barge in with the door closed, in case they might compromise the interview.

She sat down at the table, resting her head in her hands. Trying to get clear. If she could only figure out something from her visions… she went over them again and again, trying to pick out any identifying features for the street, the café. Even the station had been out in the darkness to the point she couldn't see the name.

The visions were getting her nowhere. And maybe her earlier thought had been right. Maybe she'd been relying too much on them. Getting lazy. Unable to figure anything out unless it was given to her on a plate.

Maybe it was time she tried to be a detective, not a psychic.

Laura stood up and started pacing, trying to think. Trying to clear away the visions from her mind and the information that didn't help. There was no knowing who the next victim would be, if she didn't have the visions to go on. That area was a total blank.

But the killer—that was who they had information on. They had seen him strike three times now. Laura started to think over what they had for sure: he was a man. He was bold. He was tall enough to climb the railings, and to drop the distance between the windows without injuring himself. Strong, too—enough upper body strength to pull himself up and let himself down.

And they knew, for sure, that he liked to target identical twins. There had to be a reason for that. With no link between the three victims except from their doctor—whom Laura had absolutely no reason to suspect anymore—it had to be that the attacks weren't personal. They were based on *type*, not *individual*. And the type was identical twins.

What would possess someone to go around a city, finding and methodically slaughtering identical twins?

Laura knew the answer to this. Of course she did. This was perp psychology 101. The FBI had practically invented this kind of suspect analysis.

He went after identical twins because he had a reason to. He was targeting them to either right some wrong he perceived had been done against himself, or because he was trying to recapture something. Or capture it for the first time—a fetish, maybe.

But there were no signs of sexual gratification at the crime scenes, and he'd gone after both men and women. Bisexual killers were notably rare, and while it was always possible for something to be happening for the first time or a rare case to come up again, Laura held by the old adage. When you heard hooves, you didn't assume zebras. You assumed horses.

So, what reason would a man have for wanting to kill off identical twins?

There was the possibility that he had been victimized by twins himself. Bullied, maybe. A pair of older brothers. A parent who was a twin, and who turned abusive. But it seemed tenuous. Laura had heard of plenty of cases where killers went after middle-aged women, say, because the person they really wanted to end was their mother. But for both twins to be targeted, it must have been something against two people.

If both twins were being targeted. Laura kept having to come back to that, to the idea that maybe it wasn't a given. Kevin Wurz had survived. The killer hadn't gone back to the apartment. Gausse had had someone sitting there this whole time, and they had never once reported an intruder. No one had seemingly gone looking for Kevin. If the killer knew he was in police custody still, that could explain it, but how would he know if he wasn't watching them all the time?

And he wasn't. He'd moved on. He was stalking someone else now, looking for another option. Maybe the next victims, or victim, that he had planned all along.

Laura tapped a finger against her mouth thoughtfully. Why would you want to kill both female twins, and yet leave one male twin alive?

He was a male himself.

What if he was recreating something?

If he was a twin himself...

Laura found herself standing stock-still, floored by the realization. That could really make sense. If he was a twin himself, then it could easily feed into whatever kind of mania or aggression was fueling this killing spree.

Especially if he had been a twin—but was now alone.

There was a disconnect somewhere, a reason why he'd kill both women and not both men. Maybe it was because his twin's death had something to do with a pair of female twins… Maybe they were to blame in the killer's twisted mind. She didn't know how it would fit. But it was a theory she could follow, and that made it something she needed to follow, even if it went nowhere.

Laura stormed out of the interview room and back to her desk, a purpose forming strongly in her mind. She didn't meet anyone's gaze, avoided speaking to anyone or touching anything, single-minded in her directive. She needed to go back to the research.

She needed to find a pair of twins who had been broken apart. One dead, one still alive. Based in Milwaukee.

The good news was, she didn't think she would need to spend hours combing through medical records or birth records to get this. A death of a single twin was tragic. The thought of the one left alive, alone for the first time—it was the kind of tragedy that would sell papers.

She went right to the homepage of the local newspaper and input her search term: *twin dies*.

The results were sparse. Of course they were. It wasn't exactly a common event. There was a heartwarming article about a pair of elderly male twins who had died within a few days of one another at a nursing home, in their nineties, each one only ready to go if the other was. Laura discarded it.

But the next one down…

The next one down was exactly what she was looking for.

Laura got out of her chair, grabbing her jacket and calling Nate. She needed to find out where he was so they could get over to this man's address and arrest him.

She had a feeling that she'd found their guy.

# CHAPTER TWENTY SEVEN

Laura found him sitting outside, waiting for her. He still hadn't said, on the phone, what he'd been up to. Just that he would meet her outside. And there he was, on a bench outside the precinct, his tall frame held straight against the curved metal framework.

"Nate," she said, tentatively, because she wasn't sure that he would want to cooperate with her after all.

He looked at her. His face was blank, almost carefully so. "You have a new lead?" he prompted, recalling the words she had given him on their call.

"Yes," she said. She hesitated again, then sat down next to him. He shifted uncomfortably, as though he hadn't been prepared for her to come into his space. "I found someone who could be our killer."

He frowned. "Last I heard, you were talking about twin women."

"I know, I know," Laura said. "Just forget about that. I'm talking about good old-fashioned police work. It's different."

"What, then?" Nate asked, shifting to face her a little more. She could sense he was more comfortable with this. With the idea that this wasn't related to the reason they had fallen out.

"I was thinking about the profile of the killer," she said. "Why someone would want to kill identical twins, specifically. And it hit me. You were right."

Nate frowned. "About what?"

"Kevin Wurz. The killer was never after him in the first place," Laura said. "He hasn't been back to the apartment, hasn't tried to get at him anywhere else. It's like he's given up. Or, since he never showed up that night no matter how long we stayed, maybe he was never after Kevin at all."

"I thought you didn't believe that," Nate said reproachfully.

"I didn't," Laura said. "But the more time goes on, the more it seems like Kevin isn't at risk. The killer went ahead and attacked Kenneth while the police were there anyway. Why would he hold back from Kevin just because he thought the police might also have gone to his place? He wouldn't. He would have gone to check. He would have broken in, and we would have found him."

Nate only grunted in response to that. He was clearly both annoyed that she had argued with him about it before, and vindicated now that she agreed.

"So, I thought about why he'd kill only one of the male twins. And it's basic psychology, isn't it?" Laura said. She paused to let Nate fill in the blank, but continued when he didn't. "What if he was an identical twin himself, but his brother died?"

Nate nodded, almost reluctantly. "Yes. That would fit a profile pretty well."

"That's why I started searching local news." Laura took her phone out of her pocket and showed it to Nate, already loaded up with the article ready to read. "There was a case about a year ago. Look. An identical twin was killed in a car crash. His brother survived the same crash."

"Survivor guilt?" Nate guessed.

"More than that," Laura said. "I was able to look into him a little more, through his own records. He was committed after suffering a psychotic break which saw the police called to his workplace to restrain him. He couldn't take losing his brother. It broke him completely."

"But if he's committed, then he can't be our guy," Nate said.

"Aha," Laura replied, holding up a finger. "But he isn't committed anymore. He stayed there for about eight months and was then released. His records show that he was rehabilitated, but what if he wasn't? What if he just learned to let out the grief and anger—and, yes, the guilt—in another way?"

"By killing off identical twins," Nate said. "Like he's trying to make every male twin out there feel his sorrow. But why kill off both of the women?"

"I'm not entirely clear on that," Laura said, shrugging. She had to admit to herself that it was the one flaw in her reasoning. The one thing she couldn't explain yet. "Who knows how a psychopath's mind works? Maybe he's making it so that it's only single male twins left. The women don't have a part to play, so he gets rid of all of them."

"That needs work, but I follow you otherwise," Nate said. He paused, as if trying to find a way to disprove her theory. "It's a good hunch."

She noted the use of the word. Saw how it almost pained him to say it. He didn't want to admit that she might be right about something.

Well, that was fine. So long as he was able to swallow his pride and say it anyway, it didn't make a difference. And she'd always known he would have more respect for this hunch, given that it really was one—a hunch that came from doing the investigative work and seeing connections between the dots. Doing the work.

"So?" Laura prompted, still waiting for his final go-ahead.

Nate nodded slowly, then looked over his shoulder. "Where's the car we've been using? We should head over to his address, see if we can track his guy down."

***

Laura paced back and forth restlessly, making the receptionist watch her with wide eyes. She didn't care. She was too wired up to rein herself in.

They almost had him, but now they were getting into dead end after dead end, and it was putting her nerves on edge.

"You could sit down," Nate suggested mildly, earning him a glare.

"What's taking so long?" Laura snapped in response.

"I'm sure the manager is just finishing off a call or something like that," the receptionist replied nervously. Laura felt a little bad for that. She hadn't actually meant to snap at her. She was just snapping at the world in general.

"It's only been a couple of minutes," Nate told her, from his position of leaning coolly against the desk.

"If he's escaping out the back door right now…" Laura muttered, checking the position of her gun in its holster. She hadn't intended that as a threat either, but the receptionist shifted unhappily in her seat.

"If he's not here, we'll look for him somewhere else," Nate said, an apparent attempt to calm her down. It didn't work.

"Where else?" Laura asked him. "We already tried his home, and he's not there. If he's not at his workplace either, then where is he supposed to be?"

"I think I might be able to answer that," someone else said from behind them, making Laura spin around, immediately on guard.

A middle-aged man with a prominent bald spot on top of his head in an ill-fitting suit had just emerged from a door into the office. He held up his hands as if in surrender. Laura realized she maybe was coming on a bit strong, and forced herself to drop out of a ready stance.

"You're Brady Seabrooke's manager?" Laura asked, finding her voice still harsher than she had meant it to be. She was getting too worked up. Too antsy. If she wasn't careful, she was going to get into the kind of tension where she would end up making a mistake.

"I am," he said. "I was told you're trying to track him down?"

"Yes," Laura said. "You know where he is? He isn't here, then?"

"No," the manager said, giving her a regretful look. "Actually, he was here until a couple of hours ago. He said he needed to leave early today."

"Why?" Nate asked, cutting right to the point.

"He said that an old friend was in town," the manager replied. "That he wanted to spend some time together. It seems to have been somewhat unexpected. He didn't book the time in advance. But since we already knew we'd be a little quieter today, I let him go."

"Where was he meeting this friend?" Laura asked, seizing onto renewed hope.

"I don't know," the manager said, at a loss. "But I guess it would be somewhere local. I thought he would have gone home to meet him, but I just heard you saying he wasn't there."

Laura resisted the urge to hiss in the man's face. He wasn't helpful at all. Saying he knew where Brady Seabrooke had gone, only to reveal he didn't know at all? This was a waste of everyone's time.

"Do you know his old friends? Did he mention a name?" Laura asked, her irritation only increasing as the guy looked blanker and blanker. "Do you know where he goes outside of work? Is there a bar he likes to go to often?"

"Sorry," the manager stuttered, going slightly red in the cheeks. "We don't really socialize. We're just here to work. He's always been very quiet."

Laura wheeled around, glaring an I-told-you-so at Nate, before stalking out of the office building. She had to. She was too annoyed to stay there and talk to the man. She was going to start yelling at him, and that wouldn't get them anywhere.

Nate finished up talking with him, Laura watching them both through the windows as she leaned against the car. She wrapped her jacket tighter around herself against the chill of the day. It was starting to get later already. The evening wasn't quite setting in yet, but she was losing hope that they would get anywhere before it did.

And once it got dark, the women she had seen in her vision were in danger. If her pattern prediction was correct, they could both die tonight. The killer might be waiting in one or the other's apartment, even now.

"Hey," Nate called out, jogging over to her from the doors of the office. "What was all that about?"

"I just want to get this solved," Laura said, still fuming. "Don't you?"

144

"Of course I do," Nate said. He paused, then looked at her again. "Hey, the car crash you said killed his brother."

"Davey Seabrooke." Laura nodded.

"Was there anyone else in the vehicle?"

For a moment, Laura didn't know why he was asking. But then her eyes widened in realization. She pulled up the article she had read again, scrolling through it hurriedly. "Yes," she said. "Wait, no—not in the vehicle with the twins. They were alone. Davey was killed outright as the driver's side was crushed, and Brady survived with only a few injuries. But the other car—it was occupied only by the driver, and it was the passenger side at the rear that slammed into the Seabrookes. He was fine. Just minor whiplash and nothing else."

"Is he local?" Nate asked.

"I don't know," Laura said. "His name is given as Tom Jeffries."

Nate pulled out his own cell phone, making a quick search. "There's a Thomas Jeffries listed in the online phone book," he said. "He's still local, if it's the same one."

"So?" Laura asked.

"So," Nate said, giving her a look over the top of the car as he walked around to the other side. "If I was a psychotic murderer trying to kill other random twins to make them feel my pain, I'd sure as hell want to make sure that one person suffered more than anyone else. The person who made me feel that pain in the first place."

Laura wrenched open the door of the car, almost stumbling in her haste to get in. "Give me the zip code," she said, her hand fumbling toward the GPS.

# CHAPTER TWENTY EIGHT

Laura's head ducked and whipped backwards and forwards as she peered through the windshield and both windows, looking desperately in all directions. Beside her, Nate was doing much the same, examining every property they went past and every person on the street.

"There," he exclaimed, pointing at a house just ahead of them. "That's it. Number fifteen."

Laura moved the car closer, speeding up a little to get there faster. Almost in the same moment that she hit the accelerator, however, instinct drove her to hit the brake again—to stop the car before they passed a man who was crouching behind the bushes next to the house.

The rapid movement of the car and the squeal of the brakes caught his attention, and he looked around at them. It was an almost comical moment. This thin, tall, dark-haired man staring at them wide-eyed, and them staring back at him from the car. For a moment, nobody moved.

Then he shot to his feet and ran, and Laura cursed out loud as he took off between the two houses and toward the area of their backyards.

"Stay in the car and drive around," Nate barked at her, already shoving his door open. "I'll go on foot—we can cut him off!"

Laura didn't have time to argue with him. Again, she found herself useless, untethered without anything to trigger a vision. She didn't even know for sure who the man they had seen was, although she had a good idea. He was older than the picture that had been in the paper, and thinner, as though it had been a lot longer than a year since it all happened. But he definitely looked a whole lot like Brady Seabrooke.

She clocked the map on the GPS; ahead, the road was a dead end, a residential cul-de-sac that went nowhere. Behind, though, she could get back to where the road curved around. Nate was already gone, his door slamming shut when he was already feet away, and Laura quickly put the car into drive to perform a U-turn in the middle of the street.

She shot back along the road and down the next one, taking the turn as fast as she dared while also keeping her eyes open for their suspect running right in front of her. She didn't want to hit him and kill him with the car—that would have been supremely ironic as well as the kind of thing that would get her conduct on the case investigated—but all the same, they couldn't risk him getting away just because she'd been too tentative.

She tried to make calculations in her head, working with too many unknown and unknowable variables. Had the time she needed to swing the car around nullified the time she saved by moving in a car rather than on foot? Would he be delayed by jumping a fence? Had Nate caught him somewhere back there already?

Laura flashed down the road with her heart in her mouth, one foot so ready on the brake it was like her finger resting on the trigger of a gun. That was the only thing that saved him. When he darted across the road in front of her, looking back at Nate instead of where he was going, she hit the brake so fast the seatbelt nearly choked her. She grazed him with the car, making him stumble to the side and then trip over his own feet to fall down.

He sat there in the road, looking up at her with a dazed expression, as Nate grabbed him and pulled out his handcuffs.

"Let me go!" he yelled, the second Nate's hands touched him. The shock clearly wore off fast, and by the time Laura got out of the car to help, he was writhing and flailing his arms around, shouting for Nate to stop. His words came out in such a rush of angry shouting that Laura had difficulty making them out: something about being innocent, and needing to watch, and everything being that man's fault...

"Let's get him in the back of the car," Laura said, glancing nervously around the neighborhood. People were already coming out of their homes to watch, drawn by the noise. The last thing they needed was for this to escalate, for more people to get involved. The one good thing about being a uniformed cop was, well, the uniform. FBI agents didn't exactly look like law enforcement at a glance.

Nate hauled Brady Seabrooke to his feet, reading him his rights as they went. So long as he was under caution, anything he said to them on the way back to the precinct could also be entered into evidence. And given the way he was still ranting and raving even as Nate put a hand on his head to help him inside the back seat, he was going to be saying a lot.

*\*\*\**

Laura sat back in her chair, eyeing Brady Seabrooke carefully. He was quiet now, almost docile. Laura had a suspicion that it wouldn't last.

"Brady Seabrooke," she said eventually. Nate was, apparently, letting her lead the investigation, saying nothing. The long silence had not done a great deal for Brady's nerves. His head snapped up immediately, his eyes darting to her wide and panicked. "Can you explain to us what you were doing when we arrested you?"

"Running from you," Brady said, his voice tremulous but still full of resistance.

Laura had to resist the urge to lose her patience with him. There were only a few kinds of suspects, when you got down to the interview room. There were those who were genuine and open. There were those who were genuine and open, except they were lying, because they were sociopaths. There were the nervous ones, the scared ones, and the angry ones.

And there were the ones who thought they were clever.

For personal preference, Laura would always rather not deal with the ones who thought they were clever.

"What were you doing before you saw us?" Nate asked, sounding like he was doing it through gritted teeth.

Brady looked down at his hands on the table, the cuffs between them. He seemed to be studying his fingernails, which were crusted with brown dirt. The same color as the soil outside the house where they'd found him.

"I was watching," he said, after a long moment.

"Watching what?" Laura asked, wishing he would just make this easier for them and get to it. "Or who?"

Brady moved his head in an odd kind of way, like he wanted to shake his head or toss it but couldn't. "The man who lives there."

They were getting somewhere, but it was painfully slow. Laura needed him to say it. To tell them everything, all the gory details. To admit what he was doing in full. "Who lives there, Brady?"

He moved his head in that odd way again, seemingly unable to pull his eyes away from his hands at the same time. He had started to pick at his fingernails, the cuffs clinking lightly as he did so. "The driver."

Laura suppressed a deep and heartfelt groan of frustration. "The driver of what?"

"Of the car."

Nate shifted restlessly in his seat, grabbing a file folder that sat on the table between him and Laura. He pulled out a photograph which had been taken around the time of the car accident. It was a photograph of the man who was driving the car which collided with Brady and

Davey. He tossed it across the table almost carelessly. By luck or by design, it landed precisely in front of Brady, the right way round.

"Let's get to the point, Brady," he said. "Is this who you were watching?"

A spasm of something passed over Brady's face as he looked at the photograph. Pain, maybe. "Yes."

"And why were you watching him?"

Brady paused, small echoes of things running over his face. His mouth twitched with one word, but he never spoke it, changing direction instead to say something else. "I have to see him."

"Why?" Laura pressed.

"To understand."

It was like pulling teeth. "To understand what?" she asked, fighting so hard to keep her tone steady.

"Why he's still here."

Laura paused, assessing this answer. It was easy to follow the string that Brady was laying down, however disjointed his way of laying it was. The car accident had taken the life of his twin brother. It hadn't taken the life of the other driver. He was obviously struggling with this fact, even so much time later.

Even after a long stint in rehabilitation for the mental break he had suffered—a break he was clearly not quite over. A compulsion to watch the survivor of the crash, to observe him whenever possible—which seemed like it was an ongoing thing, from the way he had spoken—was not a healthy response to the trauma.

Brady Seabrooke was still not well, and he'd turned into something of a stalker.

"How often do you watch him, Brady?" Laura asked, trying to soften her voice, to sound more sympathetic. He would be more likely to tell the truth if he thought they understood.

Brady shrugged a little, moving his head in that same way, looking away at the wall. "Sometimes."

That wasn't precise enough to give them much, but it did tell Laura something. It was probably a lot more regular than he was making out. The avoidance, the way his concentration had broken and wandered to the wall, told her he didn't want to talk about it. He was probably in denial, or at least trying to avoid getting into a lot of trouble.

"What were you going to do after you finished watching him?" Laura asked. They needed to know whether his intentions were dangerous. Whether his frustration spiraled into something else, made him violent. It would make sense. He was looking more and more like their most viable suspect so far—a psychotic break, an obsession with his dead twin, stalking behavior…

"Nothing," Brady said. He was looking at his hands again. Telling the truth, Laura decided. "I would just go home."

"What about when you figured out the answer?" Laura asked, trying a different tack.

This time, Brady lifted his head and looked right at her. "The answer to what?" he asked, clearly puzzled.

"To why he survived," Laura said. "Once you figured it out, what would you do?"

He seemed to struggle with this question for a long time, his brows furrowing down over his eyes, his mouth working without opening. "I don't know," he said at last. "Nothing. I just want to understand."

Laura watched him again for a moment without speaking, the way he kept his eyes on his hands, his fingers constantly working. He was telling the truth, she thought. But it was hard to assess. Someone who'd had a psychotic break—they might disassociate from their own actions. They might not really know what they had and hadn't done.

"Where were you last night, Brady?" she asked. She tried to keep her tone conversational, like it was a point of curiosity and nothing else. To keep it light. If it got too heavy, he might clam up.

"I was there," Brady said. His fingers traced a line on the table, a swooping circle that twisted into a figure eight. "Outside."

"Outside the house where we found you earlier today?" Laura asked, to be sure.

"Yes." Brady's fingers didn't stop moving. "He had a nice dinner with his family."

"Okay, Brady. And the night before?" Laura asked.

"Yes," Brady said, like he was just confirming she was correct.

Laura sighed, leaning back in her seat. Brady didn't look up. He was too entranced by whatever he was doing on the tabletop.

This was impossible. His alibi was useless. There was no way to prove he'd really been there—after all, the fact that he had seen someone eat dinner wasn't proof of anything. It could just be a good guess, given that most people ate dinner in the evening.

And with his state of mind, there was really no way to be sure whether or not he knew that he had done anything. They would need to get an actual psychiatrist in here to have him assessed. Then there would be a lot more work to put into tracking his movements, trying to trace down any cameras that might have caught him, before they could be sure where he had been for the last two days. It was the kind of investigation that could take a long time.

"Have you heard of a woman named Ruby Patrickson before today?" Nate asked, his voice cutting across Laura's thoughts in a low rumble.

Brady tilted his head, still for a minute, as if he was frozen. Then he shook it slowly. "No. I don't know who that is."

"How about Jade Patrickson?"

"No."

"Kenneth Wurz?"

"Who are they?" Brady asked, looking up at Nate properly for the first time.

"They're all twins, like you were," Nate said. "Do you know what happened to them?"

Brady was stilling somewhere inside; Laura could see it behind his eyes. Fear. "No," he whispered, his head barely even shaking from side to side now.

"They died," Nate said. "Do you know who did that to them?"

Brady shook his head again, minutely, silently.

Laura bit her lip. Looking at him, she didn't know what to think. When she'd touched him as they brought him in from the car, she'd felt nothing. No solid vision, not even an aura or shadow touching him. Nothing to give her a clue as to whether he was connected to all of this or not.

On the one hand, he struck her as someone who was just scared. Traumatized. Unable to cope with grief. Mostly harmless, stuck in one place. But on the other hand, she knew that conditions like this could be deceptive. That the harm could be hidden under the surface, triggered only when something powerful let it out.

She glanced at Nate, trying to catch his eye, but he wasn't looking at her. She had to make an executive decision herself here.

"All right, Brady," she said, standing up. "You wait here. We'll be back later." She ended the interview, turning to walk out of the room, waiting in the corridor outside for Nate to follow her and shut the door behind him.

"Well?" Nate asked, when it was just the two of them. His manner was blunt, brusque. "You've obviously come to some kind of conclusion."

"Far from it," Laura said, biting her lip to stop herself from reacting badly. "He's too messed up. Without a confession or solid proof, I

151

don't know that we can call this case closed just yet. It might not be him."

"He fits all the marks we're looking for," Nate said. "Deceased twin brother. Psychological issues. History of admitted stalking. No alibi."

"And yet," Laura said, letting the phrase hang in the air.

Nate sighed heavily. He glanced up. From here, just down the hall, they could see one window that led outside, to a courtyard where vans could roll up to the precinct in case prisoner transport was required. The light out there was getting dim. "We better hope it is closed. Because if it isn't, it's getting into the right time of evening for the killer to strike again."

Laura followed his gaze to the window, a feeling of dread welling up inside of her.

They had a suspect in custody. Two suspects, in fact. So why did it feel like the worst was yet to come?

# CHAPTER TWENTY NINE

Laura sat at her desk in the precinct, pressing her hands against her temples. The boxes of files were still surrounding the whole space, leaving her with only enough room to rest her elbows on top of the desk and stare ahead at the screen of the computer they'd assigned to her. She felt hemmed in, in more ways than one.

Nate was already acting like they had their man. He was organizing all the necessary strands of investigation, tasking Detective Frome and his colleagues with all the admin that would need to be done. It was a huge task, and daunting enough if they had it right.

Laura wasn't convinced at all that they had it right.

In fact, the more she thought about it, the less she believed that Brady Seabrooke was their man. He just didn't fit with the very little she had been able to see in her visions. The hand she'd seen holding the coffee cup was slim and white, the nails neatly kept and cropped short, clean and tidy. There was no dirt under those nails, and if Brady was in the habit of hiding behind bushes every night of the week, the dirt would be there.

And it was more than that. If the killer was going to strike again tonight, then the visions she had seen of him stalking the new twins had to take place today. It was daylight when they were out at the café, when they were walking around. Getting on for evening when she'd seen them meet up and head to the station together, or in the first set of visions, watching the smartly dressed one walk home.

So, if the killer had to have been stalking them even in the last few hours, then he couldn't be Brady Seabrooke. She knew where Brady had been during that time. Crouched behind a row of bushes, and then here at the precinct.

There wouldn't, surely, have been enough time for him to watch them and then head over to the house and find his hiding place.

Which meant that the killer was still out there—and all the while, Nate and most of the other cops in the precinct were switching their attention from catching a killer to investigating a suspect they already had in custody. They were letting their guard down. And that meant that the twins she'd seen were still in danger.

Either of them could be about to die. Maybe both.

Laura stood abruptly and thrust her hand down the side of the box of files she hadn't yet opened, in the narrow gap between the files themselves and the inside of the box. She gasped lightly as she felt paper cuts opening up, but that was nothing compared to the spike of pain in her head, the one she had been hoping desperately to trigger—

*Laura was standing on the street somewhere near a subway station—not the same one as before; somewhere different. She could only see it from the corner of her eye, half cut off, the sign not visible. She wanted to scream. She tried so hard to look, to read the sign, but she couldn't.*

*She couldn't, because the eyes of the person she was seeing through were fixed somewhere else. On the twins. The same women that she had seen before.*

*They were dressed the same way. Their hair the same. Everything about them the same. The waitress had just come from work in her casual clothes, her sister dressed in the smart skirt suit. They had gotten on the subway, and he had followed them—maybe beaten them in a car—come out here to wait. And now here they were, walking down the road arm in arm in front of him.*

*Laura watched them with a sinking sense of despair. She knew it was him. He didn't lift his arm into her vision, didn't look down at himself, but she knew she was seeing them through his eyes.*

*And if she was still seeing them through his eyes in a vision now, then it was still going to happen.*

*It wasn't Brady Seabrooke. It wasn't Dr. Fairmont.*

*They didn't have the right guy in custody yet.*

*Laura watched the women walking up the road, felt him beginning to follow them at a distance. How he moved with a purpose, keeping them in sight, as though he was controlling how far they went. Watching for the right moment. She strained to see some kind of landmark or sign that would tell her where to look, where she could go to intercept them—*

Laura breathed again on the other side of the vision, pulling her hand out of the box with another flare of pain in her fingers. She flexed them, looking for blood, but there was none. The paper cuts were shallow, even if they did sting like hell.

Nate was walking back across the bullpen toward their desks, flipping through pages of something in his notebook. He glanced only briefly at her as he passed by, as if she was only an inconvenience. He was probably wondering why she wasn't taking part in setting up the next phase of the investigation.

He probably didn't realize she was still on the first.

"Nate," she said, almost reluctantly, because she had to do this. They had to talk about it. She couldn't just be a loose cannon going off on her own, not if he was ever going to trust her again.

Even if she didn't, he might never. But they still had to at least pretend that they were working together. She had to keep it together for as long as she could.

"I was thinking we go in and talk to Seabrooke again," Nate said. "Put the pressure on him this time. More hardline. See if he lets it out when he's scared or angry. If we can push him, he might admit it all."

"Nate, I don't know about this," Laura said. "I don't think it's him." She knew it wasn't him. She was absolutely sure. But she wanted to approach this cautiously, to ease him into the idea.

He only stared at her. "Why are you saying this now?"

"I told you outside the interview room I wasn't sure," Laura protested. "I just don't think we should concentrate all of our resources on one theory when we haven't proven it yet."

"Just look at the facts," Nate said. "He fits everything. And it was *your* theory that led us to him in the first place. What, are you now saying your little hunch was wrong?"

"That wasn't a little hunch," Laura sighed, knowing what he was trying to get at. "That was a guess. An educated one, but a guess. And I don't feel that killer instinct from him. I don't think he could go that far. Besides, he's so obsessed with this driver, I don't think he even has the time to go after anyone else."

It was all logical, she knew. She was making a good case. But the one thing she could say that might convince him completely—that she had seen it wasn't him—wasn't good enough. She couldn't tell him that.

Whatever she did, she needed to come up with something fast. It felt like yesterday was repeating itself. She hadn't convinced him fast enough then, and Kevin Wurz had died. She couldn't argue with him forever.

She needed to get him to see, and she needed to do it fast.

"I've organized a psychological assessment, and I'm fairly sure I know what it's going to say," Nate argued. "The guy's a head case. He doesn't even know what he's been up to. I'm expecting to get a report telling us that he could be capable of anything. You saw what he's like, Laura. Would you really want to put that guy in a dark alley and see if you come out of it unscathed?"

"That's reductive," Laura said, trying to hold her tongue as much as possible to keep it civil and not insulting. "Look, Nate. I know what you're going to say even before I say this, but... I have this feeling. The next set of twins, they're still in danger. If we can just warn them..."

"This wild goose chase again?" Nate asked, shaking his head. "You're going to go after some specific women and try to track them down, without even telling me how you know what to look for? You're really trying this?"

"I..." Laura closed her mouth, realizing that almost anything she could say would be useless. Unless she was going to tell him the truth, none of it meant a thing.

"Tell me this," Nate said, his tone fierce. "You say your hunch about this revenge killing twin theory was wrong. Now you're telling me you have another hunch and that we should divert our resources onto that. Why should I do that, Laura? Why should I trust a single thing you say?"

"They're not the same," Laura said, desperately. "You're saying they're both hunches, but this... I... I *know*..."

"No," Nate snapped, shaking his head at her. "Knowing something means you have proof of some kind. And you don't know. And I'm not going to waste any more time following your wild hunches around when I don't even know where they come from or what they mean."

He stalked away from her in the direction of a group of detectives he'd been talking to earlier, leaving Laura feeling like she had been dismissed.

Which meant she was on her own. And the twins she'd seen...

If she didn't do anything, if she let Nate get to her and just shut up and put her head down, they were going to die.

Laura sat down again at her desk, slumping into the chair. The files around her fluttered lightly in the slight wind caused by her passage. There were so many of them. Where was she even going to start?

Finding the women seemed impossible. A needle in a haystack. Even though she'd been handed the haystack, it was getting late. Soon it would be totally dark outside, and from that point on the women would be in great danger. He could be lying in wait for them even now. The time it would take her to go through every file, look up every women who might fit, rule them out one by one until she found them— and then look for an address, organize a patrol...

No. There wasn't enough time to do it that way anymore. She had to think of something else.

They had the wrong guy, but maybe that didn't mean her approach had been without merit. She'd been looking for the killer, not the victims. The fastest way to catch him—to stop him. Even if she saved a life tonight, he might still slip away the same way he had with the Wurz twins. Catch the killer instead, and you'd save everyone, not just one person.

Dead twins had been a good start. The psychology fit. That was why she had been able to convince Nate to go after him in the first place—because it wasn't just wild conjecture. It was a solid theory.

Laura opened up the browser, started a search the way that she had before. Dead twins in Milwaukee. She'd seen most of the results before, but she kept scrolling, hoping. Thinking something else might be there that she had missed.

But she hadn't. She'd seen every case. Everything that was relevant. There were no other dead twins who fit the bill. Which left her right at another dead end.

Unless…

Laura's heart rate picked up as she typed in *missing twin Milwaukee*, feeling like she was on the verge of something. Something that made a lot of sense. Not every death was reported as a death, right?

Some people weren't reported as dead until their bodies were found.

She had a hit in the results. An appeal for a missing twin, over on the other side of the city. A very small local paper running a story about a man who hadn't been seen in a few days. She checked the date, and her eyes almost popped out of her skull.

The news story had broken less than a week ago. Only a handful of days before Ruby and Jade Patrickson turned up dead.

Why hadn't this been flagged up in relation to the case?

"Frome," Laura called out, right as the detective was hurrying past her desk. "Come here."

"What is it?" he asked. He had a few sheets of paper in his hand, and he gestured loosely with them. "Agent Lavoie just asked me to—"

"Never mind that," Laura said. "Have you heard of a missing person case in the city this week? Name of Clark Clifton?"

Frome frowned, shook his head. "I didn't deal with it."

"No, it looks like it was probably reported at another precinct," Laura said. "Can you check with them?" She gave him the details. She would much rather talk to the detective who took the report than look it up on the system. If this was a lead, she needed to chase it down as fervently as possible. She needed to act fast, and that meant getting the most up-to-date and accurate information she could.

Frome walked back to his desk and picked up the phone, talking into it quickly. Laura moved to join him, listening in as he asked for the details. Within moments, he was apparently talking to the officer who had taken the report, and Laura held out her hand for the phone.

"I'm just passing you over to Agent Frost," Frome said, polite as ever. "She's got some questions about your report, eh."

"Hello?" Laura said, the second she had the phone in her hand and pressed to her ear.

"Hello, there, Agent," the detective on the other end—a young woman, by the sound of her voice—answered. "How can I help you today?"

"Tell me about this missing person," Laura said. "Everything you can—and who reported him."

"Oh, that's easy," the detective said, her voice almost annoyingly cheerful. "It was his twin brother who came in. Almost caused a bit of confusion, that, the two of them looking so similar and all."

"They're identical?" Laura asked. Her eyes drifted back to the pile of files on her desk. She'd been assuming the visions were triggering for the victims. What if it was the other way around?

"Oh, yes." The detective chuckled lightly. "Anyway, he says he hasn't seen his brother for a few days and there's been no one at his apartment. Couldn't give me much more detail than that. He was distressed, poor thing. Wanted us to make sure we brought his brother back from wherever he'd gone. I had the feeling he thought he might have wandered off or something, and there weren't a lot of risk factors."

"What do you mean?" Laura asked.

"He's a healthy adult male. No history of poor health, mental health issues, or so on," the detective said. "The twin mentioned something about him having a new girlfriend. He hasn't reported in at work, but from the way I understand it, it was a bit of a dead-end job anyway. Doesn't seem likely that he would be trying to harm himself or suffering in some way mentally. In fact, when I suggested to the twin that his brother might have gone off for a week with his new girlfriend, he even seemed to relax. Like he agreed."

Laura chewed her lip, thinking. It would be the perfect cover, though, wouldn't it? Report your twin missing if you knew he was dead, and let the police think he was probably just off somewhere having fun so they wouldn't prioritize an investigation. Let the trail run cold.

"Can you give me the details of the man who made the report?" she asked, grabbing her notebook out of her pocket. She had a feeling in her gut that she was onto something here, and she needed to follow it down before something else happened.

She was going to have to pay this brother a visit—even if it meant she was going to have to go alone.

# CHAPTER THIRTY

Laura looked at the house from a short distance down the street, out of the yellow circle of the streetlights. It was fully dark out now, everything lending just that little extra bit of chill in the atmosphere. The house itself was quiet and dark too, no lights in any of the windows. It was very likely that the homeowner wasn't home.

But, glancing at the clock, Laura reminded herself that it was late fall. It was dark earlier now. There was a good chance that the man who lived here—Gregory Clifton—was still on his way home from work. Maybe still even working, if he had a late shift. The house was in poor repair, even in the dark: Laura could see weeds growing through the short driveway in front, and there was a piece of cardboard in place of one of the upstairs windows. It was the kind of place where someone might live if they were struggling to make it. Working graveyard shifts and even holding down more than one job—anything was plausible.

Laura got out of the car, stuffing her hands into the pockets of her jacket against the cold air. She stepped forward hesitantly, her eyes straining. Her breath came out in a puff of white. She wanted to walk closer, but she was wary. It would mean stepping through the circle of the streetlight.

She made a decision and surged forward, her feet moving fast across the sidewalk. There wasn't enough time left to hesitate. She didn't have enough time to be wrong. She flashed through the light and past it, onto the weedy parking space out front of the house, her feet feeling the change from proper paved sidewalk to cracked concrete. There was no vehicle here, which reassured her somewhat. No one seemed to be here.

She moved forward, toward the front door. She didn't know what she was looking for, but she needed something. Anything. A hint of a sign.

Laura reached out and touched the door handle, not heavily enough to turn it or even make a sound, but she felt the spike through her head all the same. The night air was so quiet and still, only the sound of cars on the road back a few twists and turns away disturbing it. For a second it almost felt like none of this was real—

160

*Laura was jolting along, stumbling on the uneven ground as she moved away from a car in a hurry. The door of the house was ahead of her. She was almost inside. She reached out a hand—his hand—she saw it in her peripheral vision—toward the door...*

*He brought the hand up to his face then, staring at it. It was covered in blood. He needed to clean it off before he touched anything—*

Laura blinked her eyes open back on the same scene, almost disorientated by the door standing in the darkness in front of her both within the vision and now back in reality. But the hand that was stretched out toward it was her own. She blinked a few times to try and clear her head, settling back into her own body and reality with an uneasiness that she had rarely felt before. Coming here had been a risk, maybe a mistake. Putting herself into such close proximity with him, especially when her visions were already allowing her to see through his eyes.

But she would take it as a win, because now she knew something else. She was on the right track. It was him.

And he was still going to attack, and presumably kill, tonight. You didn't get that much blood on your hands if you only grazed someone, or you failed to attack them at all.

Laura hesitated, tried touching the door again, the handle, even going to the window and trailing her hands along the wall. Nothing else came to her. Nothing that would help her see how to stop him. But at least now, she knew who she was looking for.

It was slim comfort, but if she didn't manage to figure out where he was going, at least she would have the recourse of coming back here and maybe catching him literally red-handed.

Laura walked quickly back to her car, keenly aware of how exposed she was out here. Coming here without backup hadn't been smart, but it had been her only option. The smart thing to do, even now, would be to call Nate and tell him what she'd discovered.

Or, at least, as much of it as she could to get him to back her up in her search for the killer. The killer who, she now knew, was Gregory Clifton. She had him in her sights, and she just needed to get over that finish line and find him before he attacked tonight.

But she couldn't call Nate. Not yet. Not until she had actual evidence to show him. If she gave him just one more hunch, he would be furious with her. He would probably refuse to take her calls at all after that.

Laura sat behind the wheel, her hands gripping it at either side, trying to think. How could she figure this out? How could she find him now?

She knew he hadn't been at work today, if he even held down a job anymore. He'd been at the café. If she had a warrant already she could bust into his house, see if there were any old receipts lying around or other clues that she could follow. But she had nothing, and no time to get one, and anything she did find by breaking in illegally would be utterly unusable in court. Never mind that she might save a life with it—if he was allowed to go free on a technicality, they would be back to square one, and he might have the chance to kill again.

Laura glanced around again to check there was no one nearby and picked up her cell phone, turning on the screen. The glow of it illuminated her face, made her visible to anyone who might be walking by or looking out of a window, but she needed some kind of lead and this was the only way she could think to get it. Her nerves felt like catgut, strung out for a bow. The trouble with her visions was that the timeline was always iffy. She'd felt a strong stab at the door, which suggested Clifton's return home was imminent. But how imminent? Five minutes? An hour? Three hours?

She searched his name on social media, finally coming across a new social media profile by using an email address she'd pulled from his LinkedIn (a page that was miserably empty of connections and details, pointing again to his lack of employment, just as the rundown house did).

It was an odd page. An Instagram account with hardly any pictures or information. In fact, the first post had only been made a week ago. A photograph of two small boys together, old and faded, set in a frame and clearly from years ago. The caption denoted that it was of "Me and my twin brother, when we were still cute." No hashtags, no further identifying information or tags. The username was generic, MilwaukeeTwinGuy2. Nothing to really tell you who this person was.

And yet she knew it was him, because it was connected to his email address. Either he didn't mind being found that way, or he'd forgotten to change his privacy settings after signing up.

Laura was trying to think, trying to see her way through all of this before it was too late. Why make a new profile and keep it anonymous, and yet still reference your brother with a picture from your own childhood?

So that people who were also twins would be more likely to accept follow requests and let him see their posts?

So he could stalk the people he wanted to kill?

The account's followers were low, but it was following an even smaller number. Just twenty-four people. Laura opened them up, but in the same moment her eyes darted away from the screen, following another internal train of thought.

She'd already had the instinctive thought that reporting the missing twin to the police would be the best first step at deflecting suspicion from yourself. Knowing now that Gregory Clifton was a murderer, and that his identical twin brother was missing, it seemed almost inevitable that Clark Clifton was dead. And if he was dead, then it also seemed fairly certain that it had to have been Gregory himself who killed him, setting off this whole crusade against twins.

*Crusade.* And it did feel like that, didn't it? Like he was on some unholy mission to wipe out all of the identical twins in the Milwaukee area. But there had to be a reason behind that. A reason that caused him to kill his brother in the first place. There was a chance, Laura supposed, that something had happened accidentally, causing a psychological break much like the one suffered by Brady Seabrooke. It was somewhat plausible, if you squinted, that an accidental death like that might push him to take away the siblings of all the other twins in the area, just as he had been deprived.

But he had killed both Ruby and Jade, and that didn't seem to sit right. No—and neither did his actions after the fact. To go to the police and report it, to systematically move between twins on the same night, it all seemed premeditated. Like he'd thought about it carefully and decided what to do.

Like he had killed his brother on purpose and then set another course of events into motion. Which would mean that his first victims were not Ruby and Jade. His first victim was Clark Clifton, around a week ago.

Laura put her eyes back to the list of accounts that Gregory followed, and her eyes nearly bugged out of her head. Right there: the first two accounts were ones that she was familiar with. They belonged to Ruby and Jade Patrickson, their profile pictures frozen now in a permanent reminder of how they had been when they died, never to change again. And Laura remembered what they'd been told about those accounts, even though the posts had been taken down before they'd ever seen them. That they had publicly shamed Pete Barton and sent a world of virtual hurt his way.

It was bad behavior, she supposed, if you looked at it a certain way. Perhaps Pete Barton had been in the wrong, but they had also deliberately turned the wrath of their followers on him. Allowed it to spread to the point where he'd had no choice but to turn his profile dark and hide himself away from the world. To a point, anyway.

The next victim, Kenneth Wurz, had been something of a bad boy by all accounts. A wild child. He'd even had a criminal record, one that should have been stricter. He'd gotten away with what he had done for the most part. But Kevin Wurz had been a volunteer at a local charity. A good man. And he was still alive.

It was dawning on Laura that the fact they hadn't been able to fathom—whether Kevin survived by luck or by design—was all part of the pattern.

She gasped out loud, alone in the cold air inside the car, when it came to her fully. The killer was going after not just any twins, but twins that he thought were bad. To use a clichcd phrase from popular culture, the evil twins.

The twins who were, Laura guessed, just like his own.

She scrolled down the list of followed accounts, her eyes lighting easily on both Kenneth and Kevin, both of them on the list. Again, smiling in their profile pictures in a way that at least one of them never would again. If Kevin suffered the way that Brady Seabrooke had, maybe both.

And then she saw it, and her heart almost stopped.

A picture of a pretty young woman with wild curly hair spilling around her face, her mouth open in a grin. A woman she recognized easily.

One of the twins from today's visions.

Laura tapped on her profile with a shaking hand, taking in her name. Amelia Adams, listed in her profile as employed by a local bank. Her account was full of striking, strong images, Amelia in power suits and in power poses. In a few of them, she was with her sister. Laura tapped there again to find out her name: Coco Adams, whose profile was full of images of coffee cups and wildflowers growing from the pavement and street art. Two very different sisters, despite the similarity of their looks.

And she had them now. She did. She could save them—if she got there in time.

Laura hurriedly moved to another page in her phone's browser, bringing up a search for the two women. She found addresses for both, put them into her map and searched the surrounding area. One of them was down the street from a subway station. Laura switched to street view and saw it. The same station she had seen them emerge from in her vision.

They were at Coco's home.

Laura didn't waste any time now in dialing Nate's number. There was no time to even second-guess herself. They needed to do this now.

"Laura?" Nate answered, sounding pissed already. "Where are you?"

"I've found him," Laura said, cutting through the preamble. Better to just get out the lead rather than waste time on the details that wouldn't matter until later, when they were writing up their reports. "The killer. And I know who his next victim is going to be."

"If this is just another one of your hunches—" Nate began, but she cut him off.

"No, Nate, listen to me. Look up MilwaukeeTwinGuy2 on Instagram. That's him. He's following all of the people he's picked out as potential victims, and I've found them. I can't explain right now all of the investigation I've been doing—it's too much, and we don't have time. He's either on his way there now, or he already is there. We have to move fast." She'd started her engine, and she pulled off along the street now, gunning the accelerator as soon as she was away from the sidewalk.

There was a single moment's pause, and in that horrible moment, Laura thought he was still going to refuse. But maybe something in him still trusted her. Maybe the fact that she'd used the word "investigation" to back up what she'd found. Maybe he was just looking up the account and verifying what she'd said.

Because he responded, and he gave her the response she had been waiting for.

"All right," he said. "What's the address?"

Laura rattled it off quickly for him, reading it from her own GPS. "Meet me there with backup," she said, taking a turn just a little too fast and having to fight back control of the car. "I'm closer. I'm heading there right now."

"No, wait," Nate said. "You shouldn't go on your own—wait for us to catch up with you."

"I'm not leaving it too late," Laura said grimly. "I'm not going to let him take another life."

And she ended the call, cutting off whatever objections Nate might have and leaving him no choice but to hurry to catch up with her.

165

# CHAPTER THIRTY ONE

Gregory stole through the back streets, occasionally using the odd alleyway that cut through to the main road to make sure that they were still on track. They wouldn't see him from down here. Wouldn't know he was keeping track of their progress, making sure he would still keep his timings and get to the apartment faster.

He couldn't stay following them like he had before, risk either of them to turn around and look at him. Especially not Amelia. He didn't want her to know he was there.

It wasn't that she would recognize him. After all, they were strangers. But he couldn't take the gaze of her eyes on him, even in the dark. Not until he was close enough to end her. He knew what people like her could be like, and he didn't want to get anywhere near her until it was time.

It made him shudder to think of it. He looked at the way she gripped her sister's arm. All the while he'd been following them home, he'd been mulling it over. How Coco could stand to be so close to her. And the answer had been obvious to him: it was the same way it had been for him. He'd never wanted to be close to Clark. But Clark had never given him a choice.

He was going to have to find a way to separate them. Surely, at least once they got to the house, Coco would find a moment to herself. To escape to the bathroom, maybe. It had always been that way with Clark. Having to duck into any room with a lock on the door just to give himself a bit of breathing space, always so suffocated in his brother's presence. The way he would fill the room until it felt like there was no longer anything left for anyone else. And then he would walk out and you would realize he had taken it all with him—literally, in many cases. Little things missing that had been there before. Money. Keepsakes. Things you would beg him not to take or destroy, but he would anyway.

Gregory cut down a side street, through a few alleyways, heading for the back of the apartment complex where Coco lived. He thanked himself for checking this place out previously. He hadn't thought he'd need it—it had been fairly obvious, fairly quickly, who was the one to go after. Just like it had been with the Wurz twins. It was only the

166

Patricksons who had given him trouble, working out which was which. In the end, he'd seen signs of the corruption taking over both of them. Just being connected to an evil twin was enough to make someone give up. He knew how close he'd come to that himself, so many times. To just trying it Clark's way and seeing what happened. So, unable to figure out which of the Patricksons was the original source of the evil, he'd had to take the option of protecting society at large. He'd had to take them both out instead.

But he'd checked out the place and spotted a way to climb up the fire escape as well as this route which would get him there quicker, and he knew how to get inside.

Out of sight of the twins themselves, stealing through the shadows at a run, he felt more secure in the plan. It was like he felt everything falling into place more when Amelia wasn't capable of catching him. Like he was still afraid, because he knew everything that a twin could be.

He knew what she must be capable of.

He would wait inside the room that Coco used as storage, the small box opposite the bathroom. It would be dark in there, and he could make it work, once he'd jimmied the window open and slipped inside. He would be able to watch, to see them as they moved around without them seeing him. If Coco went into the bathroom, he could slip past the closed door and take Amelia out before she returned. But if it was Amelia who went in, he could just lie in wait.

This could work. He didn't need to kill them both. Unless Coco got in the way... no matter how good of a person she may be, it was more important that he take out the evil. Twins didn't just target their siblings. They could hurt other people, too. He had to eliminate Amelia, no matter what the cost would be.

He saw the dark shape of the apartment building ahead, some of the windows blazing with light and the others dark and dormant. It was going to be a challenge, slipping up that fire escape without being seen through a window, but he was going to have to do it.

A voice came into the back of his head, a voice telling him he was going to fail. Taunting him. He shook his head. It was funny, almost; Clark wasn't even here anymore, and yet he was still trying to put Gregory down. It was seared into Gregory's memory, the way he would sneer at him. The way he would tell him how useless he was, how he was never going to get anywhere in life. And then it would start.

He was never going to be able to impress his friends enough into making them actually like him, Clark told Gregory. So why didn't Clark take over and pretend to be him, just for a while?

His girlfriend would break up with Gregory when she realized how useless he was. How pathetic. So he should let Clark step in, just for one date, or two.

And then he would come back home with that look on his face, and start talking about how it was better this way anyway, less pain for his brother. How he didn't need them around because he had Clark. How the two of them should just always look out for each other, the way Clark had looked out for him by finding out how fake those friends were, what a prude that girlfriend was.

And he'd go to school the next day and the halls would be full of people talking about him behind their backs, and he'd found out what Clark had done while pretending to be him. And none of them would believe him.

Gregory gritted his teeth, gripping hold of the bottom of the fire escape. He could only just reach it, but he'd been training, and... he lifted himself up with the strength of his arms alone, then swung his legs to scrabble against the brickwork until he could haul himself up, panting and sweating, to sit on the fire escape above the ladder, catching his breath.

That wasn't going to happen to Coco, not anymore. Just like Kevin was free now. And he was going to do it again, and again, for as long as he needed to.

It had taken him nearly thirty years to break out from under Clark's thumb and do what needed to be done. Almost thirty years of being pushed around and taken advantage of. Watching Clark take everything from him. His friends and his chance of any kind of romantic connection. His job. Even his apartment, because when Gran died there had only been one apartment and she'd had to choose one of them to get it in her will. And she'd chosen Clark, because of all the times Gregory had been bad and broken her things or stolen them and pawned them.

All of the times that it was really Clark all along.

And he'd gotten the apartment too.

That had been the beginning of the end, as it turned out. Gregory wouldn't have credited it, not at first. But losing the apartment had been something. A nail in a coffin. And when Clark had started hanging out at Gregory's place more often than he did the apartment, like he didn't even want it that much, it had been a kick in the teeth that spurred him to action.

And he'd done it. Finally, he'd done it.

It had been hard. Horrible. He'd cried, after. For a long time. But then he'd gotten up, and figured out what to do, and realized that there were others out there who needed this, too.

And he could do it again.

He braced himself, then stood up, moving lightly across the fire escape. The journey from here was easy. Just up, up, up. The vulnerable window wasn't attached to the fire escape, but it was close enough that he could swing across. He could get his hands into the frame, get his feet on the sill, then carefully bend. He had all the time he needed—he always did. It somehow seemed easy, like that. Like something out there was giving him a helping hand. He liked to think it was because he was doing something that was right, something that the world needed. The universe recognized his efforts.

He was sparing innocent people, people who had done nothing wrong. By no fault of their own, they had been born a twin. A good twin, with all the good qualities desired in a human being. They were meek and mild and could not stand up for themselves. He'd been like that once.

But now he was going to stand up for them.

He found the right window and leaned over, listening carefully for any sound of movement inside. He heard none. He'd beaten them here, as predicted.

Now he just had to get inside, and the waiting game would begin.

He pushed the window open, starting to climb through—and looked up at a noise, freezing. His blood went cold.

They'd beaten him up here.

How had they beaten him up here?

# CHAPTER THIRTY TWO

Laura pulled the car up across the sidewalk so quickly the tires screamed, ramming the brakes on and jolting herself forward in the process. It was lucky that it was nighttime, and that the front of the apartment block was brightly lit. If it had been busy day, she'd have had to slow down for fear of hitting a pedestrian.

She was out of the car before the engine had even registered that it was turned off, reaching for her gun to check that it was secure in her holster and running for the front entrance to the building. She rushed to the intercom system, found the button marked "Adams," and pressed it. She heard the tinny buzz of the bell connecting, knowing it must be ringing out somewhere above her head. She waited, but there was nothing. No response.

She could have tried again, tried some other way, been systematic. But there was no time. It was dark—darker than it had been when she'd seen the twins heading toward the building in her vision. They had to be inside already. They had to have made it up there.

Which meant she was behind, and the killer might already be up there with them.

He might have been and gone.

Laura didn't want to think about that possibility.

She hammered every single button on the intercom panel one after the other, relentlessly hitting name after name. Thirty of them in all. The building looked bigger; Laura figured there was another entrance with another intercom maybe, a different side of the building which let out onto a different street so the address could be separate. She just needed one of them to answer. Just one.

The door made a buzzing noise and then clicked, and Laura shoved it.

It opened.

After this was all over, she was going to have to ask Captain Gausse to put out some kind of bulletin about community safety. But for now, she was grateful that someone up there didn't have enough sense to check who was outside before letting them in.

For now, she just ran.

There was an elevator, but she ignored it. This wasn't some high-speed luxury hotel elevator—it would take too long for it to arrive and take her up. Instead she ran for the stairs, taking them two at a time. By the time she hit the second floor, she was pulling her gun out, readying it in her hands. She needed to be ready. If he was already there, she might need to shoot.

Laura ran down the hall, conscious of how heavy her own footsteps sounded. She heard Nate's voice in her ear, from the phone call earlier, telling her to wait. Not to go in alone. But it was better this way. He was the one who was in danger. The one who had the aura of death around him. The more she kept him away from this kind of situation, the better.

She'd never seen her own death. Never sensed it. She had no way of knowing if this would be it for her. But it was worth the risk.

There were two lives at stake here, and it was her duty to protect them.

Laura skidded to a halt at the doorway, the one she knew must lead to the right apartment. She didn't even have to check the number. It was obvious. Obvious because the door was swinging open, and beyond that Laura could see a bit of splintered wood lying in the hall—

And an arm, a hand, lying prone across the floor.

Laura kept her gun drawn and pointed ahead of her as she entered the apartment, moving forward as swiftly and quietly as she could. There was one opening on the left side of the hall. She kept her back against the wall and stepped out, swung to face it. There was nothing there, only an empty room.

Laura moved down the hall, noting the prone body of the woman stretched out on the floor as she got close enough to see more. There was no blood that she could see, except a small smear near the woman's temple. She was one of the twins. Laura couldn't tell which. She cleared the rest of the small apartment quickly, checking each room. In one of them, full of boxes and looking more like storage than anything else, the window was open.

Laura glanced out and down. It led onto nothing—but to the side, she saw a fire escape. Grimly, she understood exactly what had happened here. Gregory Clifton—he'd beaten her to it.

But why only one of the women? And why wasn't she dead?

Laura heard a groan in the hall and rushed back out, dropping to her knees beside the woman on the floor. She was coming around, her eyelids fluttering open.

"Miss Adams?" she said, since that was the only way she could satisfactorily identify the woman.

"What?" she murmured, still out of it, frowning up at Laura. "Who...?"

"I'm an FBI agent," Laura said, wanting to get to the point. There was no time to get out her badge or ease this woman in slowly. "Can you tell me what happened here?"

"Uh," the woman said, blinking and looking around slowly. She was dazed. Confused. "I was... there was someone at the window."

"Someone was breaking in?" Laura asked, trying to prompt her to move through the details faster.

"Yes," the woman said. "I went over there—I could see him halfway in the room—he was climbing—and then he..."

"You confronted him?" Laura said.

The woman tried to sit up suddenly, her arms flailing, her head bobbing on her shoulders like she was drunk. "My sister...!" she burst out.

"Stay down," Laura told her, pushing on her shoulders. "You've had a blow to the head. It's not a good idea to move. Your sister was here?"

"Yes, and he—he must have hit me—where is she?"

Laura glanced around the empty apartment grimly. She didn't want to have to answer that. She didn't even know the full answer.

"Stay here," she said. "Help is on the way. Don't try to move—you might hurt yourself worse. I'm going to go and find your sister."

Laura got up from the floor, watching Adams—whichever one she was—until she saw a flicker of agreement and understanding on her face. Then she grabbed her gun again and rushed out of the apartment, trusting the fact that Nate and the other cops were not far away. They would help her, get her the medical attention she needed. She seemed stable enough now. That would have to do.

Because wherever the other twin was, Clifton had gone after her. And Laura was sure now that that meant only one of them was going to die.

She looked both ways down the hall, seeing nothing. But the woman had been just coming round as she searched the apartment, and she'd woken up alone, showing no immediate signs of medical distress. That meant she couldn't have been out for long. All this must have happened either during or right before Laura's spring up the stairs.

172

They would have passed her, either in the stairwell or out there on the street. She'd have seen someone running in the beam of her headlights.

That had to mean they'd run the other way.

Laura set off in the opposite direction down the hall, coming to a pair of double doors. There was a smear of blood on the white paint—just a light smudge. The kind that might be on a hand, or more likely a glove, after knocking someone out with a blow to the head. He'd come this way. Laura was sure of it.

She raced along to another set of stairs. They went in both directions—up and down. Where would she go if she was scared for her life, hearing an intruder chase after her? Laura made a split-second decision. Down. She'd rather go down and try to get out of the building than get trapped up there on the roof.

She took the stairs two at a time downwards as well, feeling almost like she was flying. Like at any moment, she might lose her balance and soar down the rest of them, landing in a crumple at the bottom. She retained just enough control to prevent that, one hand clattering along the railing and grabbing it to keep herself upright, the other still holding her gun.

Laura reached the bottom of the stairs and burst out into a side-street, just as she had figured from outside. There was no sign of anyone around, the street running both ways into darkness. One way led to the road Laura had screeched up on. The other went past a second building and then out to another road that Laura could just glimpse now.

Which way?

In the far distance, Laura heard the sound of sirens. They were near, but not even close to near enough. For the time it would take them to get here and catch up on the situation, Laura was functionally alone. She had to act now. Waiting would be too late.

There was something lying on the ground a short distance away, just visible in the gleam of the streetlight that reached this far, next to the other building. Laura ran to it, checking her six and her twelve all the while, the sound of her heart beating loudly in her ears. He could be anywhere. They could be.

She reached the object she had spotted and crouched down. It was a woman's shoe, a flat and businesslike black pump. She touched it, picking it up to look, and a headache shot through her brow like a bullet, making her fingers let go of the shoe—

*Laura was standing in the hall, looking at her. He was standing there. She saw his hands in her peripheral vision—the knife raised. It was wicked sharp and glinting, but clean. No blood on it yet.*

*He looked down, and Laura could see what he was looking at. The woman on the ground. She was lying there still, unmoving, her eyes closed. Laura felt confusion welling up inside of her. No, this wasn't right. She'd just left this twin. She was awake. She wasn't unconscious anymore. What did this mean? Was the vision wrong? Was—*

*The girl on the ground moved, her hands groping along the floor as if in search of something. They connected with her cell phone and she let out an exhale, as if in relief.*

*He stalked forward toward her. At the noise of footsteps her eyes flew open. She saw him. She opened her eyes and her mouth both wide and screamed.*

*And he rushed forward to close the distance between them—*

Laura came back to herself as the shoe hit the ground with a thud, landing right back where she had found it. She gasped in a breath of the cold night air, feeling it sting her lungs.

The killer—he'd tricked them. Tricked her. Maybe not on purpose, since he wouldn't have known that he was so close to being caught. But he'd done it anyway, by going after the wrong target.

He'd knocked out the one he wanted to kill. Chased the other one away. And then when she was sufficiently far away, sufficiently terrified not to come back, he could make his move. Double back around, get to the other twin, the one he really wanted.

Kill her without any interference.

# CHAPTER THIRTY THREE

Laura spun back in the direction she had come from. The doors—they were locked to her again. She had gone outside, made the stupid mistake of falling for it. She raced back to the way she had just left, hammering all the intercom buttons again, hoping and praying that someone was stupid enough—

The door buzzed open and let her in, and she almost fell through it in her haste to get inside.

Laura thought of the killer, how he could possibly get back in. He hadn't gone in the same way she was going now. He couldn't have. She would have passed him there again. So, if she was him, then how...?

The same way he'd entered in the first place, of course. It had to be.

He would have doubled back along the back of the building, climbed up the fire escape, then shimmied over to the window...

Yes, in the vision he'd been lined up that way. Coming in from the room filled with boxes. Laura's heart was almost hammering like it would burst as she took the stairs two at a time again, cursing every day in her life that hadn't been spent at the gym, every beer or hamburger that slowed her down at this moment now. The pounding in her head became a ringing, leaving her dizzy as she spun through turn after turn in the staircase.

She reached the apartment too late. He was already there. The twin who had been on the floor was still there, but somehow she'd found the strength and the presence to fight back. They were locked together down there, a whirling and turning mess of limbs, both grunting and gasping and crying out in pain as they struggled to hit each other, to kick, to get the upper hand.

Laura held her gun in front of her. Her hand was shaking with the exertion of her enforced run, with the adrenaline, with the pain in her head. She aimed, but couldn't fire. They were moving too much, her shot too uncertain. If she fired now she might hit the wrong one, might end up killing the woman instead—

"Freeze!" she shouted, as if it was going to make any difference, and of course it didn't, because he had no reason to listen to her. He was already fighting as hard as he could. The knife had dropped to the floor but they were rolling toward it, rolling almost in arm's reach...

A blur shot past Laura, almost knocking her to the ground. She stumbled, righting herself against the wall, steadying her hands. She only just managed not to pull the trigger, firing indiscriminately into the area in front of her, hitting god only knew what it would have been. When the initial flare of shock and panic was gone a split-second later she saw something unbelievable.

Something she never would have expected if she hadn't seen it with her own eyes.

There were two of them.

The other twin, the one who had run—she had come back. She and her sister were both fighting him now, wrestling him down, pinning his limbs between them until he was unable to move.

Laura froze. She felt like she was back in that room. Back in the room where the smell of blood was still in her nose, where her hands were still wet with it from touching Mrs. Fallow. She felt herself frozen as she had been then, no idea where to point the gun, how to help. Watching Nate wrestle a killer, knowing that Amy was only feet away, so close she was in the line of fire. In the line of danger.

She couldn't breathe.

In front of her, the killer still fought the twins, fought them so wildly Laura couldn't get a chance to use her weapon in their aid. It was happening all over again. She couldn't shoot. He was snarling, twisting, throwing his weight—every time they almost seemed to have him, he threw an arm or bucked his back and slipped out again, his hand grappling toward the one he wanted to kill as if he was going to squeeze the very life out of her given one second's chance.

"What are you doing?" he yelled, and Laura heard his voice for the first time. There was a wild kind of desperation in it, a pleading, a sound that broke raw from his throat. "Can't you see I'm trying to help you? Why would you want to save her?"

It was a moment, but it was enough. As he yelled, he stopped fighting so hard. One twin, the one who had been unconscious, had his left arm on the floor, her leg looped over his left leg, holding him down. The other twin, the one who had come back, managed to get his right arm pinned at the same time.

He was there in the middle, between them, pinned and just for a moment totally still. They were out of the way, and he was right in front of Laura.

She had to wake up.

She couldn't let anyone else get hurt because of her own fear.

Laura felt a newfound ferocity bursting through her, driving her to take action. No. No! No one else was going to get hurt here, not at his hands! She sprang forward, placing her gun safely on the floor out of reach, using the same motion to drive her on top of him. To overpower him. To add a third body to the two trying to take him down.

And just like that, they had him.

They pinned him like they were a team, like this was all natural to them. They flipped him onto his stomach and forced his arms behind his back, even though he fought and shouted at every step of the way.

Laura sat up across his back, pinning him down, pulling her cuffs off her belt as she heard behind her a cacophony of voices. Primary among them, Nate's. At first they were only yelling in the hall, and then they were right behind her, and Laura heard Nate demanding to know about the blood, if anyone was injured, if Laura was all right. She got the handcuffs snapped onto Gregory Clifton's wrists at last and sat back, finding that she only wanted to sit right now, that she didn't have the strength for a moment to stand back up.

"Yes," she said at last, only after he'd repeated the question again. She looked at the doorway, at the cluster of detectives arrayed there. At the two girls, sobbing and holding each other. At Nate, leaning over her and Clifton, concern etched onto his face. "Yes, I'm all right. But we're going to need a couple of ambulances—and to read this creep his rights."

Nate took in what she'd said, and just for a second she thought he was about to smile.

# CHAPTER THIRTY FOUR

Laura looked at Gregory Clifton through the one-way glass of the interview room, her arms folded across her chest. He looked so normal. So many of them did.

"What do you think?" she asked, not turning to look as someone entered the room behind her. She didn't need to. She could see Nate's reflection in the window.

"He sounds genuine enough," Nate said. "Like he really believes this evil twin stuff."

"Well, I suppose he would be more of an expert than either of us," Laura said. She meant it to sound like a joke, but it came off grim and dark.

They stood there in silence for a while. Gregory Clifton sat there on the other side, unaware of their gazes. He was alone in the room, left with just a half cup of lukewarm coffee in plastic, his hands cuffed where he could only just reach it and nothing else. Nevertheless, he seemed comfortable enough.

Not that he seemed happy, though. His shoulders were slumped, his eyes staring down at the table. The only movement he made was to reach for the cup now and then, take a sip, and set it back down. His head hung down, like he was beating himself up about something internally.

And he probably was. He'd been caught. From the way he described it to them, it seemed like he felt he'd failed in an important mission. Something only he could do.

The scary part was that Laura could relate. Though she was fairly sure that her own mission was based in reality, while his was simply a delusion.

"You spoke to Rondelle?" Laura asked, at length.

"Yeah," Nate told her. "Plane leaves in about an hour. He's happy to let Gausse and her team handle it from here. Sounds like they won't need a trial, so we're just about done here."

Laura nodded. Clifton had confessed to everything, after all. They'd gotten enough information from him already to find Clark Clifton's body, hidden in a chest freezer in Gregory's basement. Somewhere the local police had never had cause to look, given that they weren't even sure he'd been murdered until Clark told them so.

Hours of sitting in that confessional with him had left Laura with a sore and stiff back, and the plane journey home probably wasn't going to help either. And now she had the thoughts of Clark Clifton, the way he'd terrorized and abused his brother over the years, to keep her company as well.

She doubted Nate was going to be doing much in the way of distracting her from that.

"We'd better get our things from the motel," Laura said, because it was better than standing here staring silently ahead, neither of them doing much to acknowledge the other. Looking at a man who couldn't see and wouldn't acknowledge them, either.

Besides, it was done. This whole time, Laura had wanted nothing more than to get home, and now she was going to get that chance. She wasn't going to linger here for a moment longer.

She turned and left the room, even though Nate hadn't replied. That was the way it was now. She didn't like it, but she was getting used to it. Horrible as that was. She wished she wouldn't, but there it was.

Laura got behind the wheel of the car they'd been using for the past couple of days, neither particularly surprised nor completely expecting it when Nate slid into the passenger seat beside her.

"Ready?" Laura asked, just to break the silence.

"Sure," Nate said.

Great. So the second the case was over, they were back to silent and surly.

Laura took a deep breath and started the car, pulling out before she had the chance to start screaming and never stop. She had too much going on right now to pander to Nate. She knew he was hurting, that he felt like she'd betrayed him. But she hadn't. She was only trying to keep the status quo, to stop him from hating her and getting hurt in the process.

She was probably going to lose Nate as a partner if this continued. But if she told him, she was convinced she'd lose him for sure. And every day she kept him working alongside her was another day that she had the chance to maybe, just maybe, save his life and send that shadow of death that hung over him away.

They drove back to the motel in silence to gather their things, which she knew wouldn't take much time at all. Laura always kept her bag half-packed. She was sure Nate did the same. There wasn't much point in taking everything out when you weren't going to be staying for long.

Even as they drove to the motel, her mind was ticking over, already leaving Milwaukee behind and returning to D.C. To what waited for her there.

Two things. Two little girls.

Amy, who was with someone new. Someone who might not be safe. And Laura owed it to her to try to found out where she was, who she was with. To keep an eye on her. It didn't seem like anyone else was going to do it, if not Laura.

Then there was the custody hearing, which was more imminent and in some ways more urgent. Laura only had two days left to prepare. She was going to have to go over everything with her lawyer, make sure she had the right documentation. Get her apartment cleaned up as much as possible, in case there was an inspection. Go over what she would say in court to convince the judge that she was worthy of this.

She had her sober chips, proving she'd been sober for five months now. She was going to make it to six, too. She could do this.

Now she just needed to prove it to everyone else—and hope that Marcus wasn't planning to throw her under the bus, after all the peaceful collaboration they'd been starting to achieve.

Lacey first, Laura promised herself. Then Amy.

And then Nate.

Because as much as she hated the thought of all of this, as much as she wanted to put it off forever and never deal with it, he wasn't going to let her. And she did owe him something. Not the truth, like he seemed to think, but something. In return for three years of solid partnership, of friendship, of trusting her implicitly, she owed him some kind of explanation.

What that would be, she didn't yet know. But she had to do something about the situation.

She just couldn't think about that until she'd dealt with everything else in turn, one by one. Starting with the most important—her own daughter—and working her way from there.

# CHAPTER THIRTY FIVE

Laura squatted down, her knee hitting the floor of the court building hard, but she barely felt the pain. She was too excited, too happy. Lacey skipped over to her and landed in her mother's arms, hugging her tightly.

"Mommy, does this mean I get to see you more often?" Lacey asked, her small, innocent voice so sweet that Laura wanted to cry. Just not from sadness this time.

"Yes, baby," Laura said, kissing her daughter's head and holding her, running her hand over her blonde hair to smooth it into place. "Yes, I'm going to see you at weekends from now on. Isn't that great?"

"Yeah," Lacey said, smiling affectionately. "I miss you when I'm just with Daddy all the time."

Laura smiled through eyes that were brimming with tears, tucking Lacey's hair behind her ear just for an excuse to cup her face and look at her. Her daughter.

There had been a time, not very long ago at all, when she'd been afraid that Marcus would never let her see Lacey again. Not until the girl was eighteen, maybe. But it hadn't gone that far. The judge had given her partial custody, and even though it wasn't a perfect split, it was something. It meant seeing her daughter every week. Regularly. Being a mother again, properly now.

Laura had been so nervous about the court case, about the possibility of Marcus blocking her from seeing Lacey for good. But in the end, it had been for the best. Because now, a court had mandated her visitation and custody rights—and Marcus couldn't take that away from her without authorization.

She was a mother again.

"We can't stay too long, Lacey," Marcus said, from a few feet away. He was leaning against one of the pews set in the halls of the court, a resting place for people awaiting their trials and hearings. There was a faint note of irritation in his voice. Laura couldn't say she was surprised. He'd probably expected to keep full custody, to stay in control of Lacey and whether or not Laura could see her.

But the glowing recommendation Laura had received from her supervisor—one Division Chief Rondelle—and Garth, her AA sponsor, had added up to a lot. She made a mental note that she needed to give them both some serious thanks. They'd come through, and it had been enough, along with everything else, to sway the judge. They always wanted to side with the mother, if they could. Laura knew that. And she'd benefited from that today.

"Why, Daddy?" Lacey asked, whining a little before being overtaken by the excitement of a new idea. "I want to play with Mommy. She hasn't seen my new horses yet. We should go home and play!"

"Mommy's not coming home with us," Marcus said. "Remember what the judge said, honey? She will see you at the weekend. It's not the weekend yet."

"Why isn't it?" Lacey asked, pouting.

Laura wanted to burst out laughing. The logic of a six-year-old. She didn't understand why it couldn't be a weekend just because she *wanted* it to be.

"Don't worry, sweetie," Laura said. "We'll play a lot this weekend, okay? You can bring all your horses to show me."

"Okay," Lacey said, heaving a big sigh as if she had just given the biggest concession in the world.

Laura smiled and stood, straightening up. She met Marcus's eyes. He nodded after a moment, a somewhat gruff response—and yet, she could see that he was trying. That he wasn't going to make this hard for them. For Lacey. He would comply with the court.

"See you Saturday morning," he said, and that was all, before he reached for Lacey's hand and started to lead her away.

"See you Saturday, sweetie!" Laura called out, and Lacey turned to wave before they both moved toward the stairs leading down and out of the courthouse.

Laura took a deep breath, letting it fill her lungs. It had been a good day. A good result. Maybe the best she could have hoped for.

The stress, the worry, that had been hanging over her head for all this time could finally dissipate, drifting away.

She was a mother again.

Laura walked to her car with a spring in her step, enjoying the bright yet cool sunlight of an unseasonably sunny day. It was like the whole world knew how good today was. Like even the sun was there to congratulate her.

The drive home was no less cheerful. Laura even turned on the radio, found herself singing along to an old song she hadn't heard in years. Maybe there were still things she needed to deal with, heavy things that were going to settle back on her shoulders later like huge birds of prey returning from a temporary flight. But for now, life was good.

Laura got inside her apartment and went straight for the cupboard under the sink, moving bottles of cleaning fluid and spare sponges out of the way until she found it hidden right at the back. The bottle of liquor she'd bought after walking away from the encounter with Nolan Perry.

She hadn't managed to bring herself to throw it away, earlier. She'd been too consumed by doubt. She'd thought about how she would feel if she didn't get any rights at all, if Marcus made it clear that her time with Lacey was once again over. She'd felt, very much, like she might need it.

But she didn't need it. She was stronger than this. Stronger than all of it.

She twisted off the cap and upended the bottle over the sink, watching all of it swirl and glug down the plughole. She turned on the tap to erase the smell, then threw the bottle unceremoniously into her garbage can. It was over. All of that. She was going to be so much stronger from now on.

She was going to set a good example for her daughter.

Laura's phone lit up with a call from where she'd left it on the counter, and she went over to check it out. The name she saw on the screen made her snatch it up quickly, eager for news.

"Yeah?" she said, which was kind of a joke, because that was how he always answered the phone when she called. Dean Marsters, from the FBI's tech division, was something of a friend. More than a colleague, anyway—an acquaintance, at the very least. And he always helped her out with her requests for support, no matter how strange or outlandish they might have seemed to someone else.

"I got the info you wanted," Dean said, sounding very pleased with himself.

"That quickly?" Laura asked. She'd expected that it might take a few more days, at least. "How did you manage to get inside the CPS system so easily?"

Dean made a scoffing noise down the line. "It's not like they did a whole lot to keep me out. Anyway, do you want to know or not?"

"You know I want to know," Laura said. "I'm going to owe you a serious favor for this one."

"Bring me a pizza Friday when I'm working the graveyard shift, and we'll call it even," Dean said. "So, the next of kin who picked up responsibility for Amy is a guy called Christopher Fallow."

"He's on the Governor's side of the family," Laura said, feeling her heart sink a little at that news. Not that it meant anything—not definitively. Just because someone was related...

"He's his younger brother," Dean confirmed. "Thirty-seven years old. He lives in D.C., so she's still staying local. Apparently, he's a doctor."

"A doctor?" Laura said, concern roiling in the pit of her stomach. "How is he going to have enough time to look after a little girl? Is he married?"

"Not according to the records," Dean said. "Who knows if he has a girlfriend, though. Maybe he's going to hire a nanny. I guess that's something you'd have to ask him."

"Yeah," Laura said faintly, the name Christopher Fallow burning into her brain like a brand. She was going to have to look into him. Find out everything she could about him.

And if he turned out to be as bad a parent as John Fallow, then she was just going to have to burn him to the ground and get Amy free to safety—again.

"He does have one thing on his record," Dean said. "A DUI from about twenty years ago. Looks like it was expunged, though. Of course, that was no match for my searching skills."

"Twenty years ago?" Laura frowned. "He can't have been very old."

"Sixteen or so," Dean said. "I guess they should have gotten him for underage drinking, too. Looks like someone pulled some strings. Probably Daddy's money."

Laura felt a sinking feeling in her chest. If he was the same kind of man as his brother...

He'd been raised in the same household. Given the same privileges. It wasn't wild to assume he might have some of the same vices. Anger management problems being one, potentially.

Of course, it wasn't proof.

"Nothing else flagged up on his record?"

"Nothing," Dean said. "Not even a hint of scandal on the gossip pages. Which, given his brother's run for Governor, you might expect."

So, two sides to the coin. On one hand, a record from when he was a teenager that likely meant nothing. On the other, a clean profile as an adult.

184

She wasn't convinced. She doubted she would ever be. But it felt like a good start.

"You need anything else?" Dean asked. "His home address, extension number at the hospital, social security number…?"

Laura almost had to laugh at that last one. "No, Dean. Thank you. You've done good. I'll take it from here."

"All right." Dean paused slightly. "Don't get yourself into trouble again, will you? I would miss having these little calls to brighten my day if you got yourself fired or jailed."

"Just for your sake, then," Laura joked. "I'll bring you that pizza on Friday. You want pepperoni?"

"You know I do," Dean said. "All right, then. See you, Laura."

"See you," she said, hanging up.

It was progress. It wasn't quite the same elation she'd felt when she learned she was going to get to be with Lacey, but it was a good start. She could use this information, make sure that Amy was safe and sound. Get to know what kind of man Christopher Fallow was from afar, maybe. Look for the signs. She was confident that she was going to be able to handle it.

Amy was going to be safe, one way or another.

Which left her with only one thing more to deal with. One task she'd set herself.

And with everything going so well today, she felt like it was probably the best time to try it. If it all went wrong, maybe it would only bring her back down to the ground, given how high above it she was flying. It wouldn't be so devastating.

Maybe.

Either way, she had very little choice now. It had to be this. Laura could see that now.

She knew where Nate lived. It wasn't a long drive. There wasn't any other excuse. If she didn't do this, she was going to lose him anyway. And getting Lacey back, being able to hug her daughter again, reminded Laura of one very important thing.

The people you cared about the most were the most important people in the world. And letting them slip out of your life for any reason—and especially just because you were afraid—would only leave you deeper in despair than you would have been if you'd taken the chance.

She had to take the chance, no matter how many times she'd talked herself out of it before.

She needed him. His support. His trust. His reassurance. It was everything to her.

Laura grabbed her car keys and headed for the door, stopping for a moment to look out at the sunshine again before she headed to where she'd parked. It was a good day—maybe the best day—for what she had to do.

She had to come clean. Tell him everything.

And hope that he would understand.

**ALREADY MISSING**
**(A Laura Frost FBI Suspense Thriller—Book 4)**

**Women are turning up dead, clocks found mysteriously around their necks, ticking away the seconds before their death. Can FBI Special Agent (and psychic) Laura Frost stop this serial killer before time runs out on his next victim?**

"A MASTERPIECE OF THRILLER AND MYSTERY. Blake Pierce did a magnificent job developing characters with a psychological side so well described that we feel inside their minds, follow their fears and cheer for their success. Full of twists, this book will keep you awake until the turn of the last page."
--Books and Movie Reviews, Roberto Mattos (re Once Gone)

ALREADY MISSING (A Laura Frost FBI Suspense Thriller) is book #4 in a long-anticipated new series by #1 bestseller and USA Today bestselling author Blake Pierce, whose bestseller Once Gone (a free download) has received over 1,000 five star reviews. The series begins with ALREADY GONE (Book #1).

FBI Special Agent and single mom Laura Frost, 35, is haunted by her talent: a psychic ability which she refuses to face and which she keeps secret from her colleagues. Yet as much as Laura wants to be normal, she cannot turn off the flood of images that plague her at every turn: vivid visions of future killers and their victims.

**This time, Laura's visions aren't just confusing—they run directly counter to the evidence. Following them can get her fired.**

**But not trusting them can mean a life.**

Will her gift lead her down the wrong path?

**And will this killer's sick mind games finish her off for good?**

A page-turning and harrowing mystery thriller featuring a brilliant and tortured female protagonist, the LAURA FROST series is rife with murder, mystery and suspense, twists and turns, shocking revelations, and driven by a breakneck pace. Fans of Robert Dugoni, Melinda Leigh and Lisa Regan are sure to fall in love. Pick up this fresh new mystery series and you'll be flipping pages late into the night.

Book #5 (ALREADY DEAD) is now also available!

## Blake Pierce

Blake Pierce is the USA Today bestselling author of the RILEY PAGE mystery series, which includes seventeen books. Blake Pierce is also the author of the MACKENZIE WHITE mystery series, comprising fourteen books; of the AVERY BLACK mystery series, comprising six books; of the KERI LOCKE mystery series, comprising five books; of the MAKING OF RILEY PAIGE mystery series, comprising six books; of the KATE WISE mystery series, comprising seven books; of the CHLOE FINE psychological suspense mystery, comprising six books; of the JESSIE HUNT psychological suspense thriller series, comprising nineteen books; of the AU PAIR psychological suspense thriller series, comprising three books; of the ZOE PRIME mystery series, comprising six books; of the ADELE SHARP mystery series, comprising thirteen books; of the EUROPEAN VOYAGE cozy mystery series, comprising six books (and counting); of the new LAURA FROST FBI suspense thriller, comprising four books (and counting); of the new ELLA DARK FBI suspense thriller, comprising six books (and counting); of the A YEAR IN EUROPE cozy mystery series, comprising nine books (and counting); of the AVA GOLD mystery series, comprising three books (and counting); and of the RACHEL GIFT mystery series, comprising three books (and counting).

An avid reader and lifelong fan of the mystery and thriller genres, Blake loves to hear from you, so please feel free to visit www.blakepierceauthor.com to learn more and stay in touch.

# BOOKS BY BLAKE PIERCE

**RACHEL GIFT MYSTERY SERIES**
HER LAST WISH (Book #1)
HER LAST CHANCE (Book #2)
HER LAST HOPE (Book #3)

**AVA GOLD MYSTERY SERIES**
CITY OF PREY (Book #1)
CITY OF FEAR (Book #2)
CITY OF BONES (Book #3)

**A YEAR IN EUROPE**
A MURDER IN PARIS (Book #1)
DEATH IN FLORENCE (Book #2)
VENGEANCE IN VIENNA (Book #3)
A FATALITY IN SPAIN (Book #4)
SCANDAL IN LONDON (Book #5)
AN IMPOSTOR IN DUBLIN (Book #6)
SEDUCTION IN BORDEAUX (Book #7)
JEALOUSY IN SWITZERLAND (Book #8)
A DEBACLE IN PRAGUE (Book #9)

**ELLA DARK FBI SUSPENSE THRILLER**
GIRL, ALONE (Book #1)
GIRL, TAKEN (Book #2)
GIRL, HUNTED (Book #3)
GIRL, SILENCED (Book #4)
GIRL, VANISHED (Book 5)
GIRL ERASED (Book #6)

**LAURA FROST FBI SUSPENSE THRILLER**
ALREADY GONE (Book #1)
ALREADY SEEN (Book #2)
ALREADY TRAPPED (Book #3)
ALREADY MISSING (Book #4)

**EUROPEAN VOYAGE COZY MYSTERY SERIES**
MURDER (AND BAKLAVA) (Book #1)
DEATH (AND APPLE STRUDEL) (Book #2)

CRIME (AND LAGER) (Book #3)
MISFORTUNE (AND GOUDA) (Book #4)
CALAMITY (AND A DANISH) (Book #5)
MAYHEM (AND HERRING) (Book #6)

**ADELE SHARP MYSTERY SERIES**
LEFT TO DIE (Book #1)
LEFT TO RUN (Book #2)
LEFT TO HIDE (Book #3)
LEFT TO KILL (Book #4)
LEFT TO MURDER (Book #5)
LEFT TO ENVY (Book #6)
LEFT TO LAPSE (Book #7)
LEFT TO VANISH (Book #8)
LEFT TO HUNT (Book #9)
LEFT TO FEAR (Book #10)
LEFT TO PREY (Book #11)
LEFT TO LURE (Book #12)
LEFT TO CRAVE (Book #13)

**THE AU PAIR SERIES**
ALMOST GONE (Book#1)
ALMOST LOST (Book #2)
ALMOST DEAD (Book #3)

**ZOE PRIME MYSTERY SERIES**
FACE OF DEATH (Book#1)
FACE OF MURDER (Book #2)
FACE OF FEAR (Book #3)
FACE OF MADNESS (Book #4)
FACE OF FURY (Book #5)
FACE OF DARKNESS (Book #6)

**A JESSIE HUNT PSYCHOLOGICAL SUSPENSE SERIES**
THE PERFECT WIFE (Book #1)
THE PERFECT BLOCK (Book #2)
THE PERFECT HOUSE (Book #3)
THE PERFECT SMILE (Book #4)
THE PERFECT LIE (Book #5)
THE PERFECT LOOK (Book #6)

ONCE GONE (Book #1)
ONCE TAKEN (Book #2)
ONCE CRAVED (Book #3)
ONCE LURED (Book #4)
ONCE HUNTED (Book #5)
ONCE PINED (Book #6)
ONCE FORSAKEN (Book #7)
ONCE COLD (Book #8)
ONCE STALKED (Book #9)
ONCE LOST (Book #10)
ONCE BURIED (Book #11)
ONCE BOUND (Book #12)
ONCE TRAPPED (Book #13)
ONCE DORMANT (Book #14)
ONCE SHUNNED (Book #15)
ONCE MISSED (Book #16)
ONCE CHOSEN (Book #17)

**MACKENZIE WHITE MYSTERY SERIES**
BEFORE HE KILLS (Book #1)
BEFORE HE SEES (Book #2)
BEFORE HE COVETS (Book #3)
BEFORE HE TAKES (Book #4)
BEFORE HE NEEDS (Book #5)
BEFORE HE FEELS (Book #6)
BEFORE HE SINS (Book #7)
BEFORE HE HUNTS (Book #8)
BEFORE HE PREYS (Book #9)
BEFORE HE LONGS (Book #10)
BEFORE HE LAPSES (Book #11)
BEFORE HE ENVIES (Book #12)
BEFORE HE STALKS (Book #13)
BEFORE HE HARMS (Book #14)

**AVERY BLACK MYSTERY SERIES**
CAUSE TO KILL (Book #1)
CAUSE TO RUN (Book #2)
CAUSE TO HIDE (Book #3)
CAUSE TO FEAR (Book #4)
CAUSE TO SAVE (Book #5)

CAUSE TO DREAD (Book #6)

**KERI LOCKE MYSTERY SERIES**
A TRACE OF DEATH (Book #1)
A TRACE OF MUDER (Book #2)
A TRACE OF VICE (Book #3)
A TRACE OF CRIME (Book #4)
A TRACE OF HOPE (Book #5)

Made in the USA
Las Vegas, NV
31 July 2022

52481139R00115